CONTENTS

welcome!

We are pleased to welcome you to our Academy 001.
Our mission statement here is that we will build for you - the
exceptional, empirical you - a home. You will find inside all of
the education, support, purpose, and family any Psychic could
ever hope to have. We understand the circumstances of you
arriving at our doors may not have been within the realm of
your control, but we are so grateful that you are here. Within
your manual you will find our history, our purpose, and our
duties. Your arrival here should be thought of as a gift, a chance,
and an opportunity for you to demonstrate to the entire world
your exceptional self. While here at Academy 001, we hope
you will share with us your strengths, your talents, and your
diligence.

Welcome to the Academy.

Gregory Krag, Academy Superintendent.

PROLOGUE

Tobias was less than enthusiastic about his wait. There were 19 recruits in total applying for positions in TITAN that day. The written exam had been easy, as had the physical. Now he was sitting in a small cramped office with industrial white paint that fatigued the eye. There were only 10 or 12 chairs in the room, and the remaining recruits who couldn't find seats were sitting on the floor or standing restlessly against the wall. They had all been there no less than an hour in relative silence. There were only two doors to the room they were in. The first was an entrance to the room itself, the other was to the office where the interviews were taking place. Two recruits had gone in; neither of them had come out.

"How many of us do you think they will take?" came a small excited voice.

Tobias turned his head to find its source. It was a young woman, maybe 18 with athletic features, honey-colored eyes, and a shaved head but the short growth indicated dark brown hair. She was dressed in athletic wear and was sporting a bruise on her cheek from her physical examination. It had been pretty thorough. Three hours of running, jumping, weights, endurance tests, and then five minutes of sparring with a very fresh combat instructor. Most of the recruits in the room were pretty banged up. Black eyes, injured hands, rubbing sore joints, and such. Tobias appeared one of the few recruits who'd emerged from the physical unscathed. He considered answering but was cut off by a young man with close-cropped brown hair who was nursing what appeared to be a boxer break to his left hand.

"Rumor has it they weed out about 50% during examinations, then half of that during the interview. So about a quarter if the rumors are right." He spoke with an unusual calmness for a man that should have been in considerable pain.

Tobias had heard a much different story. That the mercenary organization TITAN, the largest merc recruitment in the regions, took less than five percent of the applicants that it brought in. It would make sense. The organization was known far and wide for being one of the best paying jobs around. And despite being incredibly dangerous work, there never seemed to be a shortage of recruits.

"The written exam seemed easy. The history of the old countries and such. Did you guys have any trouble with the questions about the Psychic War?" the girl chirped, clearly trying to vanquish her nervous energy with the conversation.

"It's all the same stuff they teach in primary school. Stuff everyone knows. The questions on the Pacification Pact are the ones that were the hardest to answer. Who remembers the details of some 20-year-old document?" the young man retorted.

Tobias looked across the room at the wall. The war had ended when he was just a kid and its facts meant very little to him personally.

The door across the room swung open and a young man in a sharp, pressed uniform with a clipboard in his hand looked up.

"Marshall, Tobias."

Tobias stood up and walked across the room. As he entered the small bare room there was little to see. A plain unadorned wooden desk with no personal effects on it. A latched wooden door that led out the other side of the room, and a stern-faced man who was rifling through a stack of papers. Across from the desk and sitting close to the door Tobias had come through was a young plain-featured woman with large scared brown eyes that looked up at Tobias for only a moment then back at her lap. The young man with the clipboard closed the door behind them and pressed his back into the corner of the room and began reexamining his clipboard.

"Have a seat Mr. Marshall." The stern man behind the desk spoke. Tobias moved to the empty seat beside the frightened-looking girl.

"Marshall...Marshall...hmm. No record of education. No record of employment. No record of birth or residence..." Tobias forced his irritation away. He hated being grilled about trivialities.

"You scored high on your exam, both academic and physical. And in your combat exercise..." The officer behind the desk flipped a page in his folder. He read and then reread as if he was having trouble recognizing words.

"...you broke the instructor's wrist and collar bone. Had some experience fighting, have you?" Tobias straightened his shoulders up enough to relieve the growing tension in his spine.

"A little."

The officer raised an eyebrow and typed on his computer interface for a moment, scrutinizing the screen, then spun the monitor around to face Tobias. It was a video from a stationary vantage of Tobias during his sparring session with the combat instructor. The video showed the two of them standing several feet apart, Tobias in a relaxed boxing stance with his hands open and the instructor, who was easily 10 centimeters taller and well-built, circling closer and closer to him. It happened in the span of a few seconds. The instructor rushed Tobias, throwing a hard left hook. Tobias slipped past the range of the punch and as the instructor threw his right cross to complete the one two combo, the fight ended. Tobias used his left elbow in a sweep to deflect the punch away, caught the right wrist in his own right hand and pivoted sideways and shoved the instructor down at the shoulder using his left hand, forcing him to the ground. Tobias, maintaining the grip on his wrist and pressuring forward, forced him down hard, adjusted his grip on the arm, and with a lock then a twist, the wrist snapped. The last thing the camera showed was Tobias walking out of the room untouched.

"A little, huh?" came the officer's bemused voice.

Tobias shrugged. "Maybe more than a little."

The officer reopened the file in front of him.

"Well, your lack of history isn't an issue for us. Too many records were destroyed in those final days of the war; we have a lot of displaced individuals in our ranks, and not having any kind of family ties lends itself to this type of work. No documented education would normally be a problem, but you passed your written exam with flying colors, so obviously you're not illiterate. There is just one question left to ask ..."

Tobias wasn't patient and beating around the bush irritated him. "What is it?"

The officer considered Tobias for a moment then reached in his desk and pulled out a thick, black handgun. It was a simple design with no external safety.

"Have you ever fired a gun before, Mr. Marshall?"

Tobias maintained his peripheral on the gun while he responded. "Yes."

"Have you ever killed someone without provocation, Mr. Marshall?"

Tobias didn't answer; he just stared hard at the officer.

"Your last test is to take the gun on this table and kill Ms. Ortiz here. One shot through the head should be fine."

Tobias reached for the firearm and lifted it, examining it.

.45 Gyro, high capacity magazine, no external safety. Named Gyro for the built-in gyroscope in the barrel, as the weapon fired it would absorb the recoil and prevent the gun from kicking back. A heavy but accurate weapon. Tobias aimed at the girl in the chair. He leveled his hand, balancing the barrel less than a meter from her temple.

She began sobbing uncontrollably. "Please don't–"

Click.

Tobias had pulled the trigger. The gun dry fired.

"Not much of a test if the gun is empty, is it?" Tobias chimed as he removed the magazine from the gun to reveal it wasn't loaded. "The weight was off."

The girl in the chair sat wide-eyed with tear-streaked cheeks. "It- it wasn't …"

"Very good, Mr. Marshall. Ms. Ortiz here couldn't complete this element of the test and so she became our next volunteer. And even though I can't say this officially, Mr. Marshall, welcome to TITAN. You will be issued your uniform and 6:1k rifle, the price of which will come from your first several paychecks. Tomorrow, we expect you to be here bright and early."

Tobias walked out of the room past the other recruits and out of the entrance door.

"How'd it go?" asked the pretty girl with the shaved head tentatively.

"Quickly" was his icy response.

———————————————————————

The hallway seemed endless. Rudra tried to ignore the sound of their hard-soled footsteps as they echoed down the hallway.

The normally warm Agni was uncharacteristically agitated. "Because it makes me sick, that's why!" Agni barked, her tone frustrated and defiant.

"It doesn't matter how it makes you feel, we have our orders. And besides, if it didn't happen now it would happen in a year or two anyway" retorted Rudra, his voice echoing down the tile hallway. Rudra held back his comment. He knew his sister was too agitated to listen to reason.

The Merger wing of the Academy had always struck him as surgical and sterile, which led to it feeling deeply uncomfortable. Nothing like the actual council chamber which was warm and comfortable where they were kept to do the Wash. Maybe he should talk to the directors about a paint job or something to make it seem a little homier; after all, it was usually children who were dragged down here to be pressed into the Merge.

"But she's only 13, Ru. Even I was 16 when we underwent the Merge!"

Rudra let it go, he knew she needed to vent before they got to the merger room. It was going to be a tense enough situation without her on the verge of blowing the room up.

"Try to remember Agni, three people have already died on the table. Moreover, it still hasn't killed the girl. She's extraordinary and danger-ous, you know she has to be Leashed." Then under what could only be described as a concerned sneer, "They say she's the strongest unpaired Psychic since you."

The temperature in the hall rose several degrees.

"I couldn't care less about the girl's level of strength, Ru, she's a child. And without meaning to, she has now killed six people, three of them fully-trained Leashes. She needs to be in a care facility, not on a battlefield."

Rudra's hushed and serious tone cut her off.

"Enough, collect yourself. She needs us to be steady. Remember, despite her age she's strong enough to kill all of us, so clear your mind."

The air around them cooled slowly as Agni composed herself; it always amazed Rudra the incredible level of control his sister had to demonstrate over her emotions. But when a temper tantrum can cause a forest fire, you learn quickly the importance of control.

The room they walked into was cold, uncomfortably so, and it was mostly unadorned except for a large, gurney-like hospital bed in the center of the room, large enough for two people to lay side by side. The only person in the room was a little girl who had turned to face them. She was slight, her small stature made her look younger than her unblemished features would have suggested. And her youthful face was framed by platinum blonde hair.

Rudra immediately threw up mental shields to guard against being probed.

Agni reached out with her mind to the girl and almost immediately pulled back with a shudder.

The girl's mental presence was wild and ravenous. Agni had felt as if all the heat in her body had been ripped from her, and what had started as a gentle mental caress had turned into Agni feeling as if her very essence was being pulled from her pores. Her eyes sharpened and she stepped forward, a moment's lapse in what was normally a well-regulated mind. But Rudra's gentle fingers touched her.

She didn't mean to. His voice came like a whisper in her mind, words heard but not spoken. *I feel it, too. Like she's pulling the life out of everything.*

"Hello." The girl spoke softly, as if she were afraid of her own voice.

Rudra's face inclined toward the girl and his charm switched on.

"Hi there. I'm Rudra. We were sent to make sure that you're safe today during the procedure. Is that ok?"

The girl smiled weakly.

"No you're not. You're here to make sure I don't hurt anyone, right? I could hear you when you were walking down the hallway."

Agni was stunned, it takes even strong Psychics years to be able to read specific thoughts much less identify their source with such precision.

While Agni's face betrayed her, Rudra's smile didn't even shrink. "Close, we're here to make sure no one gets hurt, especially you."

Agni smiled at her brother. He had such a skill for putting people at ease, something she didn't have.

"Is there anything we can get you?" Rudra asked, full of genuine concern.

"I'm a little cold," she answered softly.

Agni grinned. This was her area of expertise. She pressed her palms together and cupped them in their center; she felt the familiar surge of energy, the heat rising to nearly 50 degrees Celsius in the span of a few seconds. When she opened her hands, it was as if she was releasing a small butterfly, the heat dispersed evenly throughout the room, the temperature rose several degrees around them and what was previously a freezing surgical room was now warm and comfortable. The girl on the table stared wide-eyed at Agni.

"You can make heat?"

Agni beamed warmly.

"I can use telekinesis to excite the oxygen atoms in the air and create friction within a given space, or for something more explosive I can compress oxygen molecules together until they can be ignited from almost any stimulus. So yes, I guess you could say I can make heat."

The girl looked up, her eyes full of curiosity...and something else...hunger?

"Can you make more?"

Agni nodded, inhaled deeply through her nose, and exhaled sharply into the palm of her hand. The rapid flow of oxygen made the reaction easier, even though an exhale contains high traces of nitrogen the added air current and the trace oxygen in her lungs made a pathway that was easier to manipulate with Psychic energy. Her breath came out hot from the first instant then sparks appeared from nowhere when tongues of fire leaped from the place where the oxygen began to dissipate, and a raging inferno appeared in the palm of Agni's hand.

It glistened and danced above her palm like something alive. The heat coming off of it was intense, but Agni did not flinch or try to make the fire dissipate.

"How do you maintain a constant flame with no fuel?"

Agni smiled at this inquisitiveness.

"My own energy is the raw fuel after I oxidize the air. I have to be careful though, because if I'm enhancing a flame it can suck all the oxygen out of a room if the fire exceeds the oxygen available. Now if there is natural fuel available I can use that to spread the fire at will ..."

She felt Rudra press heavy against her mind. Agni had set entire platoons ablaze, roasted men alive in their beds, and, on one occasion, burned down an entire town. Rudra didn't like it when she was glib about her ability.

The girl stared wide-eyed.

"If you're Rudra, the Tornado leash, I guess that makes you Agni, the Pyre."

Rudra chuckled, Agni smiled.

"Agni and Rudra are fine names for you to call us. Do you mind if we ask yours?"

The girl smiled weakly, the kind of smile you give when you're lying in a hospital bed and someone asks if you're ok.

"I could hear you," the girl touched her own temple, "as you were walking down, so I know you already know. But my name is Alyssia."

She held out her hand and the dancing flame that was sitting atop Agni's fingers flitted and then sank into Alyssia's outstretched finger-tips, warming the cuticles before vanishing beneath her skin. Rudra looked at Agni and saw his sister's mouth hanging open, the color drained from both her face and her fingertips.

"And I'm an energy sync, I can connect and consume any source of energy. I hope I didn't hurt you," she said as Agni rubbed her fingers together, trying to return the feeling to the icy digits.

"Any energy?" asked Rudra curiously.

"Yes," Alyssia responded. "Heat, electricity, fast-moving water. Anything."

"Even Psychic energy?" asked Agni, still nursing her fingers.

"Yes, I think that's why the three Mergers didn't happen correctly. Right?" She cast her eyes down ashamed. "I hate that people are getting hurt and that it's my fault. I wish I could change it or do something about it. I don't want to hurt anyone."

The door opened at that point and in walked the Council. Nine of the oldest living Psychics. Agni hated them, something she couldn't explain. With their empty shuffle, their tear streaked faces and confused childlike voices. She knew their condition couldn't be helped. They were simply a product of their mergers, having lost their Leashes and having half their personality ripped away must have been unbelievably painful, that was probably why she hated them so much. She was so near them in so many disgusting ways. The only thing that made their presence bearable was Gregory, a tall husky man with a kindly bass voice and hands the size of frying pans. He was the tenth member of the Council, and the only member of the Council who still had a Leash, and therefore the only one with a fully functioning mind.

"Agni, Rudra. I see you two have met our latest recruit, Ms. Alyssia, how are you?" he smiled warmly, his broad face and kind features hiding the strain and concern that must surely hide behind them.

"I'm fine Mr. Gregory I was just meeting Agni and Rudra," she responded with a more genuine smile than the siblings had seen.

"The Council has concluded..."

Rudra issued a snort of derision.

"...and we think we have discovered the primary issue. What I think we will try, if you will bear with us one more time," he said smiling down at the young blonde girl "...is we are going to try a different approach. I think we have been mispairing you with incompatible Leashes. We were picking strong and confident individuals hoping that it would put your young mind at ease. But you seem to feel threatened by them, and that is why things haven't worked out. I think we have found our solution..."

The door to the room creaked open and in walked a beautiful woman with flaming red hair and intense serious eyes in her early 30's. Agni and Rudra both reached out to her mind, Agni was trying to dig as much as she could without breaking the woman. She slammed into a mental wall that was as hard as concrete the second she made contact. The red-haired leash shot a glance at Agni and flashed a half-smirk under her stunning green eyes. Rudra, not being a Psychic, or nearly as adept as his sister, felt his mind bounce off the Psychic wall and back into his own skull, shaking his head from the recoil. It was a good sign. She was strong and full of life and concentration. She'd be a good match. It did make him wonder however what must have occurred, even the most focused of Leashes leave an imprint of their trauma on them somewhere. Rudra could still smell his parents burning skin in his dreams...

The red-haired woman moved toward Alyssia on a curved line, a simple move that strategically softened her approach to the frightened teen.

"I bet you're sick of seeing all these old farts, huh?"

Alyssia let out a shocked laugh at the comment.

All the other Leashes had approached and tried to befriend her in general ways, introducing themselves or explaining confidently how they were going to take such good care of her. Alyssia reached out timidly, her mental tendrils caressing at what she expected to be an impermeable wall of mental blocks, like the previous Leashes had been, but what she found was soft and yielding.

She saw images of the woman as a 16-year-old girl, married young and recklessly. Followed by images of a set of twins being born on a living room floor, while her handsome husband held her hand and coached her gently. Years flashed, and the woman showed her images of herself as a happy mother and wife, another baby was on the way. Then the scene shifted, it was dark, a man hovered over her, covered in blood, searing pain shooting through every inch of her body. The red-headed woman's voice reached out hoarsely screaming for her children while the bloodied man above her flashed an evil and complete smile...her husband, drenched in their baby's blood. The smell of death hanging thick in the air, the knife in her husband's hand, the instrument of their children's end and of the unborn baby in her womb. He fell upon her, and even though Alyssia was only seeing the memories she could feel his weight on her, she smelled whiskey on his breath...he was so strong...and the pain was so intense. Then both of her hands shot up, pressing her thumbs into his eyelids, gouging at his eyes and throat. He fell back, screaming. Blood streaked down his cheeks, he had dropped the knife, the pain was so intense, she was losing so much blood, she picked up the knife...her vision was going blurry, plunged it into his body, once, then twice, then a thousand times until the blackness enveloped her mind...

Alyssia opened her eyes and felt the warm embrace of the red-haired woman and the slick wetness of her own tears on her cheeks.

"You're safe, girly. I'll protect you."

In the space of a moment an incredibly intimate bond had been formed. Alyssia could not fathom the pain this woman had gone through, but she kept hearing about pain making the strongest Leash-es.

The council then spoke in their broken unison. Nine broken minds trying to form a single thought. Alyssia could feel the temperature in the room rise and smiled over at Agni; she guessed she disliked the council, too.

"We w-will prepare the m-merge now?" came the voice of one of the women on the council. She was probably in her 60's but the voice didn't belong in her mouth. It belonged to a child, lost, lonely and confused. A child terrified of the world around her, and unable to cope with the reality of its horrors. How Alyssia pitied them. The red headed woman climbed onto the table and pulled Alyssia into her lap.

"Ready to go for a ride, doll face?" the woman chirped at Alyssia. Damn, she liked her.

The council made a circle around the table, their hands extended outward. Alyssia noticed Rudra crack a half smile, she understood. Extra sensory abilities were a scientifically explainable phenomenon, not some hocus pocus magic trick that required special words and phrases or hand signs to focus. Psychic ability was simply the evolution of key parts of the brain, "telepathy" simply a physical, sensory, sensitivity to the electric currents that ran through other people's brain waves, "telekinesis" easily explained as the ability to manipulate electrical, magnetic, and thermal forces at a molecular or sometimes atomic level. There was no need for their silly hand signs.

"Shall we b-begin?" One of the males of the council stammered in an almost pathetic voice. It came first as a pulse.

A broad sweeping sensation, like a tidal wave crashing into you so it knocked the wind from your lungs, hit everyone in the room in the space of a second. The room then began to swim with Psychic energy so thick you could almost taste it. Alyssia felt the Leash who was holding her begin to flush and breathe more heavily. Even the well-controlled Rudra's cheeks were flushed and his eyes glossy. The feeling of raw Psychic energy was stimulating to a normal human, but to a Leash who used Psychic energy like sustenance, it was intoxicating. It had been months since Rudra had undergone his last Wash, not that he was running low. He always managed to conserve what he needed, and he never went on any assignments without a full tank of Psychic energy flowing through his veins, but he did miss the feeling. That nearly god-like sensation of being submerged in power, of being invincible. Of being a Leash.

Gregory spoke kind but authoritative.

"Alrighty then, we are going to stabilize the energy Wash now so that it makes a solid field, then we are going to link your minds together. This sensation will feel a little unusual at first and all Psychics experience it differently so just try and relax and remember, all you're really doing is finding each other in the dark."

"I gotchu baby just relax" the red-haired woman gave Alyssia a gentle squeeze and Alyssia snuggled down against her.

Never had she felt more cared for, and by a stranger much less. Someone who had opened their mind so fearlessly to her. She didn't want the feeling to go away, she didn't care if it was a façade, she didn't care if it could all end at a moment's notice, she didn't really care about feeling safe, just accepted, just home. Their minds touched again. They had to listen for each other, almost like trying to pick out a single instrument amid a perfectly synced orchestra.

Then she felt it. An energy that burned like a wildfire. Alyssia reached out for it. It was so warm and inviting. She wanted to caress it with her mind. She wanted it to be a part of her. She wanted to be connected to it, she reached out with her mind, her mind reaching for the wildfire gently.

Even though Rudra was supposed to be facilitating this procedure, he was lost in the torrential sea of Psychic energy that was flowing around the room. Every molecule in his body was sighing softly into oblivion and he wanted to melt alive. The feeling was pleasure, pure and uninterruptible. Suddenly a strong stream of Psychic energy slammed against his mind. He pushed it away with effort. He was in paradise, and nothing could interfere with his pleasure; he would float here forever. The same presence slammed into him again this time with more force, enough to make him open his heavy eyes. He looked around the room. The council was still pushing wave after wave of energy out of their bodies into Alyssia and the red-haired Leash attempting to meld their minds.

So everything was going as planned, right? So why was there fire all over the ground? That wasn't there before...someone should really stop playing with matches don't they know there are little kids here.... Rudra's thoughts swam through his head sluggishly.

Rudra's senses crashed back into him with weight and the nightmare that was in front of his eyes became a stark, abrupt reality. The woman on the table was screaming and writhing, her face gaunt and contorted into an inhuman shape. Her skin looked stretched tight over the bone, as if it were being pulled from the back of her body, like plastic wrap over a molding. The color was rapidly draining from her as if the blood was being poured out of her body by the pint. Agni was frantically trying to stop the council from going any further.

Gregory was pleading in vain with the all-powerful simpletons begging them, "Please stop! They could die! Please!!! No more I'm begging you."

Rudra wasn't the begging type, he pushed off the ground with his left foot using his reserves of Psychic energies and commanding his body to inhuman speeds. Maybe if he could knock the table off balance, he could save them. In the space of four feet he accelerated to over 100 kph, The Tornado Leash had earned his title. He could see the whole scene in a millisecond flash, the red haired Leash being emptied from the inside, the horrified look on Alyssia's face as her new found friend was shriveling into a husk, the circlets of fire floating around his sisters' body, Gregory's substantial chest pumping like a bellows as he heaved himself at different members of the council, his large frame halted by walls of energy so dense, gunfire wouldn't have penetrated.

Then he felt it. The wall went up. Psychic defense so substantial that it stopped him in his tracks and hurled him backwards. He slammed against the concrete wall faster than he had been running, his internal organs rupturing and then healing almost as rapidly. He fell face first to the ground as blood filled his vision. His left eye had burst from the impact, the Psychic energy in his body tickling behind the bleeding orbital as it tried to repair his failing vision. The body of the red headed woman now hung limp and lifeless off of the side of the table as Alyssia sobbed uncontrollably. Agni was rushing to his side, every exhale of her chest produced a shower of searing sparks, while Gregory slumped against the wall, his glasses in his hand wiping off sweat and frustration.

"Not again...she'd been through enough...I can't do this anymore...I can't hurt people anymore I just can't...please Mr. Gregory please don't make me." Alyssia cried out, trembling and heartbroken.

"Never again, my child. As long as I am alive, you will never have to endure this again," Gregory comforted her. "I'm sorry. The merger was a failure. Just like the previous three. Scrub the project. Alyssia, the Energy Sync, will remain the only unpaired level four Psychic in the world."

Rudra looked over at Alyssia through the one eye he had that wasn't ruptured. He looked and tried as hard as he could to see a little girl. He tried as hard as he could to see a human. He tried until the moment he passed out, to see her anyway other than an all-consuming monster. And if he gained that sight before losing consciousness, he couldn't remember it. The darkness swallowed him.

CHAPTER 1.1

The Relationship Between Psychics and Leashes

"The purpose of a Leash is to protect. If that which is Leashed is weak, it is for their protection. If that which is Leashed is strong, it is for the world's protection. This is the purpose of the Leash Protocol."

Three years later

Tobias had to choke down his anxiety. That primal instinct that had helped man survive his first several thousand years of evolution was shouting into the back of his mind. The hole he was in was black, the walls were slick and devoid of texture, and the water he was in was thick, warm, and putrid smelling. He couldn't climb out. He put his hands along the outside and pushed.

About 2 meters in every direction ... except up.

He gazed into the empty blackness hoping that his eyes would adjust; they didn't. He had been treading water for what seemed like hours, but he knew it hadn't been more than 20 or 30 minutes. He recognized his level of fatigue, but the water was so thick and the smell so awful that he nearly regretted trying to fill his lungs, and despite the smell he dared not open his mouth and risk potentially swallowing a mouth full of the liquid.

Water is just not this thick. Why can't I move anywhere?

He felt the grip. Small but strong, determined fingers wrapped around his ankle and started to pull, his head slipped below the surface. His arms surged up pushing him above the water, his mouth opened to gasp air and only swallowed a mouthful of retched fluid instead. The hand around his ankle pulled even harder, yanking almost inhumanly strong. The grip was desperate, full of need and fear; the nails dug into his skin.

Tobias dove down, determined to shake off his attacker. He struggled with the hand at his ankle. When he failed to detach the grip, he swam deeper looking for something to attack. He reached out and felt a face, small like a child's. He didn't care, he put his palms on his assailant's temples and dug his thumbs into his attacker's eyes. He felt the pop of the eye bursting, and the smooth slick outline of the inside of the orbital socket, but his attacker still wouldn't release him. If anything, the grip intensified. He lifted his free leg up and pressed it into the gouged face of his invisible opponent and tried to kick off, but his muscles failed him, and suddenly his whole world felt as if it were breaking in slow motion.

Tobias's eyes snapped open, and despite an unearthly desire to spring to his feet, he commanded his body to be still. He looked at the others in the back of the transport at a glance, five souls total. The two Greenies he had been assigned to and the pair of contractors that had been hired.

The two Greenies on the far side of the truck sat quizzing each other over the officer's test they were both looking to pass in the next week. Stein was a slight man, thin and narrow, barely out of boyhood, with close cut brown hair, freckles, and a nose too large and pointed for his narrow framed face. But Tobias knew he had passed his physical exam with flying colors. Farm boy muscle, strength that was built from labor.

"Ok so, the world was at war? Like, the WHOLE world?" Stein asked the man sitting next to him. Hernandez was his name. A middle aged man whose skin was like dark leather. His eyes prematurely showed signs of crow's feet and gray and black stubble covered his weather-worn face.

"Come on kid, it wasn't even that long ago. Back when the regions were still divided into countries and everyone had their own militaries, there were a lot of tensions, you know? Childish little squabbles that eventually led to alliances and enemies. Well, like usual, the little guys couldn't defend themselves against the big guys, so they started hiring mercenaries. That's where groups like TITAN, and AGEIS came from. We showed up and swung the fight in favor of the smaller, democratic-style countries and eventually forced everyone to sign the Pacification Pact, making all the countries disband their armies in favor of private military police forces. That's why we exist. To do the dirty work other people aren't strong enough to do on their own. Groups like TITAN make the world a better place, kid."

Tobias smirked, but one of the contractors outright laughed. The man was smooth featured and handsome, didn't look like he had seen much in the way of combat. His frame was slight and his skin appeared to be blemish free. But there was something about the way he carried himself. Cold, calculating with a permanent smile perched on his lips. It was almost unsettling.

Tobias had seen the type before. Assassins never did get very dirty in their line of work. The woman sitting next to him was noticeably more interesting to look at. Her dark rich skin, slender legs, and black hair that hung like curtains around stunning green-gold eyes. She was gorgeous.

The man began to speak, his voice smooth and confident.

"I guess you forgot the part where the Psychic Academy showed up after six additional years of mercenaries and soldiers killing each other and intervened. How the Founder showed up with his Psychics and Leashes and single handedly won your war for you."

Hernandez fired back.

"The Academy had been secretly building its own private military for years. Taking in sick kids and turning them into soldiers. Then they put pressure on the newly formed regions that were terrified of them to give them political immunity. No one should ever have that kind of power. They ain't nothing to admire. Bunch of freaks if you ask me. And the Psychics showing up is what started all the purges. All those people getting killed in their homes 'cause the Academy had them on a registry."

The smooth featured man grinned challengingly.

"Society demanded Psychics be registered and then locked up. And people have been trying to kill them long before the purges began. It was even suggested by some groups that all Psychics should be euthanized at birth so as not to spread their disease. The Academy took in society's undesirables and gave them a home. Then turned around and saved your asses. Must sting knowing that it was the sick kids, as you called them, who saved your lives." the retort had been cool and precise

Hernandez blinked twice, began to rise, set on crossing the back of the transport to the smooth featured man.

"Sit down Hernandez." Tobias issued his curt command.

"Good of you to join us, Mr. Marshall," came the voice from the woman across from him, a voice that reminded him of music he had enjoyed while he was in the easternmost region, the former Indo-China Alliance.

Instinctively, Tobias threw up a mental shield, thinking of combat tactics, chess moves, simple arithmetic. The woman began to laugh.

"How very interesting you are. Your dreams are far more telling than your woken mind, Mr. Marshall. But I didn't get your name from reading your thoughts. I got it from reading your dossier."

The man sitting next to her held up a medium-sized folder before opening it back up and continuing to study the information.

"Leave him alone, Agni. He's just a soldier. He doesn't even know what he's about to get mixed up in. Can't you feel the anxiety from the other two?"

She smiled gently.

"Of course I can, but they aren't anxious for the reasons you think."

The woman brushed her hair behind her ear and took a deep breath.

"Mr. Stein is worried about his father back home. He's sick and unable to work for himself, which is the primary reason that he signed up to work for TITAN. Because despite their awful record of fatalities in the line of duty, they pay the best. Mr. Hernandez was more concerned with his superior finding out that he doctored his physical wellness exam to hide an aggravated knee injury which probably needs surgery, but he can't confess that or he'll be fired. But Mr. Marshall over there is an iron wall, everything comes through in a haze, he must have been around Psychics before."

What had taken the considerable Psychic abilities of the woman, whom he now knew as Agni, Tobias had already discerned through perception. The way Hernandez was walking had Tobias debating on crippling him before the assignment so that he wouldn't be slowed down. And the boy Stein was as timid as they come. Afraid of his own shadow, a farm boy from nowhere who was trying to play soldier because he wanted to make an easier life for himself. Would probably get himself killed soon.

Now that Tobias was certain she was a Psychic, that would make the man next to her the Leash. He made hard eye contact. He didn't like Psychics. They were bad enough in an interrogation room when they were trying to rip information out of your head, or one of the stronger Psychics could throw a car at you. A Leash wasn't much better. Having to dump an entire wheel of .45 acp into a high level Leash only worked if you were close enough for them to stick their hands in your chest and rip your heart out. He had fought with and against Psychics and their Leashes before and had no desire for more of the same.

"Do we make you uncomfortable, Mr. Marshall?" This time it was the Leash who spoke, his now noticeably intense eyes peering over the documents in his hand, the same eyes as the Psychic.

Behind his eyes, Tobias felt the tickle of a well-trained Psychic trying to probe his mind. She was good; he would have to resort to something more drastic. He locked his eyes on the Psychic's uniform and imagined it balled up on the floor, the only thing concealing her nakedness were her crossed legs and her slender delicate arms. He made the image so powerful and profound in his mind that it absorbed all his thoughts. The tickling stopped and Agni lowered her gaze to the floor, trying desperately to hide the burning of her ears.

"A very interesting tactic," Agni muttered through tight lips.

The Leash started to laugh.

"Guess he's got you figured out, Agni."

Tobias finally broke his silence.

"Agni of the Pyre, then, I assume? A unique name, easy to pick out. And I guess that makes you the Tornado Leash Rudra. Doesn't make sense that the famous Academy would send two of their elites on a negotiation mission when our primary purpose is to just drop off money, pick up what's left of our team, and leave. So it begs the question, why are two trained killers coming on a negotiation assignment?"

It took both Psychic and Leash a moment to recover. They weren't used to not being completely in control of a situation, and this Tobias character not only seemed to have them both figured out, he also seemed impervious to his own mortality. It was just a trick, as old as the most formidable martial art.

In the face of god, resolve to be the devil.

"How did they know all that stuff about us, Marshall?" asked a very frightened Stein, not fully realizing, as Tobias had, that the two individuals in front of them were responsible for more dead bodies than any team, or dozen teams for that matter, in all of TITAN could claim.

"They're from the Academy; they aren't just contractors. They're a level four team, two of the 14 most dangerous people on the planet. I'm getting the distinct impression this is no longer a negotiation assignment."

Hernandez held his weapon a little closer. "Well, if we're not going to negotiate, then what are we going for?"

Tobias began to take inventory of his weapons. His two .45 handguns were strapped in place on his thighs with two extra magazines hanging under them for each. On his belt holster seated, rather uncomfortably on his left hip, was his custom made .357 loaded with pressurized Argon hollow points. The special pressurization process kept the Argon liquid until the round collapsed, at which point it would rapidly expand; it had once put an end to a Leash even after the Leash had nearly liquefied his rib cage.

Tobias slid into his heavy vest and clipped it under his right arm. It held several additional magazines, flashlight, and various other tools in side pockets while his vitals were protected by sewn in synthetic, fiber plates. His most recent set of smart fiber clung to his skin under his clothes and vest. It was a prototype, but it had already proven its worth. Any impact to the skin and the fiber became rigid, it softened blows from hand to hand combat, and in case of a bullet or knife wound, it would cling to the skin and add as much as 40 kgs of pressure.

It had saved his life more than once and proven that the replacement set had been well worth the money. Compared to the Greenies, who stood in full black body armor with heavy plate carriers and full sleek black headgear on, his equipment probably seemed minimal. But both of them were just recruits for TITAN, and Tobias had been working for them for the last several years and was enjoying the full benefits of his promotions.

Access to experimental protection had landed him with his smart fiber as opposed to the heavy plate lined jackets and pants with the electric green TITAN logo across the shoulders that Hernandez and Stein had to wear. Even the handguns Tobias carried had synthesized pink dust in them as opposed to the old depleted nitro loads which doubled his firepower. So his handguns packed more punch than the two recruits TITAN standard issue 6.1k rifles.

"I imagine they were hired by TITAN to swing this mission into a more favorable position. What started as a trade now appears to be a tactical retrieval."

The Leash Rudra smiled, bemused. "Not quite. We are here in an advisory capacity only. Your money will still change hands. Our job is just to make sure that all goes well."

Stein perked up. "Well, that's great then, right? I mean with two super humans working with us, we don't have anything to worry about?"

Tobias leaned back against the cold metallic transport wall.

"Don't get too excited, Greeny. They aren't here to protect us, they are here to protect assets. Hiring these two probably exceeds the credits we brought with us to exchange for the hostages. So don't get it mixed up, they don't have your back."

Rudra smirked. "Everything will be fine. Our presence alone should make sure everything goes smoothly. So, no reason to worry." He was dishonest and manipulative. Tobias liked him immediately.

Conversation dissipated with the exception of Stein clumsily trying to understand the differences between the regions as they were and the old countries. Tobias felt only one additional tickle at his mind when he closed his eyes to shut out the light. This earned Agni an image of herself bathing and shaving her legs. She retreated inside her own mind and opted to stay out of others.

After more than three hours of driving they finally arrived at their destination, what looked like a two-story warehouse covered in the red dirt from the westernmost neutral district. The building had little on the outside of it except for a large bay door for vehicles to drive into and a smaller door to its side for personnel.

"Stein, Hernandez, perimeter." Tobias instructed, trying to keep his tone level and his orders succinct.

Hernandez and Stein made a quick scan around the vehicle, then exited. Utilizing their training, they scanned windows and ledges for snipers or traps. Good soldiers, bad mercenaries. Tobias walked out of the transport, suitcase full of credits in his hand, Agni and Rudra close behind. He made the decision to leave his firearms holstered. Guns always made negotiators nervous. He wanted everyone to be calm.

As they approached the building, Tobias noticed an extremely tall man in a gray suit exit the small door, ducking to avoid hitting his head. Even at a distance it was clear he was well built and from the way he deliberately shifted his weight and kept his knees bent, it looked plain to Tobias that he knew how to handle himself. Behind him, a half dozen armed guards filed out, their covered heads and thick body armor made it difficult to discern much about them other than they were heavily armed.

The suited man greeted them with a low bow, a broad smile, and a creamy Northwestern accent.

"Welcome, guests. We have been waiting," he turned and opened the door behind him.

The Greenies anxiously crossed the threshold, nervous eyes darting back and forth. Tobias walked past the giant, pausing only for a breath beside him trying to gauge his reach and balance, then he passed. They walked down a corridor, the framing of the walls was haphazard, and the lighting was terrible. To Tobias it looked like the setting for an old horror vid, that at any moment they would be stuffed into bags and executed on camera.

There were no doors or windows so there was no need for directions, when they reached the end of the hall there were two doors, one directly in front and one to the right. Stein reached for the door in front of him; it was locked and solid. Too heavy even to break down if the need should present itself. Tobias shifted his weight so he could feel his entry weapon press just a little harder against his hip bone, if this door needed to come down, he would be the one to make it fall.

The door to the right was much less sturdy like it had been installed later. It was flimsy, poorly placed plastic with some insulation. At a turn of the handle Stein opened the door and walked in, lowering his weapon at the sight of life.

Inside the room against the wall were four men in chairs blindfolded, two heavily armed guards, and one greasy-haired man with a crooked nose.

If Tobias could read minds like Agni, he would have known that his father gave it to him when he was 12, the first time he stepped out of line. His dad had broken his nose and fearing police action had tried to reset it himself, the result had been a permanent crook in it that he would have until the day he died, which unfortunately for him wasn't far off.

Tobias noticed another man in the corner of the room. His frame was thin with small round glasses on his face. He was wearing a clean pressed, button down shirt, slacks, and a suit vest. His hands were behind his back and his eyes took the whole room in lazily as if he was watching a movie he had seen a hundred times and knew all the lines to. His clothes fit closely enough that Tobias could tell he wasn't armed, and yet his complete lack of concern about how tense the situation felt was the single most unsettling thing Tobias had encountered all day. Agni and Rudra had entered silently with the exception of a small chuckle that Rudra had let slip.

"Thought this was a negotiation," spouted the greasy-haired man, eyeing Agni and Rudra closely.

Tobias signaled to the Greenies to put down their guns. "It is."

Tobias placed the suitcase on the table and stepped away, a cautious eye watching the two bodyguards.

Tobias suddenly felt the all too familiar tickle of a Psychic trying to intrude upon his mind. Like an itch between his eyes and nose that he couldn't quite get to. He mentally started disassembling and reassembling his gun until the tickle stopped and he heard a small noise from the well-dressed man with the glasses between a chuckle and a sigh.

So he's a Psychic, but not a good one. Tobias thought as he brushed away the last of the annoying tickle.

The greasy man produced a scanner and ran it over the box. "No explosives or tracers I see. Smart. Open it!"

Despite being annoyed by his tone, Tobias remained calm. He knew that a few nasty words were no reason to shoot someone in their annoyingly crooked nose.

"I said open it, stupid, before I start plugging these hostages and just take the money!"

Although Tobias was now considering making an exception.

Hernandez was getting antsy, and Tobias knew that this trade needed to happen quickly. Agni and Rudra were standing in the corner of the room watching everything that played out very closely. To Tobias's eye they appeared entirely too relaxed, especially considering that the giant in the gray suit was now standing in the doorway with his broad smile filling his substantial face.

"If you two don't mind, I'd like you to come with me, I'm afraid we may have an unpleasant conflict of interest in this particular matter." The giant spoke gently to Agni and Rudra.

"What makes you think we have any interests that would conflict with you?" Rudra replied smoothly.

"Why, you're both from the Academy, are you not? I was hired from the Academy as well. As an advisor, I suggest we step outside and discuss the matter." Agni looked surprised, Rudra looked amused. Nevertheless, both of them left the room, and despite the exit of the giant, the Psychic, and the Leash, the atmosphere in the room became noticeably more tense.

Stein shifted his weight onto his back foot and bent his knees slightly, a move that showed he was bracing for a fight. Tobias opened the case and counted out 100 bound stacks of credits, totaling 10 million credits. A quick scan showed that they were unmarked, and he slid the case across the table where it was collected by a yellow smile with shimmering, greasy hair.

"Thank you, and that concludes our business."

Stein moved across the room to the four hostages and began to untie the first one. Everything was going smoothly and quickly, just the way Tobias liked.

"Marshall!" Stein shouted.

Tobias looked over and saw that the first hostage had been untied and was now laying in a pile on the floor.

"Marshall, they're dead!"

Weapons blazed out of their holsters. Tobias had one of the guards leveled in his barrel. Stein and Hernandez, despite the close quarters, found themselves in tactically advantageous positions, their bodies creating a pincer shape around the greasy man and his crew. The only person who hadn't moved was the well-dressed man in the corner, his only motion to incline his chin up from staring at his shoes to watching all of the action unfold.

"Easy, easy, boys. They aren't dead, just drugged. We wanted to ensure that our exit was protected. Your men being drugged is just our insurance," the greasy man stated, his voice still confident, but his slick smile significantly less comfortable.

"Stein, check for a pulse," Tobias said curtly to his team member.

The Greenie made no move.

"STEIN!"

The boy blinked several times and reached up to the throat of the first hostage, bending his knees so he could keep his gun leveled at the bodyguards.

"Slow, but there's a pulse, Marshall."

Tobias crossed the room and without changing where his weapon was aimed, pressed his heel into one of the hostages feet. A soft groan escaped his lips and Tobias was satisfied.

"Stein, walk these guys out front." Tobias unholstered his remaining sidearm and leveled it at the second bodyguard.

He hated using two weapons at once, knowing full well his aim would be cut in half, but at this range it didn't matter. He also hoped the image of it would cause enough caution in the bodyguards that they wouldn't get antsy. And while it seemed to work on them, the well-dressed man made an amused "tsk" sound.

Stein cut the ties on the hostages and stood them gingerly up, taking off their blindfolds and watching them blink emptily into the artificial light of the room. Stein shuffled them one at a time out of the room while Tobias and Hernandez held the four men in their sights.

"See. I kept up my end of the deal, boys. Just a little insurance," came the nervous swallow of the greasy negotiator.

"Leave." Tobias growled through clenched teeth, his fingers reflexively increasing the pressure on his hair triggers up to the millimeter before they went off.

The greasy haired man hastily retreated from the room followed by the two body guards; the last to leave was the well-dressed man, who lazily pushed his glasses further up his nose as he examined a still tense Tobias. He finally cracked an almost friendly smile as he strolled out of the room.

Tobias couldn't help but notice his own slight involuntary tremble as he holstered one of his weapons, opting to keep the other one close at hand. He walked into the hallway and saw Stein trying desperately to keep the nearly catatonic men in a straight line and moving forward.

"Marshall, why did they go through all this trouble?" Hernandez asked, still holding his weapon in a ready position. "And who the hell was that guy in the suit vest?"

Tobias stepped around the group, the narrow hallways dim lighting and faux walls making him feel unusually claustrophobic. His mind was racing with questions.

This was too easy, why did they bring eight armed guards for a negotiation?

Who was the fourth man?

Why did the Psychic and Leash leave with that big man?

What the hell is going on?

Beep.

It was a faint sound, but it caused Tobias to stop where he was.

Beep.

"Marshall, did you hear that? That beep noise?"

Tobias had heard it, but his mind had been too distracted to notice the location. He quickly scanned the walls and the floor looking for wires, looking for cameras, looking for anything.

Beep

The recently rescued hostages' groaning was starting to increase in volume and pace.

"Will you guys shut the hell up and put all that energy into walking?" Stein muttered anxiously.

Tobias could sense something bad getting ready to happen. What had he missed? What had he overlooked? He marched forward several more paces taking up the point position. Hernandez was several steps behind him followed by the hostages and Stein bringing up the rear guard.

"Marshall, where is it coming from?" Hernandez blurted, letting the panic in his voice shimmer through his accent.

"Be quiet," Tobias snapped.

Beep.

The groaning was now so loud it was preventing Tobias from thinking properly.

"Will you shut up!" Stein approached one of the men and pushed him forward. "Hey man, you hear me? Shut ..."

The ensuing concussion filled the hallway with a deafening bang. Tobias was hurled across the hallway, slamming into the hastily constructed wall, leaving a sizable hole in it, then skittering across the ground. His ears ringing, he felt something running down his face. He wiped his eyes, and realized he was covered in blood and viscera.

Bombs. They put bombs inside of the hostages.

He managed to get his eyes clear enough to be able to look around the hall. The walls and ceiling were black with blood and burn marks. Tobias' ears rang and his vision came to him like an old movie reel.

Five dead from the initial blast. He even managed to recognize a piece of Stein's freckled cheek floating in a pool of blood. Hernandez was still alive, his face contorted into a silent scream as he stared at his own bleeding stump of a leg. Tobias stood painfully, pieces of people scattered about the room.

He suspected the only thing that had saved him was Hernandez's body being in between him and the blast. His vision was blurry as he approached Hernandez and dropped to his knees. His screaming had subsided into a curl of biting lips and tear-streaked face. Even through blurry vision, Tobias counted no less than five wounds that in their current state, and without immediate medical attention, would prove to be fatal, and Tobias was no doctor. While Hernandez began to convulse and go into shock Tobias felt his heavy limbs steady as he took careful aim and put an end to the Greenie's suffering. Why make the dead wait for death?

He glanced toward the exit, the door swinging loosely from the one hinge, the sunlight spilling in unimpeded and the hot breeze passing occasionally by his face. It may have been 15 meters away, but to Tobias it could have just as easily been 15 kilometers.

Too far.

So tired.

He wanted to close his eyes. Besides, it was getting dark outside.

He tried to focus his muddy vision on the door only to see that it had been blocked by a giant... a well-dressed giant at that. The giant who had been wearing the gray suit was in the doorway leaning heavily upon it. As Tobias's vision cleared, it appeared to him as though half of the giant's clothes and skin were burned away. Blood was splattered all over what remained of his clothes and the grip he had on the steel door frame was bending it and flexing it. Human hands couldn't do that.

"Idiot," Tobias felt the words in his mouth even if he couldn't hear them.

A Psychic at the negotiation and now a giant who'd been sent on business from the Academy. The giant began to lurch forward, first stepping, and then striding, and then sprinting, as Tobias tried to order his heavy limbs to draw his firearm and back away for a clearer shot.

A Leash?! Tobias's mind screamed all too late.

What felt like 500 kgs of force slammed him into the nearest wall behind which a support beam stood, he felt three ribs crack and one break, as his .45 skittered across the hall. His hands lashed out, striking fierce accurate blows into the giant's face, throat, and clavicle. Tobias groaned after the third punch landed, feeling two bones in his right hand break against the steely structure of the Leash's skull. The giant threw three sloppy but powerful punches. Tobias evaded but only just, forcing himself painfully into his stance, his feet at shoulder width, his left arm low and bent, elbow out, fingers open to deflect and grapple, his right hand in a loose fist curled over his left shoulder prepped for short, sharp strikes.

Tobias raised his back leg. Not straight up, but to the side so that when he leaned into the kick and lunged out, the force would be enough to tear most of the ligaments in the human leg. He made solid contact, although it felt like kicking rebar, and while the leg did not give way it was evident his opponent was not used to being staggered by someone half his size. The giant regained his footing but not fast enough. He swung his right hand in a shapeless haymaker, Tobias rotated his left forearm over catching the giant's wrist. Normally with the engagement of small muscles even the arm of a strong man would give way.

However, this wasn't a man, it was a Leash. The arm did not move, but it did give Tobias a superior fighting position. His crescent step flowed smoothly, sending his right fist flying directly into his enemy's ear. Tobias assumed that even a Leash would have trouble fighting with a ruptured eardrum. The contact did not cause the giant to fall, it only served to make Tobias's broken hand scream in pain and his fractured ribs protested every little movement, even his breath couldn't be caught through the shocks of pain.

The giant pivoted and arched his left fist toward Tobias' face. Tobias barely had enough time to cross his arms to block before the impact crashed into his forearms and sent him sprawling across the hall. He knew his right shoulder was dislocated and his forearm likely broken based on the searing pain shooting through it. He drew his second .45 with his left hand and fired 16 rounds at his enemy. The giant covered his face with his arms, the bullets slamming into them like so many angry hornets, collapsing against a superior force and then falling to the ground.

Tobias was out of bullets and had no time to reload. The giant approached rapidly, he would be on him in three more steps. Tobias reached into his belt.

Two steps away.

He drew his .357.

One step.

He brought the barrel up, level.

Half a step.

The giant's hand covered the barrel of the pistol as the first round erupted from its mouth. As the round collapsed, the pressurized gas expanded rapidly, blowing two fingers off the giant's hand. The second shot flew past the mangled fingers and into the giants' shoulder, the third into his throat. The remaining shots Tobias couldn't see because of the landmass of a man that now covered him. He knew; however, they had pierced the body. The feeling of fresh liquid blood flowing over his already blood soaked skin, was enough proof of that.

The giant's breathing had stopped, and his dead weight laid with crushing severity on top of Tobias. He had to weigh at least 200 kg which seemed impossible even as large as he was. His broken ribs screamed with each sipped breath, and his right arm was nearly worthless to bear the weight. Tobias tried to plant his legs, but the pain was too much to move under, and he feared that soon one of his broken ribs would pierce his lung and he would suffocate. His vision started to blur, and he felt his muscles fail as tunnel vision set in.

Again, huh? Well, I guess it can't be helped.

If it hadn't been so physically painful, Tobias might have laughed. Suddenly his dull senses recognized that the monster of a man was being lifted off him and that he was being lifted off the ground. The ground moved around him, small but strong hands lifted his body.

Agni and Rudra had been sitting in relative silence for the last hour on the uncomfortable transport seat. Rudra's entertainment had ended when the man named Tobias Marshall had gone back to sleep. His sister's nerves had been noticeably shaken by him.

He's more dangerous than he seems, sis. Rudra's voice spoke inside of Agni's head.

You don't think I noticed? Agni snapped back.

Still reeling from embarrassment that her brother had shared in the images that Tobias Marshall had put there of her nude body sitting comfortably in her seat.

Did you know he's killed two Psychics and a Leash? Three neutralized teams total? Rudra said matter of factly.

The Leash he killed was a Soldier Leash. Kadeem. Not the smartest Leash, but still loyal. Rudra closed the dossier folder. *We'll be arriving shortly. We should prepare. Our target will most likely greet us in a less than friendly manner.*

Agni glanced again at Tobias. When she had tried to dig into his mind she had hit a distortion of information that didn't seem to have a consciousness. But there was something else. Many people knew how to throw up mental barriers to protect their minds. Few could make theirs vanish completely.

They arrived at their destination and almost immediately after exiting their vehicle saw their target. He was hard to miss. He was enormous, he was head and shoulders taller than the six men who stood beside him. After Tobias and his crew had checked around the vehicle they approached the building. Agni passively touched her brother's wrist, her palms were hot to the touch. She was angry. The men they were hunting had abandoned their post for selfish gain. As a result, several teams of Mumblers died, most of them teenagers, or they had just undergone the Wash.

Breathe Agni, we need to be certain before we act. Otherwise we may end up killing the wrong people. Rudra's voice was soothing in her mind. He had always been her balm. Even in her worst moments, her brother's voice could shine through. They passed the doorway, went down a hallway, into a small cramped room where the hostages were being kept.

That's when they got their confirmation. Giuseppe Corelli, a greasy and dishonest man who came to the Academy late in life after being arrested several times for gambling fraud. He had been paired with a

Leash that, by all accounts, was believed to be honest and noble. But actions do so often speak louder than words. The only unexpected turn was the unidentified man in the corner.

He was well dressed and seemingly disinterested with everything that was happening. Agni reached out her mind, three of the men were doing their best to keep their minds clear. But little is hidden with a simple shield, especially from a Psychic who could kill every person in the room with one sharp exhale. But the well-dressed man felt like an open book. He didn't even glance up as Agni entered his mind. It was always an interesting feeling, trying to read the neural networks of another human being. Many people thought that focus, or a mental "shield" was the most effective weapon against telepathy, but it wasn't. Because people generally don't have the capacity to truly empty their minds and throwing up a mental wall only works against weak Psychics who are having to use all their concentration just to get past your initial barrier and your loudest thoughts. The most effective tool was distraction, polluting the waves with information creating so much static and noise that a Psychic couldn't concentrate. Second was picking one thought, one that was powerful and prevalent and making it take up every ounce of mental energy you had. Tobias Marshall had shown her this earlier and she had to push the thought from her mind so she could concentrate on the task at hand and hide the burning in her cheeks. She pressed into his open mind and it gave way, but after she breached the initial passageway into his mind something unusual happened, she felt like she was back at the beginning. His mind laid bare in front of her. She pushed again, and again felt the first breach of the man's mental wall. And again she found herself pressing against the same wall. Something was wrong. His mind was static, cold, there was nothing there and then the pain began. Small at first and then rapidly growing like white hot pin being pushed into her temple. She withdrew her inquiry, eyes fluttering back to focus, pushing away the pain that still throbbed behind her eyes and looking up. The well-dressed man glanced up from his shoes with a hint of bemusement crossing his lips.

What the hell? She had to bite the words back to keep them from spilling from her lips. She reached out to Rudra to ask him if he had felt it, too, when they were interrupted.

"If you two don't mind," The Leash had arrived to escort them into an ambush. They were more than prepared.

Rudra and Agni had played their parts well, and everything had gone according to plan. Their target was right in front of them leading them away from their cover.

This one is clearly the target, the deserter. Think he'll put up much of a fight? Agni felt her brother's mind speak to her.

A level two Leash and a Tickler who didn't even recognize us? I highly doubt it. He either thinks he's managed to fly under the radar or suspects with the other six guards that he can get the jump on us. Either way it shouldn't take long. Agni's response was full of forced control.

She was making a point to control her breathing. If she allowed the flow of adrenaline she was currently feeling rush through her body, to increase her breath rate, she may accidently start a fire too soon. She was still shaken by her encounter with the well-dressed man, what kind of Psychic defense was that? That could eliminate the flow of thought completely and respond defensively? It would have to wait, there were deserters that needed to be killed.

When they approached the front door of the facility the large man held the door open as they both walked blinking into the light. When they cleared the side of the building they found themselves cut off by the six guards who had been stationed there, patiently waiting to perform the task they had all been instructed to perform. At a glance Rudra saw four additional gunmen stationed on the rooftop.

Surrounded, came Agni's concerned thought.

By bugs, was her brother's bloodthirsty response.

"I'm afraid this is where both of you stop," came the giant's creamy voice.

"Oh? I thought we had business to discuss," Rudra retorted snidely, all pretense abandoned.

The men surrounding them had created a semi-circle formation so that no matter which way the two would move they would be mowed down without threat of friendly fire.

"We know how fast you are Rudra, which is why we've been instructed to only fire at your sister. The Psychic dies, the Leash dies. And if she so much as yawns, we'll kill her."

The giant's smooth accent wavered as he attempted to assert his authority over two people he had watched slaughter whole battalions without ever raising an alarm. But that was when they had the element of surprise. Now he was in control.

"So, if we fight you, we die? But if we don't fight you we die? Doesn't sound like much of a reason not to fight, does it?" Rudra chided. "But if we must die, may I ask you a question first? We were sent to find someone. A deserter and his pet Leash. They stole a bunch of credits and left a bunch of Mumblers and Leashes for dead. Bunch of them were babies. Real lowlifes these two. We're trying to find them to discuss with them our deep dissatisfaction with their choices and…"

"SHUT YOUR MOUTH!" The giant yelled, falling prey to Rudra's manipulation. "The Academy sent us into an ambush. There was no way we could have survived. It was a death trap. So, we save our lives and they call us deserters and send you two MONSTERS after us to finish us off! Does that sound fair?!"

Rudra bent his knees and smiled while Agni finished her long slow inhale.

"I don't deal in fair my friend, now speak to your gods, if you have any," Rudra remarked confidently.

Then there was an earth shattering concussion, the force of which shook the ground hard enough that the six guards stumbled from their positions and the giant's head snapped back to the doorway he had just exited.

"What?! We were told not to blow the bombs until…"

Thwack.

The giant turned around just in time to see two of the six men split like soft wet cardboard that had been hit with a baseball bat. Rudra's hands still vibrated as they breached the other sides of their bodies. Their dark red blood splashed onto the red sand. Then just a glimpse of his blurry figure as he raced away, only to reappear a moment later on top of the building, cleaving his way through the sharpshooters who had barely perceived his blurry form exit the foreground before feeling their own bodies ripped apart as Rudra raced passed them.

"You can't afford to look away," the giant heard, but he looked back just in time to see Agni's wall of flame as it roared over his body.

The greasy man was face down in front of the exit vehicle, screaming and convulsing. The feeling of having half of his mind ripped from his skull was unbearable. It felt like experiencing birth while living, having all of his faculties being created instantly while simultaneously being destroyed, and knowing he possessed the power of speech and movement, but when he made an effort to command his body, it resulted in nothing more than infantile wailing.

"I am pain!" he shrieked like a child, tears and spit pooling under his face while his two horrified guards watched helplessly.

"Mind death is always so interesting to watch," the well dressed man spoke to the sniveling pile in front of him. "They must have killed that Leash of yours."

He wiped away a stray wisp of dust that had landed on his crisp white shirt sleeve. "The matter of my payment." Concise and to the point.

"I am...pain."

"Yes, so you mentioned, but my pay?" The Specialist listened for a few more moments to the whimpering and screaming before turning his attention to the still dumbfounded bodyguards. "Would one of you please reach into his pocket and retrieve my payment? If memory serves, it's in his front left pocket. Small silk pouch."

They both stood speechless, swaying forward then back, unsure of how to assist their leader. "Gentlemen, with haste please, I have other appointments."

One of the guards, regaining his senses, leaned down and shuffled through the pockets of his twitching, incapacitated leader. Pulling a small silk pouch out of his pocket and tossing it to the Specialist. He caught it with annoyance; he so disliked inelegant gestures. He opened the pouch and counted out 15 uncut rubies. He liked gems, they were beautiful, simple, and elegant.

"This will cover the protection you asked for, and the explosives that were utilized." He slipped the pouch into his pocket. He straightened his vest and approached the exit vehicle, removing the suitcase full of credits from the exchange out of the vehicle, retrieving a claymore mine out of one of the gear bags.

"Gentlemen," he began as he staked the claymore in the ground facing the two guards and the greasy man, all of them focused on each other and not on the well-dressed gentlemen who was arming the device to kill all of them. "I wish I could say it's been a pleasure, and keeping with tradition, my name is ..."

"I AM PAIN!"

The well-dressed man scoffed. "It's rude to interrupt."

He began to walk away. One of the two guards glanced and saw the mine planted on the ground, but a moment of hesitation was all that was required. The mine erupted in a conical shape shredding the two guards and the greasy haired man. Pieces of people scattered about the ground. Bodily fluids painted the sand like red and black rubies that were already soaking into the unforgiving terrain.

"Tsk, always so interested in the immediate that they ignore what's around them." He left the three corpses on the side of the road as he drove away.

Sending his short digital transmission: *Assignments complete, your credits have been recovered.*

CHAPTER 1.2

The Prerequisites of a Leash

"The first prerequisite for a Leash is a sensitivity to Psychic energy. In most humans this is dormant, only awakened by a near-death experience that forces latent Psychic energy to become active. The more traumatic the experience, the greater the sensitivity to Psychic energy."

Tobias groaned at the intense, throbbing pain in his right hand. Although a small note of comfort went through him that the wind in his lungs had been available for the groan. He looked up at the figure in front of him, his matted wet hair and the blazing noonday sun blocking his vision. His fever made focus of any kind almost impossible, and his mangled wrist wouldn't form the fist he commanded.

"You survived."

Not a question, more like commenting about something out of the ordinary but nothing that merited true curiosity. Its owner's voice was like granite - smooth, hard and full of substance.

"Help me...please." Tobias whimpered, his small frail voice sticking in his throat. He tried to reach out to the specter with his unbroken left hand, cracked and bloody fingernails grasping at the figure.

"Make it into the house and you will have dinner and a place to sleep. Otherwise be sure to die somewhere out of the way so I don't have to work around you."

The figure turned and walked briskly away, their smooth retreat almost hypnotic, long black and gray hair swinging lazily in the noonday sun.

Tobias had to control himself as the murky haze of the dream faded, he felt every muscle in his body tense at once and he tried to rise on reflex before forcing the calm back into his nerve endings. Despite the desire to open his eyes and observe his surroundings, he didn't want anyone knowing he was awake just yet.

Where am I? His first thought came quickly, but he dismissed it. *No, how am I alive?*

I killed the Leash.

I was dying, then floating.

Was I lifted?

One at a time he flexed the different muscles in his body gingerly. His shoulder had been reset and the arm, while sore, responded to his commands without difficulty. The ribs he assessed next with more anxiety, afraid that a sharp pain might cause him to gasp. But despite feeling the intense bruising, his breath came easily and without sudden shock. The twitch of the fingers in his left hand let him feel the I.V in his wrist and the slightest spasm of his pectoral muscles let him feel the monitor on his chest.

Still fearing making his conscious state known, he tried to listen instead of relying on his eyes. He heard the whir of machinery, the hissing of pressurized locks and the beeping of at least three monitors near his head. Everything smelled sterile and dry.

Hospital.

At least he hoped. He laid in silence for several more minutes until the pressurized hiss of a door opening got his attention.

"Sir, you can't be in here," an urgent but professional female voice commanded.

"This bastard belongs to TITAN and is responsible for millions of missing credits and several of our soldiers' lives. He will be coming with me now," a gruff and angry male voice responded.

Tobias flexed and released all his muscle categories in succession, preparing himself.

"We've already told you that within the confines of this Academy no authority exists but our own, and you should know better than to test this with us." Tobias recognized that voice. Smooth and smiling.

"I don't give a damn about your supposed authority, this man is property of TITAN and he's coming back with ..."

It was at that moment Tobias felt a hand around his left wrist just above the I.V. and his well-trained reflexes took over. He broke the grip with a simple twist and pinioned the off-balance hand under his forearm while reaching his right hand across the bed and removing the I.V. needle from his left arm and pressing it against the man's carotid artery.

"I'm not going anywhere, with anyone."

With his eyes adjusting to the lights, Tobias started to make out the three figures in the room. The man whose arm he had pinned was a battle captain for TITAN named Blaine. He was tall and thin, his skin yellowed from a 20 year drinking problem that often left him malnourished. He had been promoted through the ranks based on his connections with the Upper Captains and some small combat success, but was unable to promote further due to his complete lack of actual leadership ability. Career officer if ever there was one.

The voice he had thought was female was in fact a man. Slight, thin, and panicked looking with long shaggy brown hair and a gentle face that hid his extensive battlefield experience. His eyes were saucer wide at the exchange between the two men. The third, familiar voice was Rudra, the Tornado Leash. He was leaning lazily on the door to the room and smirking absently.

"Listen Captain, I'm going to save you the bloodshed. The Academy is immune from the jurisdiction of the regions and their governments. So it doesn't matter how much you've been paid to be here, if you attempt to enforce outside rules within these walls it will result in your ejection or death. There is an army of Leashes and Psychics roaming these hallways and, if nothing else, the man you're so eager to arrest seems fairly opposed to being arrested. So why don't you leave. If it means that much to you to have him back, you can always make a formal request to the Academy. But as of now Mr. Marshall is under our protection and as far as the rest of the world knows, is already dead."

Blaine began to speak but Tobias applied additional pressure to his throat until a trickle of blood broke the skin and Blaine forced his muscles to relax. Tobias loosened his grip slowly, and the Battle Captain backed away reaching in his pocket for a silk handkerchief to clean his still bleeding neck.

"You will be hearing from us soon," he muttered with a failed tone of authority.

"Can't wait. Love fan mail around here," retorted the ever-steely Rudra. His bright eyes smiled defiantly.

As the Battle Captain quickly exited the room Tobias nearly collapsed as the slight brown-haired man approached him and began the process of cleaning his wrist and replacing the I.V. Normally Tobias would have protested, but he was entirely too weak. Add to that the exertion of trying to make himself a threat, and he had nearly collapsed from the strain.

"You certainly know how to make an impression," Rudra mocked.

"Look at all this blood, I'll have to change your bandages. We had the situation under control there was no need for you to yank out your I.V.," the brown-haired man continued to grumble as he went about his work of replacing the line.

"How long have I been out for?" Tobias asked, allowing himself to close his eyes. If these people wanted him dead, he'd be dead already.

The man working on his arm responded.

"10 days. You were in bad shape when they brought you in. Four broken ribs, your whole right arm was a mess, torn ACL in your right leg, extensive burns on your hands and face, and your left eardrum was ruptured."

Tobias reflexively made a fist and bent his knee slightly. "How am I still alive?"

Rudra walked further into the room and stood over Tobias, his charming smile taking the edge off the horrendous statement he was about to make.

"You aren't. At least not completely. You died on the table, but Luke here was able to bring you back to us. He's quite the surgeon. I'm still a little stunned that you went toe to toe with a level two Leash and survived the encounter. Not many can make that boast."

Tobias felt an intense itch and burning in his left hand and glanced over. The young man, Luke, was massaging the skin around the I.V. puncture and as he did so the skin became red and inflamed, but the wound itself that Tobias had ripped open by pulling out the I.V. was closing rapidly. When the tear had closed the inflammation dissipated and faded away until all that was left was pink skin.

"You can heal people?"

"I can encourage human cells to multiply or decay faster. But it's usually dependent on the body itself, how healthy it is. I didn't think

I was going to be able to help you at first. Thought you might be too far gone," responded Luke while he expertly redressed the I.V. and checked the rest of the machines. "And you should really try to lie still for a while longer. You're not ready for any kind of movement for the next few da-"

Tobias was sitting up as he spoke. Slowly, painfully.

"Where's my gear?" Tobias was now regaining most of his mental faculties.

"Maybe you should focus on trying to get better before you worry about your..."

"Where are my guns?"

Rudra opened a small medical cabinet. Inside hung Tobias's gun belt. His two .45s, his .357, his vest and his smart fiber, all there in a row. All traces of blood and violence had been cleaned from them.

"All of your equipment that could be salvaged is here. Anytime you want it. But for now, I suggest you do what Luke says and get some rest. No one will disturb you for the next several hours, and it's not like you can leave anyway. There's a half dozen TITAN vehicles sitting outside waiting on you the minute you walk out the door."

Tobias shook his head. "I don't understand..."

"Evidently the whole thing was your fault. Your men dying, the money going missing. All of it."

Tobias pressed his right hand to his face covering his own eyes. He was incredibly aware of every space his tired, weakened digits touched.

"The Leash I killed. He was the mission, wasn't he? We weren't there to collect our people, we were there to get the Leash."

"To an extent. The Academy had an issue it needed to sort out. TI-TAN was a convenient scapegoat for us to use to acquire the assets we need. So, we included ourselves in a contract capacity. And the mission could have been a failure had it not been for you finishing the job for us. Had the Psychic or the Leash escaped it would have been a problem. You did our job for us. So, as a thank you we brought you back here and patched you up." Rudra spoke, his nonchalance would have been frustrating had Tobias had the energy to care.

"So why did everything go to hell in the middle?" Tobias asked wearily.

"There was an unforeseen element there. Someone contracted a third party to guarantee the job got done. We couldn't trace exactly who, but whoever it was, they were brought in to make sure none of you made it out alive."

"That greasy haired guy? He planned all of this?" Tobias asked more than a little skeptical but entirely too exhausted to be able to feign real interest.

"No, that was the Psychic we were sent to eliminate. His name was Giuseppe Corelli, his Leash's name was Havi. They had been sent on an assignment in the Southern sector. They weren't paying attention and walked into an ambush. Must have been a good-sized group based on the amount of gunfire and explosions that were there, but either way Corelli and Havi were put in charge of their squad and when the fighting broke out they ran."

"So you hunted them down for saving themselves?"

"No, we hunted them down for not completing their assignment," came Rudra's cool retort.

Tobias wasn't interested in hearing anymore. He was tired, and his body ached. He just wanted to go back to sleep.

The mural spread out on the ground had been a long time coming. The kids had been working every day on it. The thing was massive, three and a half meters in every direction. And every age group had contributed.

Alyssia smiled at the children as they were putting the finishing touches onto it. It was a portrait of Mr. Gregory. His broad dark face and warm welcoming smile painted with his two enormous hands outstretched in a welcoming gesture and behind him the silhouette of the Academy. All the children had wanted to get him a gift for his upcoming birthday ceremony, and they had decided on an interclass mural and some songs they had practiced.

Alyssia had come up with the best way to complete the mural. Separate the children into their assigned age groups and then grid off the mural, assigning each age group a block. It had all really come together quite nicely and had given the children a break from their usual studies. She watched them with a contented smile for a few moments until her concentration was broken by a familiar voice and smell.

"Your idea was perfect, Alyssia. I think Gregory will love this gift. He always likes it when the children do things together."

It was Agni. Alyssia would have known her even without her voice. She always made the air taste like heat and spices. Alyssia would have been embarrassed to tell Agni that she could taste her when she was close by. They had grown close the last three years, and it always brought Alyssia a great deal of pleasure to hear praise from her role model.

"Thank you. But the kids did all the work, and Xiphos and Ms. Teresa were the ones who came up with the songs for the kids to sing."

"Xiphos? I didn't know he could sing," Agni chirped with a smile. "I'd pay a month's wages to hear that!"

"No, you wouldn't." Alyssia muttered under her breath. Agni heard and laughed.

"Did I hear my name?" The rich earthy voice of the Sword Leash, Xiphos, came up from behind them.

He was tall, strikingly so. His outfit was close fitting, barely containing his well-formed and sculpted body, and his blue, black and gold Academy uniform was adorned with his rank bars. His hair was dark brown, cut short and plain but it was perfect for highlighting his dreamy blue eyes. Most of the women at the Academy had to do a double take when he walked by. Alyssia thought he tasted like earth, hearty and rich.

"Alyssia was just telling me what a fantastic singer you are," Agni said, her voice full of mischief.

"Then Alyssia lied to you, I can't sing at all. I can play the piano, though. Fairly well or so I'm told. But I'm not here to play. Dr. Luke said he needs to see Alyssia in the medical bay. Something about that mercenary that you and your brother brought in."

"Dr. Luke needs me?" Alyssia wasn't used to being called away from the education wing. She had shown an affinity for students; she was able to teach them and understand their needs. Despite most of the adults in the Academy being afraid of her, the students at the Academy had taken to her immediately. "And what mercenary?"

Agni's face was intense and serious. "Is he sure? That man is very dangerous, he killed a level two Leash in one-on-one combat, and his tags suggest he's killed a level three Leash before as well."

Xiphos shrugged one shoulder, an incredibly masculine gesture and even Agni allowed her eyes to divert from his handsome face for a moment to admire the way his muscles flexed under his uniform before returning them to his steely blue eyes.

"He also tried to kill that officer from TITAN this morning with an I.V. needle." Xiphos said, with a hint of amusement in his voice. He admired creative combat tactics. "But he hasn't shown himself to be a threat to the Academy. Anyway, I'm just the messenger. I've got to get back before Aspis sends out a search party. We've got an assignment up north. Some dignitary is paying top dollar for protection, so she and I gotta go baby-sit. Should be back in three or four days."

"Be careful, Xiphos." Agni spoke softly.

Xiphos and Aspis were never called away to "baby-sit". Whoever they were guarding must be either doing something incredibly dangerous or incredibly reckless. Either way, if the Sword Leash and the Shield Psychic were being sent, it would be no picnic.

Xiphos gestured absently as he walked away, his broad shoulders the crowning plateau of his perfect form. "Always, Krisha."

Agni watched him walk away until Alyssia cut into her daydreams.

"You know if anyone else called you by your first name, you'd rip their tongue out. Although when the tongue is attached to that face..." Alyssia left the end of the statement hanging in the air.

Agni the pyrokinetic, who could hold fire in the palm of her hands, who had incinerated entire towns, who had roasted battalions of men alive and never felt the sting of the flame, had to fight the impulse to bring her own hands to her ears to stop the burning. "Nobody asked you for your opinion. And besides, I just like to watch him walk, don't pretend you weren't looking," Agni spat, flustered.

"You know I can read your mind, right?" Agni suddenly noticed the tickle between her eyes and had to start trying desperately to think about anything other than her arms around his perfect shoulders and a deep, earthy voice whispering "Krisha".

In the medical bay Tobias was sitting on the edge of the bed, his shirt off while the young man he now knew as Luke was examining him.

"Heart rate: 45 bpm. Blood pressure normal. No fluid in the lungs, and there doesn't seem to be any infection in your hand or arms. All good news so far," the doctor said as he crossed the room to record the information on his chart.

"You sound disappointed, Doc," Tobias said as he stood slowly and began to get dressed.

"You should be dead, Mr. Marshall. You were dead. I can reset and mend bones. I can close wounds and have them heal. I can even reverse the growth of cancer. But I can't unstop a heart. I can't wake a brain up that's been shut off. You being alive is a medical miracle and that's coming from someone who has reattached limbs with his bare hands."

Tobias cracked a half smile, remembering his mentor.

"Should be dead, huh? Well, it's not the first time."

The door to the medical bay opened with a hiss. A young girl with waist length, platinum blonde hair on a narrow boyish frame walked into the room. She looked so incredibly out of place. All the other women, even the girls he had seen roaming the hallways, all had their hair pulled back into ponytails or tight buns, but hers flowed free.

She was dressed in a uniform similar to the ones he had seen many members of the Academy in, but her uniform was less tidy, like she had gotten ready in the dark without much attention to detail. She glanced at Tobias, and he felt a tickle start in his sinus, he began mentally listing the arteries in the human body in order of which ones were the easiest to rupture without a weapon.

The girl's face went rigid for a second, then relaxed. Tobias no longer felt the tickle behind his eyes. "You wanted to see me Dr. Luke?"

Luke didn't look up from his paperwork, but he did touch the bridge of his nose thoughtfully. "Yes, Alyssia. I need your help with something. Do you mind?"

"Well, you haven't really told me what you need yet Dr. L-"

Luke cut her off. "Oh! Right, sorry. Lost in thought. Come with me, please."

The doctor and the girl walked into the space behind the privacy curtain with Tobias.

"Alyssia, this is Tobias Marshall, a former mercenary that worked for TITAN. Tobias, this is Alyssia, a gifted young Psychic and one of the Academy's teaching assistants."

Alyssia attempted a friendly smile while Tobias stared stone-faced at the girl. "What is this about, Doc?" Tobias asked.

"How much do you know about Psychic energy, Mr. Marshall?" The doctor responded in a rapid-fire matter of fact manner.

"What?"

"Psychic energy. I'll just get to the point. All humans possess a level of Psychic energy inside them. Usually it's evenly distributed throughout the body. Blood, bone, muscle tissue all have minute, trace amounts of Psychic energy. It remains latent in most people their entire lives but-"

"But some people are born with a sensitivity to it," Tobias cut him off, having little patience for long winded explanations. "Which causes their dormant Psychic energy to become active. We call those people Psychics."

Luke continued on, clearly annoyed that he'd been interrupted and his flow of thought severed.

"Yes, but there is more to it than that. When a human being is in a life or death situation, and I mean REALLY life or death situation, their bodies will concentrate that energy to try and keep your vital organs and such alive. Now usually when a situation that traumatic or dangerous occurs it will kill the person who is encountering it. But during those rare instances it doesn't, the human body uses a portion of its latent Psychic energy while also developing a sensitivity to it."

Tobias cocked an eyebrow incredulously. "What are you getting at?"

"When this void occurs, the human body becomes more receptive to Psychic energy. Have you ever wondered why you found it so easy to tell when someone was trying to read your mind? It's because you have a sensitivity. Almost like an illness that most people have an immunity to, but when a person must expend their Psychic energy their immunity, so to speak, is weakened. Although in this case the side effect is that it generally makes you stronger. The catch is that when someone reaches this point of sensitivity, they are usually dead."

"You're beating around the bush, Doc." Now it was Tobias' turn to sound annoyed.

"Almost done. Your body reacts differently to Psychic energy than any other person I've ever met in my life. So, I was wondering if you would allow me to conduct one more, tiny test. It won't hurt, and it won't take up much of your time."

"What is it?" Tobias asked, officially annoyed with the hyperactive doctor.

"I want to test your Psychic sensitivity. I want to see how much latent Psychic energy you have. That's why I've asked Alyssia here to join us. She has a unique ability to sniff these things out."

"You want me to let some kid invade my mind?" Tobias didn't make the edge on his voice a mystery. Alyssia winced at his sudden outburst of aggression.

"No nothing like that, just do a quick once over. You've already shown a prowess for stopping mental invasion anyway. So if she starts trying to read your mind, just boot her out."

"No." Tobias's answer was flat and hard.

"But if you would just think about-"

"I said, no." Tobias squared his shoulders and allowed the menace to seep into his voice.

Alyssia was progressively getting more uncomfortable as the tension in the room rose. She wasn't used to adults fighting. And this man, Tobias, made the air taste like salt and acid.

Dr. Luke sighed. "Alright, I'd prefer not to play this card, but you're going to make me, I see. If you don't agree and comply, I will instruct Academy security to remove you. They will turn you over to TITAN and you likely won't survive the trip to prison. It's your choice, Mr. Marshall. Five minutes of your time or head out the front gates. Your call."

Alyssia didn't know how to react to Dr. Luke making threats. He was a smart and kind man. He had always seemed to her to be fragile and over-excitable. This was definitely a different side of him.

Tobias stared hard at the doctor, then at Alyssia, then back to the doctor.

"Whatever, let's get it over with." He muttered.

"Wonderful! Now just relax," Dr. Luke instructed. "Alyssia, here is what I need you to do. I need you to delve into Mr. Marshall and tell me what you sense as far as quantity of Psychic energy. Can you do that for me?"

Alyssia was hesitant. This sounded too much like attempting a merge. What if she killed this man? He wasn't particularly nice, but if he died, she'd always remember his angry face and his calloused looking hands. The same way she still remembered stunning green eyes and long red hair...

"Alyssia, please begin," the doctor interrupted her thoughts, not allowing her the chance to voice her concern. "And remember, this is just an examination." Dr. Luke directed his attention to Tobias. "Mr. Marshall, try and relax."

As the doctor stood back to watch, Alyssia took a step forward and closed her eyes. "This shouldn't hurt, but I will need you to open up to me just a little bit," she said, addressing Tobias for the first time.

Alyssia reached out with her mind expecting a steel wall of mental resistance, but when she felt her consciousness touch his mind it was instead a shadow. It evaded her touch, the mercenary's subconscious mind dancing around her inquiries and slipping out of her field of vision. Alyssia opened her eyes and met Tobias's intimidating gaze.

"Having trouble?" His voice sounded suddenly dangerous.

"I...I can't seem to find you."

Tobias exhaled sharply through his nose. "Try again,"

Alyssia obeyed, and she found it again. His elusive psyche, it felt like a wild animal. She knew it was dangerous, but not like fire. Not ferocious. It was dangerous because it didn't growl, it didn't snarl, and it didn't look like a threat.

She reached out to the shadow and it held its ground and opened to her. She immediately felt like she was drowning in an ocean of thick, putrid fluid. Her eyes snapped open, and she began to convulse and cough. She sat up, eyes watering.

"Dr. Luke, I don't think I can do this," she whispered through a strained voice.

The doctor spoke, his voice soft but insistent. "Try to sync."

Alyssia had heard the words but couldn't believe them. "You want me to sync?"

Luke nodded. "Just for a moment. Just to pull the consciousness into you."

Tobias looked annoyed and angry. "This experiment isn't working, Doc."

"One more try. Please, Mr. Marshall."

Tobias resigned himself with an irritated sigh.

Alyssia paused for a moment. The mental cage she kept her Psychic power in was deep and strong. She was always afraid of it, always scared she was going to hurt someone and now she was being asked to let this monster out of its cage.

Just a little. She heard the small, hungry voice in her own mind whisper.

She opened the mental prison she had locked her abilities in. It rushed out, chasing a rabbit down a dark hole and dragging her with it. Back into Tobias's mind where she saw the elusive creature again, the shadow waiting for her quietly. Now it looked more like a threat than anything. She reached for it and it pulled her in. The voice of her hunger speaking clearly and softly.

Feed.

She stepped into his mind. It felt murky, heavy, like walking in mud. She stretched her mind out, looking for the heat that most people gave off, that life energy that they possessed, but there was nothing. Just cold and black and empty. She was beginning to panic when the small voice at the back of her mind whispered.

Feed.

She knew the sensation. The energy sync remembered that need. The feeling of wanting to pull and consume.

But maybe... she thought.

Alyssia expanded her presence and began to pull gently, using her power to hunt down this man's inner fire, the Psychic energy that dwells in everyone. She pulled tentatively, and more and more it felt as if a weight was on her chest. She pulled again, and her throat became dry and filled with ice. The voice at the back of her mind began to surge forward.

Feed!

She felt tendrils of energy swell in her limbs as she dove into the furthest parts of his consciousness. Her mind reached into the shadows of his subconscious. Her muscles stretched and strained; she could feel physical exhaustion taking over her body as she became weak and felt empty. The voice that lived in her hungry mind, that she so often attempted to lock away and keep hidden, was shrieking at the top of her sanity.

FEED!

She opened the floodgates of her own substantial Psychic energy and reached into the emptiness for any trace of life. The murky liquid she had been swimming in was now around her shoulders, and she felt the air being forced from her lungs.

Suddenly, she was gripped by the throat. A hand, made of ice-cold and bone thin digits clasped around her neck. In the blackness in front of her, she saw an orb of dull light. Flat and pale and graven, a pale face of a child. Starving and hungry, his icy fingers squeezing her throat as he pulled her close to him. His eyes were black and empty, and his mouth was an inch from hers. She opened her mouth to scream as the child opened his mouth and pulled her into it, engulfing her entire being.

As the empty black crashed away, Alyssia was painfully aware of a hand around her throat. As her vision cleared, she realized her feet were off the ground and ferocious eyes looked up at her. His hands were inhumanly strong, holding her aloft, choking the life from her thin body.

Luke rushed forward and grabbed Tobias by his forearm; instantly the skin underneath his fingertips aged decades. Tobias released his grip and backed away. Luke stood between the two of them, poised to fight. The bay door hissed and an athletically built woman rushed in, slamming Tobias into the wall with her forearm, choking him efficiently and painfully.

"It's fine Catha, let him go." Dr. Luke instructed her.

The strong woman hesitantly backed away from Tobias, releasing him to the floor but maintaining her position between Luke and the former TITAN mercenary.

Tobias rose to his feet, choking.

"What kind of game are you playing, huh?! You ask me to sit still for an experiment then you try to kill me?!" Tobias spit his words through gritted teeth.

Luke spoke up, his voice full of anxiety and fear. "I'm sorry. It was my fault. I told her to do it. It won't happen again. Please calm down. Please," Luke stepped in front of the woman named Catha. "I'm sorry, but I had to know. Alyssia, what did you feel?"

Alyssia, who had been pressed against the wall in a terrified heap, was still trying to catch her breath through sobs when she finally found the words to speak. "...Nothing. It's like he's completely empty inside."

"That's what I suspected, but I've never heard of it before," said Luke, his fear giving way to tentative curiosity.

"What?!" Tobias tried to hide the rage in his voice, but it slipped through.

"You're devoid. Your body has experienced so much trauma that it has emptied itself of Psychic energy," said Luke, more fascinated now than frightened.

"What do you mean? I thought you said human beings can't survive without Psychic energy?" Tobias responded, now painfully aware of the fatigue in his muscles.

Luke touched the bridge of his nose and adjusted his glasses. "They can't."

Tobias turned his gaze to the blonde girl currently piled in a heap as far away from him as possible. He wanted to speak. He felt like he should apologize. But it was her fault. She had reached; it wasn't his fault she had found what she was looking for.

"Alyssia, breathe?" The odd and confused question came from the woman named Catha.

Alyssia nodded. "Yes, Catha, sorry to have worried you."

Catha nodded and turned her attention to Tobias. He braced himself for a fight. She was tall, over 6 feet and well built, with deep lines by her eyes and mouth. Her silver white hair was pulled back into a tight bun. If Tobias had to guess, he would have said she was in her 60's but her build and ferocious green eyes made her look deceptively younger. Her face was square and hard, and the Academy uniform she wore was form fitting and perfectly pressed. Tobias knew a soldier when he saw one. "You, calm?" she asked. Same confused voice, same unusual cadence.

"Yes, my love, he's calm," came Luke's still-shaky reply. She turned her attention to the doctor as her form relaxed. She looked at him for a long moment, then nodded and exited the room with all the practiced precision of a battle-hardened veteran.

"Catha is my Leash, and an exceptional one at that. Sorry if she hurt you," the doctor explained.

Tobias stood up. His muscles now wearing the full fatigue of his still-healing injuries. He leaned against the wall and held up his arm, the one Luke had grabbed and forced to decay. It looked wrong. Liver spots, flesh hanging loosely off bone, and the muscle weak and fragile. He touched his fingertips to his thumb and noticed that the sensation had dulled like he was feeling his own touch from far away.

"Sorry about that, I can fix it right up." Luke approached Tobias and put his hands on his ancient arm and almost instantly the skin began to lighten and plump. The thin dermis thickened and became more elastic, and the muscle began to swell back to its former strength. It itched and burned, but Tobias didn't protest, happy to have his body back to the way it was before.

"I am sorry, Mr. Marshall. I should have told you what my intention with the experiment was." The doctor sighed deeply. "I had intended for Alyssia to show you around the Academy, since you will be spending some time with us. But after all that just happened I think–"

"I don't mind, Dr. Luke," Alyssia cut in.

Tobias snapped his gaze at the young Psychic, perplexed at her quick response.

"Sorry. I didn't mean to interrupt you, but what happened was an accident and I'd like to try and make amends for it." She turned to look Tobias in the eye. "That is, if you don't mind, Mr. Marshall."

The statement had come as a surprise to both men. Only moments before Tobias had this girl off the ground by her throat and, in all likelihood, would have killed her. And now she wanted to give him the tour? Luke was equally surprised because he knew Alyssia was shy around new people. It had only been in the last year or so that he had occasionally gotten her to call him Dr. Luke instead of just Doctor.

Alyssia had her own motive for wanting to spend time with the mercenary. The taste of his energy, or lack thereof, in the air was still acrid and bitter. But when she had delved into his mind and had opened herself to find nothing, it made her feel something that she hadn't felt since she arrived at the Academy: fear.

Not since taking her first life and feeling the ravenous animal that lived inside her breathe its first words to her had she been afraid. She had felt concern, regret certainly, happiness, and even anxiety, but not fear. Her stomach was still queasy from the encounter and something in her mind told her she needed to understand its source.

"Mr. Marshall?" She was still waiting for him to agree, noting his hesitation.

"It's Tobias, kid."

CHAPTER 1.3

Measuring Compatibility

"The Leash and the Psychic must have personalities that are compatible. Sometimes this means they are completely the same or completely different. Two strong willed individuals might rip each other apart, or they may see it as a competition with each other. Two submissive personalities might not be strong enough to form the merge at all, or they may support each other in a loving manner. This manner of compatibility must be measured on a case-by-case basis."

The Academy training facility was built on the lowest level of the Academy. State of the art, the training facility had the newest exercise equipment, ropes courses, and weights, some as light as 20 Kg and some as heavy as 1000 Kg.

The training facility was built to withstand a nuclear explosion, the perfect training ground for super humans. All around the room young Leashes were training, and even some of the more athletic Psychics.

Physical fitness was encouraged amongst Psychics and Leashes because even though it was a Leash's job to protect their Psychic, a Psychic was often responsible for protecting their Leash. More than a dozen Psychics were running the ropes course and trying to lift the lighter weights. Several Leashes were there as well, but none of them were working out. They were all too busy watching the spectacle in the center of the facility.

Rudra blinked the blood out of his eyes, it had been a lucky shot. As fast as he was, it was difficult for him to change directions without hurting himself. He also needed space, only a few feet to accelerate, but in a three-against-one match, space usually wasn't a luxury.

"You kids have been practicing," smirked Rudra, quipping to catch his breath.

The three young soldier Leashes knew this trick and rushed in again. The first, a short stocky man with blonde hair buzzed nearly to his head, rushed in. He led with his legs striking out hard with his forward left leg aiming at Rudra's knee. Rudra opened his pool of Psychic energy and outpaced the young soldier, striking faster and slamming his heel into the young Leashes hip. He hit the mat with a flat thud, the gathered crowd erupted with laughter, cheers, and sympathetic "oohs".

The other two Leashes rushed in. A tall dark-skinned leash, who fought left-handed, forced Rudra to adjust his fighting tactics to match the alternative striking pattern. The second was an athletic young woman who lashed out with mid- and high-level kicks without ever putting her foot back on the ground.

Rudra decided leverage was his best option. Rudra wasn't a martial artist. He had very little training in actual combat, so he utilized his accuracy, speed and calm demeanor to win fights. Well, that and enough foot speed to generate a sonic boom. But without space to run or time to reset, he was having a hard time doing anything besides evading and keeping his feet under himself.

The southpaw boxer was striking fierce, accurate blows aimed at Rudra's face and upper torso. Rudra managed to evade most of the punches until one surprise right hook forced him to block. His left arm bolted up to block the hard-right hook and that's when the female Leash, who Rudra could no longer see with his arm blocking his field of view, whirled her body in a circle, lifting herself elegantly off the ground before sending the ball of her foot crashing into Rudra's right cheek.

He wasn't used to being staggered, and while the blow wasn't nearly enough to knock a level 4 Leash out, it was certainly enough for him to feel. Rudra felt the calm that normally made him so deadly slip under a murky red curtain of rage. He planted his feet and pivoted, driving his right fist forward, slamming into the boxer's chest like an anvil. Rudra felt the sternum bend and then crack under the blow, and the well-built Leash was thrown ten meters back through the crowd of onlooking Leashes, curling into a whimpering ball on the floor when he landed.

Rudra turned his attention to the girl who had shaken off the stun of the violent action and got back in her stance and attempted to lash out with her powerful back leg. Rudra's left hand jabbed into her thigh before it connected with his face. He unleashed a flurry of punches that wracked her torso and chin with concrete busting force.

She collapsed, breathing through her broken jaw and into the mat. Two of the Psychic trainers rushed over to help the fallen Leashes.

The boxer was taking slow deliberate breaths as his concave chest was reforming and healing. Sweat and tears dotted his face from exertion. When the bone had reset, he took a long ragged breath of relief. The young woman was whimpering as one of the Psychics pinned one of her arms, and the other took her detached jaw in his hand. She released a guttural shriek, but the two Psychics, utilizing all their mental concentration, worked between holding her in place and assisting with the cells regrowing.

"Concentrate." The Psychic's command was soft. The female Leash whimpered then closed her eyes. With a sickening squelch, her jaw reset as Psychic energy began the rapid healing process.

After a few moments the three Leashes stood up and exchanged humble glances before braving a glance back at Rudra.

"Sorry you guys. I didn't mean to get carried away. Are you alright?" Rudra's wrath had subsided, and he was back to his charming and considerate self.

"Yes sir, we're fine," the boxer replied confidently, glancing at his sparring partners. "When we asked you for a sparring match we knew there might be consequences. Just didn't know how severe they were going to be."

Rudra blushed and made an apologetic gesture. "Why don't you guys all go to the med bay and get Dr. Luke to check you out. And tonight, drinks are on me."

The other Leashes attempted to smile through the pain as they all walked away, talking quietly about how the Tornado Leash's brutal reputation had been well earned. As the small and pitiful group walked away, Rudra's charismatic smile faded as he began mentally chastising himself.

Stupid, you could have killed them. Over a sparring match. How much is your ego worth?

It had always been the greatest contradiction between his sister and himself. He, normally calm and collected, always able to smile at any situation, known for his deliberate cunning in battle, and unable to tolerate having his ego bruised. His sister, on the other hand, who fumbled in social situations and was always passionate about this or that injustice, became a pillar of stone in battle and was full of laser-focused calm. Agni knew that a slight burst of emotion or a moment of lost control could be disastrous.

It's a good question Ru. How much is your ego worth? He could hear the smugness in Agni's voice even before he turned to face her.

Rudra didn't block his sister out. Even though her invasions into his mind were irritating at times, the closeness and connection they shared was well worth the moments of annoyance that came with it; besides, it did lend him plenty of ammunition to use in sibling rivalry contests.

"It got exceptionally warm around here earlier. You run into Xiphos?" He retorted.

Agni let out a small noise of embarrassment as Rudra's mind was flooded with images of the handsome Leash, some a great deal more suggestive than others.

"You know Agni, at this point I'm having a hard time telling your fantasies from your memories. Why don't you just go up to him, tell him you want him, and get it out of your system. If I have to be subjected to one more of your mental fantasies of you two in candlelight I'm going to lobotomize myself," her brother teased.

Agni's temper flared and as she spit out her response, her breath raining sparks. "You're one to talk, every time you pick up a girl I don't get any sleep. Worse, I'm subjected to weird memories that aren't even mine!" Regaining her composure slightly and taking a page from her brother's book, "Or is that what you're into? Want me to drag Xiphos to bed so that you can live out some deep dark fantasy about the big strong Sword Leash?"

Rudra laughed. It was nice to hear his sister stand up for herself even if it was against him.

"He is big and strong, isn't he?" The voice was curt and authoritative. Agni winced. Rudra smiled.

"Hello there, lover. You come to visit me at work?" Rudra replied smoothly to the approaching Psychic.

She was young, no more than 22, but had the form and discipline of an experienced soldier. Her Academy uniform was well pressed and fit close to her athletic build. Her brown hair was pulled back into a tight bun. Her rich, dark, skin looked like silk in the training facility lights. Rudra always had to fight the urge to stare when Aspis was around.

"You wish, Ru. Only way you're getting me in bed is if you've got your sister under the sheets."

Rudra laughed, Agni blushed.

"Xiphos told me this morning that you two had an assignment to go on? I thought you would have already left," Agni sputtered, trying desperately to change the subject.

Aspis made an annoyed noise. "Has Xiphos ever been on time for anything?"

"So what did you come down here for? Need a stretch? Maybe a little physical activity?" Rudra's playfulness got the better of Aspis and she surrendered a smile to the charming Leash.

"I bet you do everything fast, don't you, Ru?" Aspis retorted, more than used to the flirty Leash and his charisma.

"Want me to go slow? I'll go as slow as you want ..."

Aspis set her jaw against this response so she wouldn't react, but her burning ears and averted eyes was a dead giveaway for the Tornado Leash, who just smirked.

"What are you doing to my partner, Rudra? I could feel her blushing from the elevator!" Xiphos had stepped into the gymnasium. His tall, powerful form was impossible to ignore.

Rudra grinned at his best friend. "I hear you guys have to go baby sit. Anyone I know?"

Aspis shook her head "That information is classi–"

"Some northern dignitary," her Leash said, cutting her off. "He wants to make his way to the Southwest region and try to renegotiate the trade routes with them or something. The concern is he has to pass through the Center region. They've given him permission to do so, but they are also well known for assassinating dignitaries just to start a conflict. Anyway, our job is to make sure he gets there and back again with no issues."

Aspis glared at Xiphos while he deliberately avoided making eye contact with his Psychic. The four of them stood for several more minutes joking, exchanging information that wasn't supposed to be exchanged. Flirting and trying to avoid being seen staring. Trying their best to be human, even if it was just for a little while.

Alyssia was noticeably distracted. Her heart was still racing from the encounter with Tobias. She could still feel the impression of his hand around her throat, her pulse pounding behind her eyes.

Why did I agree to give him the tour? Am I out of my mind? He was just trying to choke the life out of you, stupid... Her hands traced the lines across her throat.

"Alyssia."

Her eyes snapped up and refocused on Dr. Luke who was looking at her, half curious and half concerned.

"You alright, kiddo?"

Her focus changed to Tobias who was now shirtless in front of the storage closet. His exposed back was covered in scars. Some looked like animal claws, others like small round holes. He pulled his smart fiber out of the closet and pulled it over his head. The skin tight black material clung to well-trained muscles. As he reached for his gun belt the doctor spoke up.

"I don't think you should carry your guns. For starters, they might make the younger Psychics nervous, and secondly, the stronger Psychics might kill you."

Tobias hesitated a moment then removed his hand and closed the closet door.

"Alyssia, why don't you take Mr. Marshall to meet Gregory? He'd probably like to meet our guest since his stay will be...extended." Dr. Luke suggested.

Alyssia nodded absently then headed for the door. Tobias followed wordlessly. They exited the med bay and entered into the main hall; it was massive in scale and lavish in taste. There was an ever-running stream that circled the entire Academy floor, a beautiful fixture with a natural temperature regulation system. It also fed into the gardens of the first floor where many young Psychics and Leashes could be seen studying or eating. The walkways of marble glistened and gleamed beautifully. It was truly a masterpiece of architecture.

Alyssia's pace was quick and nervous, as was her voice. "The first floor has the dormitories, library, motor pool and the cafeteria. Oh, and of course med bay, but we just came from there. Um, second floor classrooms and the student lounges. Third floor administration. Oh yeah, and the basement is the training facility and our holding facility."

She rattled off information in staccato fashion, as if she was afraid of the silence. Tobias was half listening as he examined the interior of the famed Academy. The ceilings were enormous and ornate. There were fountains that traced the entire outline of the first floor where fish swam. There was even an indoor park with trees and birds.

There were markers for each of the areas indicating what they contained. Each area of the academy jutted off like spokes in a wheel, and stairwells lined the outside of the facility every 40 to 50 meters. Above were massive glass ceilings that let in sunlight to illuminate the ground level naturally. Two glass-tubed elevators stood at the center of the Academy leading up to the administration level or down to the training facility.

The air was warm and full of life as students in regular dress rushed about with data pads, shoveling sandwiches and other food items into their mouths. Full-fledged Psychics and Leashes walked around in their uniforms, looking official and busy. There were several groups of small children walking in straight, single file lines with their hands behind their backs and their eyes facing straight ahead, being led by a professional looking individual.

On more than one occasion Tobias had noticed some of the children look at Alyssia and break their composure to wave at her excitedly before being chastised by the Psychic leading the group.

"How old are those kids?" Tobias asked, noticing the near-running pace the children had to maintain to be able to keep up with their instructor's brisk walk.

"Hmm, oh um, well, the Academy collects students as soon as they show Psychic ability. Usually that's around puberty. But sometimes they are as young as two. Some who are born in less developed regions come to us when they are a little older because they aren't noticed as soon," she said absently, still trying to maintain her focus through her anxiety.

"Two? What good can they do at two? Why would the Academy even be interested in them that young?" Tobias responded, surprised.

Alyssia stopped her walk and turned to face him, looking into his sunken eyes. She hadn't noticed before how his body was slouched but he didn't limp or wince when he stepped. She had almost forgotten that he had been bed ridden for the better part of two weeks.

"The younger Psychic ability manifests, usually the more powerful the Psychic will become," she explained. "So if we get them young, we can cultivate their ability, we can take a child that would normally live their lives as a Mumbler and can have them trained up to Ticklers by the time they are ready to merge. A very strong Mumbler can even be trained all the way up to a Soldier if they work really hard. Although not all Psychics become operatives of the Academy, some end up working within mechanics, agriculture, that sort of thing."

Tobias stared at her blankly. "Oh! Um, a Level One Psychic is called a Mumbler. A level Two is called a Tickler. A Level Three is–"

"I know that." Tobias cut her off. "But what are you?" He asked curiously.

"Me? Oh, um...I'm...Well..." It had never occurred to Alyssia what her rank was. She was such an oddball at the Academy. An unpaired Psychic at her level of power was unheard of even in the most exceptional circumstances. "I'm a Level Four Psychic, I guess." She had finally found the words, but they sounded odd finally coming out of her mouth.

Tobias looked incredulous. "You're the same rank as Agni and Rudra?"

Alyssia had never thought about it like that. But she was in fact at the same Psychic level as Agni, her telepathic ability in many ways far exceeded Agni's, but that was probably in part due to her unique ability to read people's energy like it was a menu. Agni, on the other hand, was a much more powerful telekinetic. "I suppose I am..."

Tobias looked amused, and this made Alyssia's ears burn with a mix of embarrassment and indignation. "So what is your –"

Alyssia became self-conscious and cut him off before he could finish his question. "I don't have a Leash," Alyssia blurted.

Tobias's smile faded into his normally stony expression, but at the corners of his eyes there was a slight apologetic crinkle. "I meant your name."

Alyssia's ears burned. "Oh, um. Alys–" She stopped, realizing that wasn't the name he wanted. "Wait, you meant Psychics, like Level Four Psychics, what are we called, right?"

Tobias inclined a nod.

"There are so few of us they never bothered to name us," Alyssia shrugged before continuing. "There are only eight Level Four Psychics in the world and only seven Level Four Leashes. Before the war ended there were only three Level Four pairs, and two sets were lost during battle. The only ones left from that time are Angel and Melania."

An involuntary shiver went down Alyssia's spine at the mention of the Nightmare Psychic and the Shred Leash, the two most brutal members of the Academy. There was a long silence.

"Tell me about them." Tobias inquired gingerly.

Alyssia began to walk and talk, trying her best to ignore the odd dualities of his personality or the strange flood of emotions that she had felt. Tobias Marshall was an interesting character. One minute he was cold as ice, the next smart and interested. He seemed completely apathetic then without provocation he wanted to know everything. She was intrigued, but then that nagging feeling came back into her mind.

He was empty. He wanted to kill me. My death was written on his face. And that creature that lived inside him...what was it?

She shook the thought away and began to think about the other Psychics. "All of the Level Four teams have a specialty. Agni and Rudra are our crowd control team. They specialize in eliminating large groups of soft targets..."

Tobias smirked. One minute this girl could barely make eye contact, and the next she cites large groups of dead people as "soft targets".

"Xiphos and Aspis, the Spartans, they specialize in protection details. Dr. Luke and Catha are our medical team and they are also our primary training team alongside Mr. Zander and Mr. Gregory. Dr. Luke works with all Psychics and Leashes on teaching their bodies how to heal themselves and Catha assists in the training of Level Two and Three Leashes on forward combat details. They only came to us a few years ago, but they've been amazing additions to our team."

"Why do only your Level Two and Three Leashes receive combat training?" Tobias inquired, though despite the question his attention seemed distracted by a young Psychic who was reshaping a grapefruit sized piece of iron into different configurations while it floated a meter and a half off of the ground.

"Everyone who goes into the Leash program receives basic combat and weapons training, but our Level Twos and Threes spend most of their time in combat situations, so they have to maintain a steady regimen even after they have been paired with a Psychic." Alyssia was now speaking happily. These questions made her feel like she was back in her classroom with her children.

"You said weapons training? Why would an army of superhumans need to know how to use weapons?"

"Psychic energy is a finite substance. A Leash is someone who has a naturally depleted supply of dormant Psychic energy, so they undergo a Wash which fills the gap in their passive Psychic energy with active Psychic energy. That's what gives a Leash their strength. But it can be depleted, so they learn weapons and combat training as a secondary option." Alyssia had often prided herself on her near encyclopedic knowledge of Parapsychology, and this was a rare opportunity to show off what she knew. She was definitely going to take it.

"But even a Leash that relies heavily on weapons and combat training has to undergo the Wash fairly frequently, because their bodies are in a constant state of use. Becoming a Leash is devastating to their bodies. Increased muscle and bone density can cause certain tissues to splinter and deteriorate, so they need a constant influx of Psychic energy to keep their bodies from falling apart."

Tobias scoffed. "I guess that's why I haven't seen a retired Leash yet."

Alyssia lowered her gaze. Thinking about what happened to older Leashes was almost too sad to think about. Partial mind death. Catha was showing increased signs of fatigue with age. Her mental faculties had been waning slowly but steadily, in a few more years she would probably be a near vegetable.

Tobias noticed Alyssia's downcast eyes and realized he'd struck a nerve. "So tell me about your Level Four teams."

Alyssia took a breath and then perked up a little bit. "We have a team for everything from interrogation to person-to-person combat."

Tobias raised an eyebrow "Person to person? A sniper team?"

Alyssia smirked. "More like a hunter team. Syn and Dian, they've been gone for about a week. They should be home tomorrow."

The forest air was full of humidity. Dew dressed the leaves like small gems, the smell of life was fresh and heavy. A small group of elk walked freely in a glen, damp fur glistening in the early morning sun. On a rocky outcrop surrounded by trees, laying on a fur roll, a rifle barrel protruded from cover.

Syn lined the largest female elk into his scope. He probably didn't need it, but the routine brought him an element of peace. He dug his feet into the ground, pressing himself into his rifle, and smelled the breeze. It was quiet and still under the tree canopy. He increased his finger pressure on the trigger; the elk didn't seem to notice, but at a distance of nearly two kilometers, even with a strong wind the animal would have had a hard time smelling him.

Syn inhaled slowly, filling his lungs with fresh air, then released half a breath, still using the tricks his father taught him when he had taken him hunting as a boy. Long before the military, long before his stint as a mercenary, and a lifetime before he had become a Leash. His hypersensitive touch felt the click of the trigger. The hammer fell into place, struck the casing, and the propellant in the round casing ignited before the round erupted from the barrel. Two and a half seconds later the animal fell to the ground. A perfect shot.

The jog to the animal was short. The elk was easily hoisted off the ground as Syn removed a rope with a metal spike from his pack, laced it through the ankles and then over a high tree branch. He set to work expertly gutting, skinning, and cleaning the animal, all the while humming a song he couldn't remember the words to.

His rifle laid against the tree trunk reminding him that he needed to go police his brass and clean off his shooting perch. Despite her many talents and abilities, his Psychic, Dian, was not terribly adept at hiding her presence. Syn, on the other hand, had decades of practice becoming invisible and leaving no trace. He wrapped all the good meat into his leather wrap and cinched it at both ends. Dinner was going to be excellent.

Later that evening he was sitting at his campfire atop a large log that had fallen close enough to their camp it hadn't been much effort to drag it near the fire. His kill was cleaned, and the valuable pieces had been set aside. The meat had been salted and wrapped to preserve it.

His hunting rifle had been cleaned and stowed. His 950 Judge was laying across his lap as he wound the hydraulic pressure clip down to load in the quarter kilogram rounds. The 90 kg weapon, with a 10 kg magazine, was far too heavy for any normal human to use; even most Level One and Two Leashes struggled to handle it, yet Syn wielded it with ease.

After the last round had been loaded, he stored the weapon back into its bag and turned his attention to the meat cooking over the fire and the small figure wrapped in furs at his feet. As he turned the spit and tested the elk with his fingers, the figure stirred.

"For the love of God Syn, please tell me we're not having rabbit and mushrooms again," the sleepy female voice said grumpily as she pulled down her covers.

Syn smiled, the smell of her hair caught on the breeze. "Better. Elk, onions, and wild garlic."

The lightning Psychic Dian groaned. "Why doesn't ice cream roam around in the forest waiting to get shot?"

Syn laughed softly. "We completed our assignment. We will be home by tomorrow."

Dian pulled the bear skin blanket up to her chin. "Home, huh? Don't think I've ever thought of the Academy that way."

Syn pulled the meat off of the fire and added it to a pair of metal plates from his bag, along with the vegetables, and placed it by Dian's head. He shrugged. "The Academy is home. Good or bad, it's where we belong."

Dian sat up, her flaming red hair shadowed by the evening and falling just above her shoulders. Her slender torso and toned, tan arms were covered by an oversized shirt, a clear sign of her comfort on the road. She picked up her plate and began to eat greedily despite her earlier complaint. "Home doesn't make you kill people for room and board, Pops."

Syn didn't respond as he chewed on his elk meat thoughtfully.

"I'm thirsty," said Dian in between mouthfuls. When she didn't receive a response, she spoke again much more petulantly. "I said I'm thirsty, Pops".

Syn swallowed and stood up, reaching into his pack and pulling out a canteen. He swished it around and then unscrewed the top before handing it to her. She drank and tasted the orange, lemon and honey mixed with spring water and a hum of liquor.

"What do you call this stuff again?" Dian asked, taking another gulp.

"My dad always called it dragonfly milk," Dyn remarked. "It's good for you."

She laid her empty plate on the ground and propped herself up on her knees and laid her arms and head across his lap. "Can we have fish tomorrow?"

He smirked, picking his canteen up and swallowing several mouthfuls before wiping the excess liquid from his salt and pepper beard. "Only if you catch it."

She made an annoyed noise before closing her eyes again; shortly, he heard her snoring softly.

He sat back on his log and looked up at the tree canopy and sighed.

"I've never had a home," he said as he looked down at the fiery young woman who was asleep with her head in his lap. As he looked at his petulant, surrogate daughter, he continued. "Except with you. You're my home, little one. And yes, we can have fish tomorrow."

He closed his eyes in his reclined position. And while not the most comfortable place to be, he still managed to drift off to a peaceful sleep. He didn't want to wake up, he just wanted to stay right here. Home.

CHAPTER 1.4

Understanding the Leash

"A Leash must be aware of their new enhanced supply of Psychic energy. With the enhancements that massive reserves of Psychic energy bring, it also comes with its fair share of drawbacks. Leashes must always be diligent in their self-care, just as Psychics should be diligent in caring for their Leashes. Remember once merged you are of two bodies and of one consciousness."

Blaine walked down the hallway, his hard-soled shoes giving a sharp echo off the polished marble floors. The walls were lined with posters from past recruitment campaigns that promised great opportunities and rapid advancement through the ranks. The elaborate light fixtures that seemed to float in the air were held aloft by thin wires that ran to a ceiling displaying heroic scenes of soldiers saving villages and protecting the defenseless. Only the Public Operations branch of TITAN had this kind of decoration. The rest of the buildings were much less appealing.

Blaine continued down the hall, passing all the recruitment offices and public relations workers until he found himself in a wide lobby, sparse in the way of decorations. His pace didn't slow as he crossed the room to a door at the far end. He stopped only for a second to steady his nerves before opening the door. The room he entered was populated by a single desk, which was occupied by a TITAN operative in uniform. The young man, more of a boy, was wearing standard issue TITAN gear, complemented by a sidearm on his hip. He straightened at the sight of Blaine entering the room.

"Sir." The young man stood, giving the standard respects to a superior officer.

"Carry on." Blaine had little time for this boy right now. He had somewhere important to be.

"My name is Battle Captain Blaine, I have a report to give upstairs." Blaine said, getting straight to the point.

"Yes, sir," the boy responded. He approached a digital intercom mounted on the wall. Tapping a few buttons brought up a command prompt that the operative confirmed before taking a single step back.

From Blaine's position he couldn't see the screen, but he heard the voice that came from it.

"Yes, what is it McCoy?" The commanding voice came through the screen.

The young man threw up a salute. "Sir, you have Battle Captain Blaine reporting in. Should I let him up?" The young man reported.

"Yes, send him up." The intercom clicked and the boy pressed a few more buttons on the screen, turning it black. The young man turned around and motioned Blaine forward.

"This way, sir." As the boy gestured for Blaine, the wall behind him rose up to reveal a hidden elevator door. Blaine stepped into the elevator, letting the door slide closed behind him.

As the cabin of the elevator pressurized, a robotic female voice came over the speaker. "Please hold still for a scan." A panel on the wall opened to reveal a mechanical eye. The entire elevator was designed to confirm someone's identity with a full body and biometrics scan. Even the floor of the elevator was a pressure plate to identify body weight and shifts in weight. It was also good encouragement for officers not to get lazy on their training regimen when they had achieved a certain level of success. It was hard to respect an officer whose stomach spilled from their uniform.

"Scan complete. Identity confirmed." The voice gave its programmed response.

The elevator began moving, taking him to the only floor it accessed. A minute later, the elevator hissed to a stop and the door slid open. Blaine stepped off the elevator and hit his stride, strutting his way down the hall.

There were no other doors in this hallway except for the elevator and a single door at the far end. The simple wooden door had a name plate on it that read Commandant Caylen. Blaine gave three quick knocks on the door.

"Come in," came the immediate response. It was the same voice that was on the intercom downstairs. Blaine opened the door and stepped inside, closing the door fully before stepping into the room.

Commandant Caylen sat behind his desk, looking all the part of a born and bred military man. A short haircut and a clean shaven face, a jaw strong enough to break rocks, and muscles so defined that you could make them out under his uniform jacket. His pressed uniform showed the attention to detail that only a man with years in service would develop. Blaine had once heard a First Commander quip that no man in TITAN was more disappointed about the end of the Psychic War than Commandant Caylen.

Blaine made a quick stop two paces before his desk and saluted. "Battle Captain Blaine, reporting as requested, sir."

"Blaine. Tell me how stupid you have to be to let this disaster occur?" The Commandant wasn't known for mincing words, but his tone took Blaine by surprise.

"S-sir?" Blaine asked hesitantly.

"If half of the preliminary reports I've heard are true, you'll be lucky if you don't face demotion over this. How hard is it to keep one gun squad, a gun squad that's not even at half capacity I might add, under control?"

Blaine tried to find his spine. He extended his report to the Commandant, who snatched it out of his hands. After clearing his throat, Blaine tried to regain a modicum of vocal control as he reported in his most professional fashion.

"Sir, inside you will find the full report of the operation details. The main points of the operation: three TITAN operatives with two negotiators from the Academy, were dispatched to recover a four man team that had been taken hostage on a separate mission by the AGEIS organization. The ransom was ten million credits in small bills for the safe return of all four hostages. The mission ended with the loss of the ransom credits, the hostages and two of the operatives sent in on the mission."

"On a simple retrieval? How could this have gone so wrong? Routine negotiations never go this badly. Which of our operatives survived?"

"Sir, it is believed that the one surviving member from the extraction team is the one that took off with the credits after killing a Level Two Leash and shooting one of his surviving team members in the head. Sir, I–"

"Excuse me?" The voice came from behind him, cutting him off.

Blaine hadn't known that there was a third person in the room. A chill crept up his spine at hearing the voice. Blaine turned his head to see a well-dressed man standing behind the doorway he had just entered through. His demeanor was calm and relaxed. His suit vest and form-fitting custom shoes made him out to be anything but a mercenary.

"Did you mention a survivor?" The well-dressed man spoke, and though he still seemed a quiet shadow, there was something ominous about him, like a storm front being seen from a great distance.

"I would answer him if I were you. This is the specialist who was hired by AGEIS that took our men hostage. And was then contracted by us to recollect our credits and eliminate the hostage takers. He came to us with information that we have deemed valuable and therefore will be treated as an expert in this situation," the Commandant said in an all-to-serious tone.

Blaine was irritated at the idea that an outsider with no affiliation to the organization was suddenly his superior, but he knew better than to argue with the Commandant.

"Tobias Marshall was unaccounted for when we recovered the remains of the six operatives," Blaine said as if in a trance, still looking at the Commandant.

Caylen sat forward in his chair. "Do we know where he is? Was he by himself or did he have help?"

Blaine finally came to and regained some of his composure. "Sir, he was located at the Academy. I was granted access to the facility and found Marshall in their medical bay relatively unharmed. When I attempted to retrieve him I..." Blaine was suddenly reluctant to reveal any more than he already had; the pinprick sting in his neck still hadn't totally faded, and he hated to illustrate his own failures with any more clarity than necessary. "I was prevented from doing so by Academy personnel."

The well-dressed man let out a snort of derision. "I'm certain you were a very courageous Battle Captain."

Blaine had had enough of being mocked by an outsider. "And were you not hired to get our men and our credits back? You evidently got back our money, but six of our men are dead and you're standing here like everything was a complete success."

The well-dressed man smirked dangerously. "Unfortunate losses. But I have no control of the AGEIS organization or rogue operatives from TITAN. How could I possibly be held accountable for actions taken without my knowledge. I did exactly what I was hired to do. I retrieved your money and facilitated your exchange. Everything that happened after that was beyond the bounds of my contract," he mocked the Battle Captain.

"So he's at the Academy." Caylen interjected, knitting his eyebrows and rolling the mental difficulty around in his head. "We have no jurisdiction over the Academy, no one does. And if we try to use force it could result in an inter-regional incident. I need to conference with the other Commandants about this."

"Allow me," the well-dressed man interjected. "This Marshall charac-ter intrigues me. Truthfully, no one should have survived the disaster at the facility, yet this man did. I only saw him for a moment, but he didn't strike me as nearly extraordinary enough to emerge unscathed as you claim. So allow me to clean up *your* mess."

"And how did you manage to survive the incident? There were enough explosives detonated to kill everyone there. How did you manage to get away without a scratch?" Blaine asked indignantly.

"I completed the assignment I was hired for and then left. A profes-sional always gets their job done," the specialist retorted while pushing his glasses further up on his nose.

Blaine scoffed, his rage now outweighing his hesitation. "Sir, let me go and retrieve Marshall. We don't need to use this outsider to help us."

The well-dressed man made no attempt to hide the disdain in his voice; he reminded Blaine of a serpent, coiled and venomous. "Ridiculous. You want to go to one of the only places in the world where you have absolutely no power and influence and try to throw your weight around? Any one of thousands of Leashes could rip you apart, and your plan is to what – go in and make demands of these people? To what end? To try and gain a few pats on the back and a promotion? Know your place and stay there."

"Hold on, Blaine may have a good point," the Commandant chipped in, deciding to try and calm the situation. "This debacle is a TITAN issue, and TITAN should work to solve it."

"You're supposed to tell me what I will and won't do, Commandant?" The well-dressed man's voice dripped honey and poison.

"Blaine will go as an official TITAN representative, and you will go in whatever way you please. This is something you are doing on your own time anyway," Caylen stated flatly, his years of military training making him virtually unshakable. The well-dressed man looked at Blaine, a predator evaluating his prey.

"Well, if you insist. But I won't be held responsible when he dies."

The fact that he hadn't specified how he might die wasn't lost on Blaine. As well as the fact that he had said "*when*" instead of "*if*". The Battle Captain straightened his uniform and cleared his throat in an attempt to help him gain his composure. "I will leave immediately and be back in a few days, sir. With Marshall."

The door opened and the well-dressed man exited while Blaine followed close behind.

"Blaine."

The Battle Captain turned to face the Commandant. "Sir?"

The Commandant stood, crossing the room toward Blaine. He was imposing even for a man in his mid-50s. "I cannot begin to stress how bad this has been screwed up. That team was your responsibility, and they are dead. You are a leader with no one left to lead. That makes you useless. I encourage you to prove me wrong. Do I make myself clear, Battle Captain?"

Blaine focused all of his energy into preventing his superior from seeing him swallow before he spoke. "Sir."

"Good. Now get out of my office. And remember, if you die, any company loans you may have taken out will be billed to your family."

Blaine left the Commandant's office shaken and confused. He crossed the administrative recruit's desk and back down the corridor, his mind swimming with questions. But the most pressing and disturbing was this: the Commandant was a military man and had seen multiple tours, had fought countless engagements, and had a higher confirmed kill count than many veteran gun squads. He was a man of duty, action and violence, but the tremor in his hand and the hostility in his normally calm and controlled voice had led Blaine to wonder what it was about this Specialist that made the Commandant so nervous.

The lift to the third floor dinged and opened. Tobias and Alyssia entered a large, handsome corridor., with a floor that looked as if it had been cut from one solid piece of dark blue marble. The ceilings vaulted up into a cream painted dome. They walked out from the flat edge of a semi-circle arch, mushroom shaped with the room itself being the cap. There were several doorways along the outside curve of the circle.

"All of these are our administrative offices," Alyssia spoke while leading Tobias to a large wooden door in the center of the semi-circle. "Mr. Gregory is the headmaster. He makes most of the administrative decisions for the Academy."

She knocked four times musically on the door, her disposition becoming noticeably more chipper. Tobias could only assume that she liked this man Gregory. The door was opened by an older gentleman with mocha-colored skin and salt and pepper hair. He was dressed comfortably, and his physical demeanor was completely at ease. His eyes, however, spoke to Tobias of danger and intelligence.

"Hey Al, how you been kid?" The gentleman smiled warmly at the young girl.

Alyssia smiled broadly. "I'm good, Mr. Zander. I was sent by Dr. Luke to introduce Mr. Gregory to someone. Is he busy?"

The man turned his charming smile and serious eyes to Tobias. "Probably not, but you know administrative types. The only thing that ever really wears them out is hiding from work. Is this the gentleman he's supposed to meet?" Zander extended his hand while maintaining his scrutinizing eye contact.

Tobias reached out and grabbed it, feeling the steel in his grip. They shook hands for just a moment but to Tobias it felt as if his whole arm was being crushed under the weight of the interaction. This man was obviously not a normal human. Zander turned and walked away from the door, inviting Tobias and Alyssia to follow him inside.

The room was large and warm and comfortable. It looked to Tobias more like a lavish apartment than an office. At the center of the room was a broad, beautiful wooden desk, behind which sat a man studying his computer screen quietly. He glanced toward the three as they approached.

"Alyssia, good to see you. How have you been?" The man rose to greet the trio. He was tall but not imposing. His dark skin and large hands made him look more like a friendly stuffed animal with spectacles rather than the head of an Academy for super humans.

"You must be the guest I've heard so much about. My name is Gregory Krag, Level Three Soldier Psychic and primary administrator of this Academy. This is my Leash and assistant, Zander Krag. How are you feeling?"

Tobias raised an eyebrow in mild amusement but decided not to be sarcastic. He didn't enjoy false sincerity, nor did he have patience for professional kindness. "I'd like to know when I'm allowed to leave."

Gregory didn't attempt to hide his amusement. "You seem to be under the impression that you're a prisoner here. You're not, you're free to go anytime you see fit. You were simply discouraged from leaving on the grounds that you will be killed almost immediately."

Tobias let the irritation fill his voice. "You seem awfully confident in your information. How do you know they even want me dead?"

Gregory adjusted his round glasses on his nose and leaned back in his seat.

"Mr. Marshall, I don't have you pegged as a stupid man. TITAN has accused you of killing their operatives and stealing their money. Now we know you didn't do this, but they don't. Even when they came to collect you, we attempted to explain the situation that had occurred, and they still refused to listen. At this point you have become their scapegoat. The person they are determined to blame for a debacle that even we here at the Academy are having trouble sorting out the details of. You think they won't kill you just to make an example of you?"

Tobias didn't have a response. The headmaster was right, TITAN didn't tolerate failure. People rarely got fired from the organization; they were just sent on enough assignments that eventually they didn't come back. Tobias controlled his tone because he knew the anger he felt at the helplessness of his situation wouldn't serve him. "What do you suggest?"

Gregory stood up and crossed the room to a bar next to Zander and opened a decanter, pouring himself a glass of water from it. "How many Psychics and Leashes have you killed, Mr. Marshall?"

Tobias didn't know how to take the question. It wasn't in his nature to discuss how many of someone's allies he had put in the ground. "Why does that matter?"

Alyssia caught a mental flash inside Tobias' mind. It was a Psychic. He was on the ground, hot, ragged breath on his cheek, and the feeling of a trachea being crushed under his forearm. She had caught a glimpse of a memory Tobias had involuntarily recalled. She was suddenly scared to look at him, afraid she might see the featureless monster she had encountered when she first delved into his mind.

"Psychics are thought to be gods among men, Mr. Marshall," Gregory explained. "Their Leashes almost as much so. But these last several months there has been a dramatic uptick in the number of our people who are dying while on and off assignment. So I ask again, how many?"

"Two Psychics, two Leashes." Tobias responded, still uncertain of where this conversation was leading, but ready for a fight nonetheless.

"At the same time?" Gregory asked, his tone measured and even

"No, at separate times. During four separate encounters" Tobias responded

"So four teams total. How did they die?" Zander asked, laser-like focus on Tobias. It was almost as if he had seen Tobias flex and shift his weight.

"Most recently? With bullets." Tobias quipped.

"If you would, Mr. Marshall, explain to me the tactics you used to kill a Level Two and Three Psychic and two Level Two Leashes," Gregory inquired, appearing unfazed by Tobias's sarcasm.

"You're looking for tactics? I almost died against both Leashes," Tobias retorted.

"But you didn't." Zander spoke this time, his words were soft, enticing an explanation.

Tobias hesitated before responding. "At close range, a high caliber weapon can penetrate a Leash's skin, even though they are faster and stronger than normal people. Human body mechanics are the same. Joints still only bend certain ways, balance can still be affected in the same manner as a non-Leash. As for the Psychics, the first one was honestly just a lucky shot. He threw one of my gun squad into me and when I hit the ground I had just enough space to fire a shot. I got lucky, bullet hit him in the throat. The last Psychic..." Tobias was remembering his first ever encounter with a Psychic in a hand to hand situation. It had been alarming how his body had been twisted and thrown like a rag doll. He would have killed Tobias had he not approached him after he had thrown him to gloat over his victory. "... I grappled to the ground before crushing his throat. I figured if he couldn't breathe he couldn't defend himself."

"I see." Gregory's deep voice resonated as he turned to Zander. "It seems you were right, implementing basic combat training for Psychics seems like it would be an effective course of action."

"Our Psychics grow to rely so much on their abilities that whenever they meet someone who can evade or distract them, they become helpless. Implementation of combat directives has been in the works for a while," Zander spoke, clarifying the line of questioning for Tobias.

Gregory returned to his desk and began to type at his computer. Took a long deep inhale before he began to speak. His sharp intelligent eyes staring hard at Tobias "Mr. Marshall, we have ourselves a dilemma. You are responsible for the death or decommission of eight operatives. Given two of them were going to be dispatched anyway. With that being said, we have every reason to kill, imprison, or turn you over to TITAN. Unless, perhaps, we can come to some other arrangement."

Tobias didn't like being outmaneuvered. Even if he wasn't sure how yet, he knew he had just walked into a trap. Alyssia shrunk away from him, feeling the rage flowing off of his body like a torrential river. "And what do you suggest?"

"We think you should join the Academy." Zander stated with a smirk.

Shock didn't quite sum up what Tobias felt. "You want me to join? I'm not a Psychic."

"Neither am I," came Zander's cool response.

"No, you're not saddling me with a Psychic." Tobias felt his muscles coiling to fight. His eyes sized up the two men, trying to decide what the best course of action would be if he had to try and fight his way out.

"We wouldn't dream of making you a Leash. I don't believe there is anyone that would make a good match for you. We've merged soldiers and mercenaries before and the results are hit or miss. And your record doesn't bode well for being a good match with anyone. We were thinking more of utilizing your skills here as an instructor."

Alyssia had to hide her surprise. Tobias felt his lips part in shock before he resealed them and unclenched his fist. "What would I be teaching?" He finally managed to ask.

"How would you feel about teaching armed and unarmed combat to our Psychics?" The silence was pregnant. No one moved, no one spoke.

Tobias stared unblinking at Gregory. Gregory returned the gaze, his fingers laced in front of his face obscuring his mouth while his deep thoughtful eyes were making hard contact with the ex-mercenary.

Zander was watching anxiously, knowing that if this man refused it would lead them to a potentially violent situation.Even though he knew Tobias was weakened and unarmed, there was still something about him that was dangerous.

Alyssia had to hide the fact that she wanted to squirm out of her own skin and run screaming from the room. When the silence was finally broken it wasn't with the thunderclap she had expected, but instead a voice of resignation and weariness.

"I don't have a choice, do I?" His response finally ended the awful quiet.

"No, Mr. Marshall. You don't".

CHAPTER 1.5
Understanding the Merge

"When a Psychic and a Leash are merged, their minds become linked. Their feelings, even memories, are no longer entirely their own. For this reason, both Psychic and Leash must be diligent. If a trauma is experienced by one, it could very well be experienced by both."

Syn and Dian could see the Academy ahead of them. It stood like a great metal coliseum shining in the distance. Its rounded outer shell that curved and domed near the top, high walls that masked the sprawling courtyards and the younger Academy students who tended to the gardens. They had known they were getting close when they passed the solar and wind farms that generated electricity for the Academy and the surrounding area. The envy of all the regions, the Academy was truly a self-sufficient establishment.

Dian exhaled long and slow as she hiked her pack further up on her shoulders. "Finally. My feet are killing me."

Syn smirked to himself. Dian was probably carrying a 20 kg pack; his easily weighed 140 kg, and he carried it like it was nothing. He had to remind himself that despite his superhuman strength and stamina, Dian could flick her wrist and knock the power out to an entire city. If she was really putting her mind to it, she could fry an entire region for a short period of time.

As they came over what they knew to be the last hill of their journey, they saw several armored vehicles with heavily armed men inside. They had set up small canopies off of their vehicles and some of them were sitting in chairs playing cards, smoking, or talking quietly. When they caught sight of Syn and Dian they paused in their conversations and observed them carefully. Syn discreetly placed himself in between Dian and the men and concentrated his internal pool of Psychic energy. He preferred to fight from a distance, but at this range, just a few meters, he would be able to get close and engage in hand to hand. Normal humans posed no threat to a seasoned Level Four Leash.

The hair on his arms and the back of his neck began to stand on end as he felt Dian focusing herself. He could feel the natural energy currents around her flowing, preparing to direct a bolt of lightning directly at anyone who made an aggressive move. They passed by them without incident, but it took several minutes for the electricity in the air to settle.

Who are they? Dian's mind spoke softly behind Syn's eyes. He enjoyed the way it felt when his Psychic spoke to his mind, intimate and quiet, like something old and correct.

Are you nervous? He responded thoughtfully.

She snorted with a temper as he smiled. The rest of the trip was quiet except for the occasional groan of discomfort from Dian. They arrived at the Academy entrance and both set their packs down. The door was opened by a young female Leash in a well pressed uniform and a chipper male Psychic who, while in uniform, was sloppily put together.

"Welcome back, Mr. Syn. Ms. Dian. So glad to see you both back in one piece. Anything we can do for you?" The young Psychic spoke with all the enthusiasm befitting his post.

"Our packs, will you please make sure they make it to our dormitory? And inform Zander that we are back and prepared to deliver our report whenever he's ready to hear it," Dian instructed.

The chipper male Psychic bowed low, nearly every tooth in his head showing as he smiled. "Of course, ma'am. Immediately. And as always, welcome home!"

Syn and Dian walked past the boy as he and his Leash picked up their supplies, one with a great deal more difficulty than the other, and began to walk their supplies to their dormitory.

Welcome home, he says. Dian whispered sadly to Syn's mind. *Home is where the cage is.*

Syn didn't know how to comfort the young Psychic. Hunting, cooking, building, breaking, and shooting were his main areas of expertise. *What can I do?* He mentally mustered his response.

Dian reached up and scratched Syn's beard playfully, a gesture he had always found amusing. It reminded him of a good hunting dog he had as a child and how he would sneak him into his window on cold nights.

The dog would paw at his face affectionately while he scratched his ears. He didn't mind being treated like a pet.

"Nothing, Pops. I'm gonna go get a bath. You should, too. You smell like nature...if nature died three days ago."

Syn inhaled deeply. He could smell blood and smoke on his clothes, as well as the gun oil on his fingertips, but he couldn't smell himself. He had never understood what all the fuss with bathing was anyway. It only made you easier to find in the wilderness. He watched for a moment as she walked away, before turning and heading to his own dormitory. He was tired. Maybe a bath would be refreshing.

Dian headed to her own dorm; she traced the long circle around the Academy's first floor until she came to hers. She passed more than a dozen rooms, many of them shared dormitories with a number of Psychics or Leashes living in them. Dorms were split up by gender and from there by rank. Mumblers usually ended up in quad dorms. Four separate rooms with an adjoining bathroom and a shared kitchen. Ticklers and soldiers who worked were in dual dorms with usually just one other person, most often their Leash. Children were housed in an entirely different area with round-the-clock security for their protection.

A large transparent glass sign with letters embossed in gold read Women's Dorm A. She crossed the broad causeway and through an archway into her hall. Psychics and Leashes who were in training stayed in the mass suite. Two beds to a room, two rooms adjoined by a bathroom and shower. Merged Psychics' and Leashes' dorms were designed more like apartments, with two bedrooms, two bathrooms, and a common area, normally with a kitchen.

Soldier Psychics and Leashes usually had much nicer facilities because of the nature of the work they tended to do. Lavish comfortable apartments often with windows and more access to creature comforts. No Soldier team had to share rooms. All enjoying the benefits of privacy and autonomy, something was often missed when your mind is shared with another individual. There was a time when they were even allowed to have pets, but it had caused a number of problems with the upkeep of the facilities so now only animals that worked were allowed.

Level Four teams enjoyed an unprecedented level of comfort. Their rooms were more like giant suites, with fully equipped dining and living areas and bedrooms that sprawled as large as some of the lower level Psychics' entire dormitories. And despite Dian's' displeasure with some of the Academy goings-on, she was quite grateful to be reaching for the door to her private suite. Dian passed three doors in her hallway before she came to hers.

"Dorm 6. Home sweet home," she muttered with a tired breath.

As she reached for her door handle, she suddenly felt her senses slow as the air around her warmed. The scent of wildflowers filled her nose, and she heard a honeyed voice next to her ear. It was soft, just above a whisper, but it felt as if it was the only sound in the universe. "Hello."

Dian felt a warm breeze slink and curl around every inch of exposed skin which was impossible in the enclosed hallway. It caressed her cheek and lifted her chin. "Melania..." She felt the word escape her lips almost involuntarily.

"Mmm. My name in your silk voice," Dian felt warm fingers run gently across the small of her back as if the contact was skin to skin, despite her wearing her traveling clothes. The backs of fingernails traced across her throat before coiling around her slender neck seductively.

Dian turned to see that the hallway was empty. She shook her head and turned the key in the lock to her room before entering. The feeling of hands and smells evaporated as she walked into her suite. She had to spend a moment catching her breath and shake off the sensation of a person's hands on her body. She lazily threw her keys and the contents of her pockets onto her counter before heading into her bedroom, ready for a nap before her shower, even if it meant dirtying her clean sheets. But as she crossed the threshold to her bedroom she saw her there sitting, siren-like, legs crossed, leaning back against her slender, alabaster arms.

Melania looked like something out of a dream. Her skin was soft and pale, her jet black hair framed her perfectly symmetrical features, and her full pink lips parted slightly in an enticing way. Melania. The Nightmare Psychic. Able to make whole battalions fall victim to their own dreams and imaginations, able to induce any image she chose, able to manipulate the mind into seeing, hearing, or smelling whatever she wanted them to. A living nightmare for her enemies, a dream to her lovers.

"I've missed you, my pet. You're not allowed to leave anymore."

Dian felt as if Melania's arms were coiled around her slender body like pale, smooth vines, despite the fact that she was clearly across the room. Dian shook involuntarily; it had always been unsettling to feel Melania close by. She had a way of twisting feelings until they matched her wants and needs.

"Mel I– I didn't know you'd be here. I thought they had you away on an assignment ..." Dian choked on her words. Even as powerful as she was, 18 was still a raw age, and she was not always the master of her own feelings.

Melania pouted a little with her eyes before brightening up her smile to lure the young woman closer. "You mean you're not happy to see me?"

"That's not what I..." Dian couldn't hear her own words leave her mouth. Her senses failed her in the midst of the scent of flowers and the sound of free running water. She could still feel Melania's fingers all over her skin, even though the nightmare Psychic was clearly sitting on the edge of her bed.

"So you did miss me then?" Melania purred as she stood slowly, her movements slinky and confident. She walked across the room and stood less than a breath away from Dian's face. "I wanted to be here when you came home, give you a welcome home present."

Dian felt the little hairs on her arms stand on end as the electricity in the room became palpable. She had to fight her discomfort and anxiety. Melania was too close. Her words were sweet, but her presence was threatening. She wished for a moment that Syn was there; he would make her feel more confident. He would keep her safe.

"Home just isn't home without you here, my love" Melania's voice melted into a thousand different frequencies and swam inside Dian's veins. She felt her tension easing. *That's right*, she thought. *This is right. I need more of this.*

She was so entranced she didn't feel Melania wrap her arms around her waist. "Tell me all about your adventures, pet?"

Dian looked up into the deep, dark eyes of her seducer. Dian felt her fear and anticipation rise. She was terrified of disappointing Mel. Mel, who treated her so well. Mel was safe. Mel was home. Melania gave affection and love in high quantities but expected obedience in return. Dian needed Melania to need her.

She stood on her toes and kissed Melania's cheek gingerly. "I did miss you."

Melania's face warmed. "Mmm. May I have a kiss, pet?" The Nightmare Psychic didn't wait for a response before leaning into the redhead's trembling lips.

"Mel, don't," Dian attempted to turn away. "I haven't had a bath–"

She was interrupted as perfect, pink lips grazed hers in a ghost of a kiss. "No bath? Well, we can't have that can we?"

Agni passed the mission dossier over the desk to Zander; he flipped through it, glancing at the information.

"The deserters are dead then?"

Agni would never get used to the way Zander spoke. No double talk, no collateral damage, no soft or hard targets. Just dead traitors.

She winced a little as she responded. "They are, but we only confirmed the one target ourselves, the other had already been disposed of. An anti-personnel mine evidently."

Zander pulled an ornate fountain pen from the holder on his desk and began to sign the mission dossier in the designated area, not even glancing up at her to respond. "So someone did your job for you? That's convenient," he quipped absent-mindedly as he continued signing the mission paperwork.

Agni had to hide her irritation from seeping into her response. "Ru took care of the security team while I killed the Leash, the Psychic had already experienced mind death. The mission was a success."

"You didn't kill the Leash, though, the mercenary did," Zander countered.

Agni exhaled sharply through her nose. Had it been through her mouth, it might have resulted in a shower of sparks. "No one stands in a wall of flames and lives ..." Zander's fierce eyes looked away from the documents to sharply lock with Agni's in a warning glance. "...Sir," she continued, leveling her tone to a more respectful register as he returned to signing the final pages of the mission file.

"Either way they are dead, so I guess we mark this down as a win, no matter how convoluted it may have been," he offered. "Did you get to witness Mr. Marshall dispatch the Leash?"

Agni was officially annoyed. What was with all these questions about a prisoner? The Leash was more or less dead when Marshall had shot him. What did it matter if he had been observed doing so? "No sir, I didn't see it first-hand, but it looks as if there was something of a duel between the two based on the shell casings found there. The fight, though brief, must have been intense."

Zander allowed a rare smile of amusement to pass his lips. "An intense duel between a dead Leash and a half dead merc, what a sight that must have been."

"Sir, the mission was a success. Why all the questions about it? Are we not holding the mercenary as insurance against the organization he works for?" Agni finally inquired, no longer able to contain her annoyance.

Zander leaned back in his chair and took his glasses off in contemplation, his right hand pressing gently against his temple. "TITAN has disavowed Mr. Marshall; he is now under our protection...and employment," he said, pausing only long enough for Agni's eyes to widen. "He has been asked to stay on with the Academy as a combat instructor, of sorts."

Agni nearly came out of her seat in disbelief. "An instructor?! He's a savage. You've seen the reports, sir. He's killed Psychics, and you want him here teaching Leashes how to fight? How is he even qualified to do that? Even a Level One Leash could pull him in half with their bare hands."

"Not just Leashes, Psychics as well." Zander's response was flat. Agni blinked several times, as if the action would somehow make his statement more sensible to her. "Psychics, sir?"

Zander placed his glasses back on and turned to face the Level Four Psychic. "Who better to teach our Psychics how not to die than someone who has had experience killing them?"

Agni was baffled. "When does this training begin?"

"Tomorrow. We already have a small group selected. Recently merged Mumbler teams, a promising group," Zander responded in his usual steely fashion.

"Might I be permitted to observe the lessons?" Agni inquired after some hesitation.

"Are you questioning our judgment, Agni?"

The Psychic straightened up. Even though Zander wasn't considered a Level Four Leash, she had on numerous occasions watched him put Level Four Leashes flat on their backs. His experience was extensive, and his focus was superhuman. Even her brother couldn't fight him one on one.

"No sir, but I know most of the new merges. I would just like to be present in case something goes awry."

Zander stared at Agni hard for a moment. "Gregory suggested the very same thing. I don't think it's wise, but it seems I'm outvoted. So yes, you've been assigned to monitor these early training sessions, as long as you aren't being called away to other assignments, to make sure they go well."

"So tomorrow then?"

"Too soon for you?" The familiar caustic tone that Agni had grown accustomed to made her uncomfortable, especially when paired with that smirk.

"Entirely," she responded flatly.

Hours of riding in silence had done little to curb Blaine's temper and less to improve his general demeanor, which on a good day was unpleasant. "How did we manage to get the one driver in TITAN who goes out of his way to hit every pothole in the road?"

The Greenie in the driver's seat set his jaw against the captain's verbal abuse and opted not to respond. This was, after all, fairly typical behavior from the Battle Captain.

The Specialist was seated comfortably with his back against the wall. The modified military truck had been expanded and improved upon, allowing him space without having to sit next to anyone. His eyes were closed, a bemused smile perched on his lips, a small metal briefcase resting against his calf.

"I never did catch your name by the way," Blaine remarked out of the corner of his mouth, more uncomfortable in the silence than he was with the tense conversation between strangers.

"And I never gave it," came the amused response.

Blaine snorted derisively. "Is that your idea of intimidation? The Man With No Name sounds like a kid's story. This is the real world, you know. Everyone's got credentials; that's how they get hired. And you're some kind of specialist, right? So there must be some kind of resume to go along with that. How many confirmed kills do you have?"

"Zero." The Specialist retorted, now finally opening his eyes only to observe his well-manicured nails.

"How many successful assignments are on record?" Blaine continued his questioning.

"None."

"What experience and training have you had to qualify you as a specialist?"

"Never had any," he was now making eye contact and smiling playfully at the captain.

"Then what qualifies you to consult on this assignment? What was your connection to AGEIS? What possible reason could the Commandant have for sending you on thi–"

"Your name is Blaine Kavinsky, 38 years old, a member of TITAN since 25. Solid academic scores. Modest physical fitness scores and a passing combat score. You were promoted faster than most through the ranks, which has earned you the respect of some of your peers but not of your superiors, who feel you are riding the coattails of a certain First Commander who happens to share your last name."

Blaine Blinked 3 times before he shook off the shock. "Anyone with moderate computer skills could find that information in a matter of minutes. It's a good trick, and you almost had me, but it's nothing that couldn't have been found by any–"

"Only your name isn't Kavinsky at all, it's McKellen. You changed it to your mother's maiden name when you were 16 because your father was dishonorably discharged from the military for embezzling funds from his platoon. Your academics are only on par because your uncle paid for you to have a private tutor until you were 20 because you have undiagnosed dyslexia which makes it nearly impossible to read without assistance, and the region you grew up in had a very strict policy on not educating undesirables such as yourself. You qualified for TITAN by taking your own test and passing, but your physical and combat exams were doctored by your uncle, a First Commander, the same uncle who paid for your tutoring. You have a drinking problem that causes you to lean too heavily on your right side, resulting in a wince. Your liver damage is probably irreparable."

Blaine sat speechless. He didn't even remember breathing for several seconds afterwards. When he finally could formulate words, they spilled stupidly from his mouth and without coherence. "How could ... there's no way that you ... son of a b–"

"And that's why I'm the Specialist. Information is power. And I have access to all information." Blaine sat baffled, afraid to speak, almost afraid to move. Satisfied that he had successfully earned silence for the remainder of their trip, the Specialist sat quietly, contemplating what was ahead.

Someone surviving isn't just unlikely, it's statistically impossible, the specialist reflected. *I assumed that the Leash would be killed by the Academy operatives. But between the explosions, the guards and the security, Marshall shouldn't have been able to survive. Tobias Marshall. My first failure in a long time. I hope he doesn't mind if I take it personally.* A pleasant smile traced his lips while he contemplated something he had considered impossible.

The remainder of the trip was silent. Only the roads and the poorly suppressed groans of the Battle Captain filled the otherwise empty truck. They passed the Academy's power plant on their left, right before pulling up into the TITAN convoy. Blaine jumped out of the vehicle and was approached by a fresh-faced Gun Squad leader.

"Sir, we've been waiting on you. We've been instructed to prepare for your arrival. Your tent is set up," the young soldier directed Blaine toward his temporary accommodations.

"Good. Show me there and give me your report on the way," barked Blaine, attempting to assert his authority over the clearly subordinate Gun Leader.

"I - I've been asked to take you to the Upper Captain, sir. As soon as you arrived," the soldier responded with confusion.

"Then move it," barked Blaine.

The Gun Squad Leader was doing a sharp about face and leading them both to the makeshift command tent. As they entered, there were a number of recruits working diligently behind what looked like mountains of electronic equipment. "Cap Montez, Captain Blaine is here, sir." Blaine could have reprimanded the young man for naming him second, but missed his chance, too distracted by the other captain's approach.

They were approached by a sloppily uniformed man. His physique was hardened and tall, his unshaven face nothing like you'd expect from anyone in senior command, and yet his subordinates were careful and efficient, regarding him with respect and adoration.

"You must be the expert the commandant told us would be assisting," the sloppily-dressed man spoke, addressing the Specialist. "Well, you got here right in time. We've been monitoring, as ordered. But despite 24-hour surveillance, we haven't gotten any readings from inside," the man reported while the Specialist leaned over the screens, examining what looked to be highly convoluted and encrypted lines of code.

"What do you mean 'no readings'? This is the most sophisticated equipment in the world!" Blaine spat, his indignation no longer contained.

"Mind your tone, Battle Captain. We've been running into some kind of heavy disruption, but we can't tell if it's electronic or something else," the unkempt senior commander named Montez warned.

"As per the Commandant I'm in charge until the end of this assignment" Blaine barked out, shedding the last of his composure.

The Battle Captain became aware that nearly every set of eyes in the room was locked on him even as they all continued to do their work. Blaine fought the urge to swallow hard at his own anxiety. "Besides Montez, we can pick up heat signatures through steel walls. There is no electronic equipment in production anywhere in the world that could cause this kind of disruption."

"You're not accounting for Psychic disruption," quipped the Specialist. He reached in his pocket and pulled out a small black box with grated lines on the top of it like a small speaker. He flicked the small flat switch on the side and all at once an intense high frequency buzz filled the room, then abruptly stopped.

Several of the analysts were covering their ears, mouths opened in a silent scream, eyes clenched shut against what their minds had told them was a life-altering screech, only to fall silent and lift their heads to examine their monitors.

"Every human sense is just electricity altered by the right frequency or the right flow. Introduce the proper stimulus and even the strongest Psychic becomes a schizophrenic with migraines," the Specialist explained.

They all sat looking amazed; the information on their screens was what they had been hunting for days, and it was now plainly in front of them.

"Your senses have lied to you. You are no longer the top of the food chain, homo sapiens. Better learn to make spears." The Specialist wandered over to one of the recruits who was still staring stupidly at his monitor.

Blaine wiped his eyes and fought to catch his breath before staring up at the screens. Even with his untrained eye he could plainly see thousands of small red heat signatures moving about the Academy like ants inside of a hive structure. "How could they have done that on such a scale?"

"Always the wrong questions," the Specialist chided. "Computers can be infected. Computers can be tricked or manipulated. So we make firewalls and protections so we don't have to think about potential problems. But humans, we beg to be lied to. Our reality wants to be shaped by outside information. Even color, sound, weight, and speed are all just clever fabrications that we enjoy believing but collapse around the slightest scrutiny. You were fooled because you wanted to be fooled. It takes very little persuasive ability to convince people they are right, and a great deal more to convince them they are wrong." He turned his attention back to the screens.

"What exactly are you looking for?" Blaine asked, officially tired of being made a fool of at a command post he had been assigned to.

"Food," remarked the Specialist.

Captain Montez made a noise akin to sucking air between his teeth, a habit he had picked up as a child when he had made a mistake and someone had called attention to it. "Of course you are."

"Food? All the available information in this room, the most sophisticated technology in the world, and you use it to look for food?!" Blaine had had it with this upstart.

He crossed the room, not caring what the Commandant had said, ready to teach this skinny punk a lesson. He reached out, hands tense and angry. A millimeter before he felt his fingers brush the cloth of the Specialists shirt, the heel of a shoe struck his knee and a well-practiced hand gripped his wrist, twisting the Battle Captain's arm nearly to the point of breaking.

If he could have turned his head far enough, he would have seen a smug smile ghosting across the Specialist's lips. "I encourage you to not try to sneak up behind me again, Battle Captain. Especially when I can see your reflection in the computer monitor," he said soothingly while applying additional pressure to Blaine's wrist and shoulder.

"But I am sorry," he continued. "I shouldn't have assumed you would understand. In this context it comes from an early military expression from the 20 Year War, when the Psychics started ripping entire militaries apart. The countries that were in charge of the largest armies developed a tech that did active brainwave scans on a given area that worked well with existing infrared tech. As it turns out, Psychics and their Leashes produce large quantities of certain brain waves. It's one of the reasons they are so strong; they literally leak energy."

With his free hand the Specialist pressed his thumbnail into the now profusely sweating captain's cheek until a thin line of blood appeared. "You see, much like this cut, all humans pulse Psychic energy. Though the read is small, Psychics and Leashes produce substantially more. So teach your machines to read for the particular waves that the brain produces, and you could see a Psychic coming from further off and know when a threat was going to arrive. It assisted with military hit and run tactics. But ..."

The specialist then pressed his hand hard to Blaine's cheek and smeared the blood across his face in a progressively fading red streak. "If you're looking for a non-Psychic in a pile of Psychics, then you just look for the void instead of the droplets. Fairly simple concept. But incredibly effective."

He released Blaine's wrist and exited the command tent. Blaine had all of the bluster stripped from him as he rose shakily to his full height again. The computer monitors were now a swirl of colored dots. Some points of light were incredibly bright, some more faded. Walking toward a large open area inside the Academy was a smudge, faded and dull, barely noticeable in the wake of all the other bright colors and swirls on the screen.

"Marshall," Blaine said softly.

"Bit of a wildcard, isn't he, Blaine?" Montez spoke, trying to break the incredibly strained silence that was still hanging heavy and damp over the rest of the tent.

Blaine rubbed his wrist quietly while he tried to hide his embarrassment. He glanced at the door the Specialist had just exited through. "Something like that."

Chapter 1.6

Understanding the Wash

"The change in a Leash isn't just mental, it's also physiological. The extreme quantities of Psychic energy that are required to give a Leash their exceptional abilities also take a physical toll. Leashes must undergo their Wash regularly to maintain a full contingent of Psychic energy or the consequences could be irreparable."

Along the two separate entrances to the cafeteria were what appeared to be identical restaurant windows serving identical food. But one line was entirely populated with Psychics and the other with Leashes.

"Why the segregation?" Tobias inquired.

"Leashes have to maintain a high-calorie diet, so their food is enhanced," Alyssia responded.

Live trees and the ever flowing river that traced the perimeter of the Academy's main floor ran through the middle of the dining area.

There were several recessed areas along the outside of the cafeteria, covered by glass screens with broad slide spaces for trays. Inside, cooks worked frantically to prepare meals for the many hungry Psychics and Leashes. Tables and trays were scattered throughout with baskets of breads and fruits for those who got hungry in between meal times.

In the midst of it all, Alyssia stared with a mix of horror and admiration as Tobias ate. He was currently consuming his third sandwich, breathing only between mouthfuls and swallowing hard. He wasn't making a scene, just eating, but he couldn't be deterred, and he attacked his meal with starving efficiency. He swallowed a mouthful of bread, meat and cheese.

"You just gonna watch me?" Tobias asked, not looking up from his sandwich before taking another monstrous bite.

Alyssia laughed, she hadn't realized she was staring. "I've never seen a non-Leash eat like that before." Tobias glanced around and noticed an odd trend permeated throughout the room. Groups that Tobias assumed were Psychic and Leash pairs were sitting near each other. While this didn't strike him as unusual, one individual in each pair would have a tray in front of them with portions that seemed equivalent to their size, while the second appeared to be carrying a tray large enough for several people. If they were eating sandwiches, they were eating five or six of them. It looked like an insane amount of food, but it dawned on him.

"Because of the high physical demands of their bodies," Tobias commented, suddenly realizing the source of the odd dichotomy.

"Leashes eat like slobs, right?"

Alyssia's eyes snapped up at the unexpected visitor's remark, then immediately back down at her tray of food. Tobias turned his head to see the black hair and bright, smirking eyes of Rudra. He watched the Tornado Leash as he sat down across the table, his plate piled high with a variety of fatty, high calorie foods. Even the salad that was on his plate had nuts, fruits, cheeses, and a variety of other toppings that made the item's classification as a salad ambiguous.

"Leashes have to have special diets to access all of our physical potential," Rudra continued. "The Psychic energy in our bodies increases the density of both bone and muscle. That's why we are so much heavier than the average human. We have to stay loaded up. I just got an uptick - 30,000 calories a day."

Tobias looked incredulous, but based on the absurd amount of food Rudra had loaded onto his plate he was having a hard time contesting the new information.

"Our nutritional needs are offset by the Wash, but we still have to keep in the protein powders and nutrition supplements to maintain us," Rudra finished explaining before his intense quantity of food began disappearing off of his plate and down his throat.

With his hunger satiated, Tobias turned his attention back to the rest of the room. Being in the hospital must have made him lax, because as Tobias attempted to candidly glance around, he suddenly realized there were a large number of eyes focusing on him.

"Feeling popular?" Rudra quipped without looking up. "That's because of your company."

Alyssia spoke, her voice just loud enough for Tobias to hear. "I usually eat alone or in my classroom and Rudra, well, he doesn't come down here often."

Tobias glanced around the room again. It did occur to him that half of the people looking in his direction weren't actually looking at him.

"That's right, Mr. Marshall. You're sitting at the monsters' table with all the scary people." Rudra chuckled.

Alyssia winced.

"Most Psychics get sent on recon missions, interrogations, or intelligence operations," the Tornado Leash continued. "Soldier Psychics and their Leashes usually deal with direct combat. But Level Fours like me, well, we kind of have reputations as Boogiemen. We almost exclusively get selected to high casualty missions."

He twirled his fork between his fingers and added a toothy grin before digging into another one of the many bowls on his plate, a particularly delicious smelling bowl of thick, white soup that appeared to have chunks of sausage and onions in it.

"Then what about you?" Tobias turned his attention to Alyssia who was receiving the exact same amount of tense glances and shameless gawking.

"Vampires out in the daylight tend to draw the eye," Rudra remarked, a little icier than most of his usual banter.

Alyssia looked as if someone had punched her in the stomach. "I'm an energy sync, which means I feed on energy, including Psychic energy.

It's the reason I haven't been paired yet. Every time we tried, it ended badly."

Rudra made a sound that could have been a scoff.

"So I hear you're gonna be working with some of our Mumblers starting tomorrow," the Leash said, clearly done discussing Alyssia. "Should be fun. There aren't many criers in that group."

Rudra had somehow managed to clear his tray and was now sitting back in his chair eyeing Tobias with mock scrutiny. "What do you plan to teach a room full of Psychics, Mr. Marshall? How to talk good and look at people mean?"

Tobias knew when he was being patronized. He watched the Leash as he tossed an olive in the air, leaning back to catch it in his open mouth. The olive never made it. Tobias snatched it out of the air and rested it between two skilled fingers. "Something like that," he said as he popped the olive into his own mouth.

Alyssia tried and failed to hide her smile. Rudra let out a surprised laugh.

"Alright tough guy, you don't have to prove anything to me," the Tornado Leash said. "I've seen you in action. But you are going to have a hard time convincing those who haven't seen it that you're qualified."

"I couldn't care less what a bunch of special needs children think of me," Tobias retorted, not enjoying being the object of ridicule.

A flash of anger caused Rudra's eyes to narrow and then, almost immediately, flutter back to their typical playful light. "Well I guess that's enough stuffing myself for now, you two kids stay out of trouble."

Rudra glanced around the room before standing up, leaving his tray on the table and crossing to one of the benches that were scattered amongst the live trees. He sat by a pretty, olive skinned girl with glasses. She was crunching into an apple juicy enough that she had to chase the stray drops down her wrist with her lips, before she refocused on reading her paperback book.

She appeared to be lost in her own thoughts, immersed in whatever world she was discovering on the page when Rudra interrupted her. She went through several expressions in order: surprise, then a swipe of fear, and finally a small flattered smile kissed her lips.

Tobias watched for a few moments. Rudra flirted effortlessly with the pretty woman. She would blush, and he would lean into her laugh. His posture was so relaxed and easy.

"Is he always that smooth?" Tobias remarked as he and Alyssia stood up and walked away.

Rudra stole a glance at their direction.

Tobias Marshall, just who the hell are you? The Leash wondered as he watched the former mercenary leave the dining hall with Alyssia. He decided to turn his attention back to olive skin and a delicious smile.

As they walked out, Alyssia was still smiling; her tense, uncomfortable demeanor had melted into teenage glee. She walked with a particularly satisfied bounce.

"Nobody talks to Rudra that way. And I mean NOBODY, it was glorious." Alyssia couldn't seem to contain herself. "Do you always make a habit of picking fights with people who can rip you in half?"

Tobias had to hide his smirk. "I take it you two don't get along?"

The girl's smile shrank several molars. "Oh, I'm used to it. Rudra is a good man, he has his reasons for disliking me, I guess."

Tobias didn't respond but watched the young Psychic intently as they continued to walk together. He saw the barely perceptible regression to her previous demeanor. Shoulders slumping, eyes down and apologetic, shrinking into herself as if she was afraid she was taking up too much space.

Alyssia narrowed her eyes as she stared at some imperceptible spot down the hallway. "Rudra and Agni sat in on one of my attempted merges. It...it went poorly," she explained, not realizing that she was now several steps ahead of Tobias.

"Poorly?" Tobias inquired.

Alyssia was making the circle along the Academy walkway away from the cafeteria and toward the dormitories. Her feet carried her back into her memory.

She could still smell the pulses of energy from the council. Gregory roared as he tried to throw them off balance. The heat from Agni's fire burned all around her as she tried everything in her power to disrupt the Psychic merger. And the beautiful, kind woman who was supposed to be her Leash writhing and screaming in what she could only imagine as the most painful death possible. "I ate the Leash they tried to merge me with," she answered Tobias's vague question.

Her swift steps had taken her to the visitor dormitories and she had stopped at the door to Mr. Marshall's room. "This is where you can stay, Mr. Mar – Tobias. "

Alyssia couldn't look up at him or meet his gaze. She was terrified of what she might see. Hate? Disgust? Fear?

Why did I tell him that? Why would I be honest with this stranger? The Psychic was mentally chastising herself.

"So because you eat energy, you can't be paired?" She noted that his voice was full of something, but it wasn't hate or fear. It was a curiosity.

"Sounds like you got off easy," he continued. "I can't imagine many things worse than being stuck with another human being. You're better off."

Alyssia stared at Tobias with a wide-eyed expression. Was it that he didn't understand what had happened, or was he just that cold?

"Thanks for the tour, Al." Tobias entered the room and closed the door gently.

Alyssia stood there staring at the door, wanting to knock but not knowing why. Tobias Marshall was unlikeable, arrogant, indifferent, and had absolutely no empathy. And she wanted so badly to know more   about   him.

Syn always felt a little uneasy when he was back at the Academy. He had spent most of his youth working or hunting outdoors, often sleeping without even a shelter overhead. So to be confined to a facility of steel and stone often felt stifling. He made the broad half circle around the outside of the Academy's first floor holding his satchel.

He made it to the elevator that led down to the training facility and stepped inside. He reached out with his knuckle and rapped the button, the lift moving seamlessly and smoothly down. He felt the change in the climate, the stiffness in the air that reminded him that the oxygen was now artificial, filtered and treated.

The doors dinged, and he stepped off. Everywhere he looked, young Leashes and several Psychics were working out or sparring. Some spared glances in his direction. While he was known by name and reputation, Syn was one of the few Level Four members that was widely liked by most everyone in the Academy. He was friendly and easy going which was why no one ever questioned him being paired with the incredibly excitable Dian. He cut a line across the training facility to the large steel door at the southernmost edge of the large rectangular room. It was guarded by two Soldier teams. He approached and the two Leashes stood up a little straighter, and eased their grips on their weapons.

"I'm here to see Number 12. You fellas mind if I go in?" Syn asked simply.

One of the Psychics, a young bespectacled female with strawberry blonde hair, stepped forward and spoke. "Sorry sir, but we will need to do all the normal scans as well as check your pack."

Syn lowered his pack to the ground and watched as one of the Leashes unclasped and unrolled it. The Psychic stepped forward and looked up at the Hunters Leash. "Sir."

Syn held out one hand and closed his eyes to relax his mind. He felt a small prick on his finger as the DNA scanner took effect, and he felt the tickle behind his eyes of a Psychic perusing his thoughts and recent memories.

After several moments, he heard the Psychic grant his approval.

"Approved, sir. Thank you for your cooperation."

Syn opened his eyes and smiled at the young guards.

"Sir, can I ask what kind of meat that is in your pack? It smells really good," asked one of the Leashes doing little to hide his hunger from Syn.

The Hunters Leash laughed as he ripped off several strips of meat before rerolling his satchel up and handing the guards all a strip.

"Help yourself, Cassius. You need to build some muscle anyway," Syn said jovially.

The large steel door opened and Syn walked through. The stale air smelled of stone walls and bleach. The hallway was well lit but adorned by nothing, branching off to the left and right. Syn pivoted and began walking to his left. He passed a number of steel doors on either side of the hallway, each one with a number over them in ascending order. At the very back of the hallway was a large poly fiber wall, behind which there was a cot, a toilet, and a collection of charcoal drawings scattered about.

Syn knew the wall to be harder than steel and a great deal more flexible, designed to be airtight in case the oxygen in the room needed to be cut off for any reason. On Syn's side of the wall was a single stool, and a tray slide carved into the steel wall. The opening measured only about a third of a meter in every direction.

Syn pulled down the tray door and unrolled the satchel. He deposited the package of smoked elk meat into the slot and pushed it, with some force down the chute, before closing it again.

"Brought you a treat," Syn said as he sat down on the stool and began to eat from his own pouch slowly and thoughtfully.

The cot stirred and moved before the figure on it rose. Had the figure been wearing anything it would have been impossible to identify as man or woman. The nude body was all but covered in tattoos, some clearly defined and easily identified whereas others were covered and marked over, convoluted.

The man was tall and slender, his arms and legs appearing emaciated. His head was shaved as were his eyebrows, an appearance that gave his face a gaunt, skeletal look. This was exacerbated by his slouching posture and thin features. He opened the tray door tentatively with two fingers like a lover opening a gift they knew as precious. He pulled the small package out of the opening and carried it over to the wall at the front of his cell, sat down, and opened it.

"I hope you like it. I know you prefer raw, but it wouldn't have kept that way for long," Syn spoke in between mouthfuls.

The figure reached his fingers into the package and pulled out a long piece of the meat and held it over his head, examining it in the light before dropping it into his mouth between tattooed lips. He chewed and slurped wordlessly, the thumb of his free hand petting the hide pouch affectionately. The two men sat in relative silence for the better part of 10 minutes.

"Where were you sent?" The skeletal form behind the wall spoke in a voice that was graveled from lack of use.

"North," Syn's response was less than detailed.

"Snow?"

Syn paused for a minute before taking another bite of his meat. "It's late spring, Angel, it hasn't snowed south of the Barrens for a while."

"I like snow. Fresh, soft powder. Kill anyone worth mentioning?" Angel spoke as he pressed the hide pouch to his nose and breathed in deeply, still appreciating the smell of tanned flesh.

"Not on this trip. Some upstart mercenary group that was making too much noise, the local money didn't want them getting any stronger. We fried a power station and killed a few of the key players. But no, no one worth mentioning," Syn remarked quietly as he put away his own pouch and watched the skeletal form enjoy his gift.

"Any screamers?" Angel inquired as he laid flat on his back, the leather pouch still over his face breathing it deeply in between raspy words.

"From two kilometers?" Syn chuckled. "Who could tell."

"Me." Angel planted his feet flat on the ground and pushed, his legs went rigid and dragged his body forward until he appeared to be folded in half, backwards at the waist. He then began to straighten himself, his spine coiled and bent at sickening angles making his form appear boneless but the squelching of organs and the popping of joints inside of his thin frame was unmistakably human. He continued to contort himself until he was slumped forward, his face pressed against the poly fiber wall.

"How have you –" Syn began before an awful grating noise cut him off.

He looked up to see Angel pressing his fingernails into the nearly indestructible wall, his nails cracking and bleeding with the effort. The sound was like fine glass sheets scratching against each other. It was unpleasant.

" ... been?" Angel chuckled a dry, mirthless laugh, finishing Syn's sentence.

"Was the creature you brought me female?" Angel continued in his raspy voice, closing his tattooed eyelids in concentration.

Syn found this question perverse, although he wasn't sure why, so he shrugged lazily. "Can't remember. All taste the same once they are cooked I guess."

Angel made a tsk noise as he lowered himself to the ground to lay sideways in front of the wall. "Must have been a lady. She tastes like a lady. Young."

Suddenly Syn felt the need to reach out. He opened his mind, looking for the small warm thread of Psychic energy that he knew belonged to Dian. When he did find it, it was blurry and convoluted, blended with something else. Like the shadow of a great tree obscuring the sun where only peeks of light would shine through the branches.

"Melania has taken a liking to your child, Rifleman." Angel turned his gaunt, sunken eyes toward his visitor, while he lowered himself to the ground and resumed a seated position giving the closest thing he had to a friend his full attention.

Syn had noticed a different smell lately. Something on Dian had seemed different, like she had found a new joy but it also seemed to strain her. He suspected she had a lover but was surprised to learn it was the Nightmare Psychic.

"A robin and a spider in love. How quaint." Angel spoke without blinking, his vicious gaze locked on Syn's face.

"They are adults. They can do as they please," Syn shrugged.

"How will you feel when my spider eats your robin?" Angel taunted quietly.

Syn chuckled.

"Dear Rifleman, have I offended you?" Angel asked, his tone mocking.

"Not at all," Syn mused. "I was just wondering how a spider would stand up to a bolt of lightning."

Angel laughed, an unpleasant grating sound, like gears of a motor that didn't quite mesh. "Do you remember the first?"

"Every time I see you, you ask the same question."

"You've yet to answer," Angel replied.

"What makes you think I will this time?"

"I remember my first." Angel's dark eyes glistened. "I was 18 years old–"

"Last time I heard this you were 19," Syn's bored tone spurred Angel on.

"That was my first paid assignment, this was my *first*. I was 18, money was hard to come by at that age. So I was..." Angel licked his lips, "...entertaining for my dinner."

Syn was used to these kinds of stories. Angel was always trying to shock him, tell a story that would disgust and horrify him. He had yet to manage it despite his best efforts. That, however, hadn't stopped him from trying.

"He was my third John of the evening, a pleasant enough gentleman. He invited me into his car, was fairly straightforward with what he wanted and easy enough to please. But when we had finished he refused to pay," Angel smiled as the memory swirled in his mind. "He held a knife on me. I can't remember if it was the rage or the challenge that finally motivated me, but when he finally leaned in too close I bit his face. You should have heard him. He dropped his knife. We fumbled for a while, but I got the knife before he did. I can't remember how many times I stabbed him, but I do remember how disappointed I was when he stopped screaming."

Syn stood up and placed the stool back against the wall of the cell.

"Do you want to know how I know you're lying, my friend?" Syn smirked. "You've never forgotten how many blade strokes it took to kill a man. Never."

Angel licked his lips. "Do you ever miss the war, dear Rifleman?"

Syn stowed his pouch in his pocket as he began to leave. "Which one?" He walked away from the cell waving over his shoulder. "I'll be back tomorrow. Any requests?"

"Robin eggs."

Aspis flicked the cherry off of her cigarette after her last drag then concentrated on her mental task. Focusing her energy inward, she could feel her body working to heal her scorched lungs as fast as she could inhale.

Being a high level Psychic definitely had its perks. She loved to smoke; she had started when she was 13 and had been doing it ever since. Her excuse was that her genius level IQ needed some balance. She was ahead of her classmates in every academic medium, but she didn't even get a nicotine buzz anymore. She just enjoyed the ritual of the habit.

The southernmost part of the Northern region was rugged and vegetation was sparse. The potash and cobalt deposits are what kept the people calling this unpleasant slice of hell home. The area was arid and hot during the day with rapid cooling in the evening, making the environment uncomfortable at best. Why anyone would live here was beyond Aspis' understanding.

She could see Xiphos walking toward her from between their caravan, probably on his way to give her a report. She could have reached out and spoken to him telepathically, but she liked interacting with her Leash. While he could be infuriatingly easy going, he was an intelligent, reliable, and fiercely loyal friend. Besides, even if men were not her inclination, he was a masterpiece of physical form and watching him move was art in motion.

"Hey, the scouts made it back. The road ahead looked clear," the Sword Leash reported.

She could hear something in his voice waver slightly. "Problem?" she asked.

He shook his head. "We were contracted specifically for heavy resistance? I mean, I get being over cautious, but this seems excessive. We haven't even seen another vehicle in almost 100 kilometers."

She admired her partner, but she'd never let him know that. "You're probably just being paranoid, so bored with babysitting these diplomats that you're dreaming up some action."

Xiphos shrugged. He pressed his palms together, an old habit from a former life, and then looked back at the vehicles.

"We were running on time, why did we stop?" Xiphos inquired.

He wasn't being impatient; he trusted his partner's judgment, but sitting in one place too long was dangerous, and deviating from a plan was even more dangerous. They were presently doing both.

"Client requested we stop for a rest evidently. I don't like it any more than you do, but we have orders." Aspis looked over at the stationary caravan. Five vehicles in total with 18 guards, one Psychic and one Leash.

"Anyway, we're getting ready to leave. You good?" Xiphos finished up his report as Aspis let an irritated sigh slip.

"I suppose. Would you do me a favor and scout ahead? I don't trust the eyes of these guards. And I'd rather have some warning ahead of time if something is coming our way."

Xiphos nodded as he turned to walk away. Aspis watched him take several steps as he broke into a jog and in a few steps he had vanished from sight. She reached out with her mind and touched his, maintaining a comfort that only Psychics and Leashes would ever know.

Aspis walked down to the caravan and remounted the second vehicle in line, climbing into the gun nest at the top of it and glancing past their little caravan at all the neighboring hillsides. All was quiet.

It had only taken them about 12 hours of travel to meet up with the dignitary, some politician's heir apparent, and begin traveling southeast. All in all, it had been a quiet enough trip. They hadn't had a run in with any hostiles, and even the dignitary had been quiet. As a matter of fact, he hadn't made a single demand of anyone, other than the request to stop, which was unusual for someone of his station.

Xiphos looked back from his new position at the small caravan of vehicles approaching behind him then forward with his binoculars. Even though it was early in the evening, there was little daylight available and the cold in the air made everything seem a little hazier. Still, all looked clear.

"Paranoid." He turned his binoculars forward and caught the shadow of a figure. Just one from the look of it, and entirely too far off to be a threat. Whatever it was, it was clearly moving toward them.

Aspis, unknown approaching, he projected to his partner.

A threat? His partner replied curtly.

Doubtful. Unknown is moving slowly, and as far as I can tell, alone, he replied.

Investigate, but don't get too far off. If it is a hostile, I'd rather engage it together. Aspis always spoke with authority, even if it was just inside his mind. It made Xiphos smile in a most rebellious manner he was glad his partner couldn't see.

Xiphos reached into his store of Psychic energy. He was still fresh from his most recent Wash, so when he reached into his own stored energy it felt like an ocean. He scooped it up and forced it to every corner of his body; his muscles pulsed and grew, preparing to fuel the demands he was about to place on them. His bones became dense and heavy enough to stand up to the rigors he was about to force on them. Even his organs became thicker and more durable as vast quantities of Psychic energy poured through them.

As he broke into a run, he left the road and cut a half circle in a broad arch around the unknown, making long calculated strides so as not to raise a dust trail. He stopped his run approximately 100 meters behind the target, pincering it between himself and the caravan. As he got closer, he observed the figure had stopped moving and was holding its position on the road. It felt wrong.

Aspis, something's off. Prepare to engage. He didn't need to see her face to know she had just nodded and was currently expanding her range of Psychic awareness.

"Govorit'!" Xiphos shouted. The term literally translated to the word "speak", but in the Northern Region it translated closer to "identify".

The figure took a startled half-step forward then stopped again, their focus still straight ahead.

"Govorit'!" Xiphos shouted again, breaking into a jog. There was no way this person posed a threat to a caravan at this distance, but something was wrong. There was no reason for anyone to be out here, there was less reason for them to stop.

What could they be–? His thoughts were interrupted by the figure's arm as it came above its head, and a stream of hot red light shot straight up in the air, accompanied by a high-pitched whistle.

"Screech Flare!" Xiphos felt his eyes involuntarily follow the red magnesium trail straight up before his head snapped toward where he knew the caravan to be. A tail of smoke and light raced from a hilltop toward the road. Before he could form a thought, it detonated just behind the rearmost vehicle, flipping it onto its side with a violent shock.

Aspis SHIELD! Xiphos felt his mind and voice scream at once as the smoke stream of three additional RPGs raced across the sky.

He took off at a sprint, trying desperately to beat the impending impact. He planted his feet and pushed his body forward; he felt the Psychic energy inside him flare, intensifying everything from his physical strength to his lung capacity. His sprint ramped up to over 300 kph, running past the lookout, shredding his body like wax paper with a swipe of his hand. Even as he felt his bones shattering and rebuilding under the pressure and speed he still had to watch helplessly as the second volley of RPGs erupted.

Xiphos exhaled hard, relieved as he watched the ensuing explosions splash like water off a rubber ball, and he saw the unbroken eye contact of Aspis. Her Psychic shield was dissipating and she was standing defiantly, glaring in the direction of the rockets, swiveling in her seat atop the 50 caliber machine gun, her mouth open in a mute scream.

The heavy rounds erupted from the muzzle of the weapon and smashed against the hillside, sending dirt and stone rocketing skyward. The guards of the caravan were quickly maneuvering the more heavily armored vehicles between the diplomat's car and the would-be ambushers.

"Keep us moving! Cover the client and move," the small, serious woman commanded her driver in between volleys of shots into the icy hillside. Her gunfire was the North Star to Xiphos as he raced toward the hillside, the impact of the large caliber rounds painting his target like a beacon. His lean frame flew over an embankment and for a brief moment he was airborne, then he saw their assailants. 12 armed men, some taking cover while others were leaning over to fire at the caravan. They were heavily cloaked, comfortable with the ice and sand of the desert in day or night. These were citizens of the Northern region.

Why are they attacking their own? Xiphos wondered, but it was a mystery that would have to wait for later. The moment Xiphos' feet felt earth under them from his brief flight, he dashed toward their attackers. He accelerated, leaning his shoulder down and slamming his body into the back of the first unsuspecting insurgent, the spine and ribs of the man turned to pudding as the two made contact. The now very dead insurgent was turned into a 80kg projectile that Xiphos sent hurtling at a second gunman.

Smarter not harder. Xiphos smirked to himself. The exchange caught the attention of the remaining assailants who whirled frantically to deal with the new threat. They fired in a panicked manner at the Sword Leash, but his agility made their bullets all but worthless. He raced forward, his body leaving the ground as he twisted his torso, using the momentum to snap his leg around in a spin kick that removed the head from one of the gunmen and left his remaining torso as a pile of twitching nerve endings. He landed in the middle of the remaining nine, bent both knees as a hail of gunfire split the air in his direction. He pushed off the ground with considerable exertion, his body rocketing up and forward while two of the gunmen behind him were shredded by friendly fire. He landed in the midst of another group that was screaming in the clear and unmistakable dialect of the Northern district: "Ubey Urod!"

Kill the freak, huh? Xiphos felt his lips split into a blood thirsty smile. *You can try, Suka.*

They were bugs to be killed. He jabbed his fiercely accurate left hand forward. The strike easily pierced the body of one of the assailants. He again flung the pierced and broken frame at the others with enough force to shatter bone and split muscle. He felt a gunbarrel pressed against the back of his neck; some very brave or very foolish man had decided that the risk of missing his shot was greater than the risk of being striking distance from a super human.

But before the trigger could be pulled, Xiphos whirled on his heel and split the gunman from shoulder to stomach, sloshing blood and viscera all over the sand. He whirled around to see who remained, but before he could make a movement, he heard a *pop* and was floored by an otherworldly feeling of weakness and pain, as if he'd grabbed hold of an electrical wire.

His eyes involuntarily closed and his muscles refused to obey his instructions. *What's happening to me?* He felt himself gagging and choking. In an instant he had gone from being a superhuman to being completely helpless. The weight of his own frame was unbearable, crushing him alive. He used what small strength he had left and tried to look up. Through blurred vision he saw one of the gunmen approaching him tentatively, his rifle pressed into his shoulder. The hand he used to steady the barrel was holding a small black box.

All at once there was a loud crunch and the pain stopped. He watched as all of the remaining gunmen grabbed their heads screaming. A figure stepped in front of him moving forward at a steady pace. In the dim light he could see all the men's faces begin to contort, their eyes appeared to bulge from their skulls, and their tongues wagged far past their chins. It appeared as if they were exploding, but Xiphos recognized the change.

"Aspis," choked the Sword Leash.

"Will there ever come a time I don't have to save your ass?" Aspis inhaled deeply. As she exhaled the men's skulls caved in on themselves, blood gushing from their now barren necks. Compression: the weapon of the Shield Psychic. The ability to compress molecules in a given space, the most precise of all the Psychic abilities. The pain those men had experienced before they died was beyond excruciating.

"Aspis ... they were from the north ..." choked Xiphos, still trying to regain his composure as strength slowly returned to his shaken form.

Aspis walked back over to examine her partner. "Never mind where they're from. What the hell happened to you?"

"Some kind of weapon. I heard a *pop* and then it felt like my body went to war with itself. I'm not sure," Xiphos muttered as he shook his head to clear it. When he stood he felt considerably drained of energy. "I need to get a bite."

Aspis shook her head and smiled. "Humans everywhere split into pieces and you're thinking about food?"

Xiphos smirked at his beautiful, fearless, incredible partner. "No, I'm thinking about steak."

Agni knocked on Tobias' dormitory door, not looking forward to the coming encounter with the mercenary. She found him unsettling; a human who could kill a Physic and Leash pair was unheard of, and this man had killed four. Not to mention his mental blocking capabilities.

She shifted uncomfortably at the thought of the last time she had tried to read his mind. She heard movement on the other side of the door seconds before it cracked open. A single eye peered at her through the opening, the same eyes she saw that day on the transport truck.

"Agni of the Pyre. Something you need?" Tobias spoke without opening the door any further. She felt uncomfortable hearing him address her by her full title, but she refused to let it show.

"I'm here to take you to your lesson with the Psychics and Leashes you'll be training," she said curtly, feeling her flat responses would make her appear more in control of the situation. She was one of the most powerful people on the planet; one average human would not unsettle her.

Tobias paused for only a second before opening the door fully, the sight that came nearly put Agni on her heels. There was hardly any skin left that wasn't scarred.

"Come in." Agni held her position in the door frame, not moving at his invitation. "Or don't," he said as he turned to walk back into his room.

The scars that covered his back were now visible as well. Agni watched at first, but then deliberately looked away as he donned a simple pair of pants and a long sleeve shirt, pulling his thigh holster around his leg and his .45 into it. He finished off the ensemble with a pair of boots, tucking his pants into them, an old practice that was second nature to Tobias at this point. He rose from his chair, tapping his boots on the floor to check and make sure they were secured before exiting the room, closing the door behind him.

"After you," he said.

They walked in silence through the corridor until they reached the elevator. As the door chimed they entered and Agni tapped the button to take them to the basement where the training area was located.

"Eight pairs," Agni said.

"What?" Tobias replied.

"You will be training eight pairs for the next few months. This will be the test group to determine if this program will be worth continuing. All of them are Level One pairs of varying degrees–"

"Varying degrees?" Tobias interrupted.

"Pairs are usually determined by the advancement of the Psychic. Level One Psychics, what we commonly refer to as Mumblers, are capable of hearing the strongest thought in a person's head. This makes them ideal for interrogations and assisting in criminal investigations," Agni explained, slightly annoyed at being interrupted. "When the Psychic's abilities advance beyond this, the pair is advanced to the next level."

Tobias chuckled. "So I've gone from working with Greenies to training Greenies. Fantastic. Well, we might as well start somewhere."

Just as Agni was about to say something else, the elevator came to a halt. The doors slid open to the training room. As they stepped off, the group of trainees came into view. Sixteen sets of eyes turned toward the pair exiting the elevator; most appeared happy to see them.

As they approached, Tobias began to take measure of them. Nine women, seven men. Some were clearly paired off, while others sat in such a gaggle it was hard to tell.

"Good morning everyone," chirped Agni, conjuring an enthusiasm that was a far more impressive feat than the inferno that came so naturally to her. The Psychics and Leashes responded with mutters and nonchalant nods. "This is Tobias Marshall. He's been recruited to help train some of our Psychics and Leashes in ... alternative combat methods."

Several in the group looked Tobias up and down, one or two scoffed, and one, a tall, athletically built woman with the sides of her head shaved and the top length dyed an alarming shade of purple, outright laughed. Ignoring the remarks, Agni pressed forward.

"Some of you may be apprehensive about working with someone from outside of the Academy, but it's been deemed by the administration as an appropriate measure to help diversify our Psychics by–"

"So we're supposed to take instruction from someone that most of us could kill with a flick of our wrist? What qualifications does he even have," spat the purple-haired woman.

Agni pressed her lips into a hard line. She wasn't a fan of Tobias Marshall, but was even less so of arrogant children who had yet to grow into their Merge. "Mr. Marshall is responsible for dispatching three Level Two teams and a Level Three team from the Academy. He did so without the aid of heavy weapons or the aid of Psychic abilities."

There were several seconds of stunned silence before the purple-haired woman sneered. "Impossible. I'm almost a Level Two Leash; my partner and I could mop the floor with this clown."

"Give it a shot."

Agni turned to look at Tobias. His blunt comment had been issued with just enough venom to make it a threat.

"You and your Psychic - I'll take you both on."

The purple-haired Leash was momentarily taken aback before allowing her sneer to return. "You can't even beat me, much less me and my Psychic."

A small-framed woman with tightly braided blonde hair and a full Academy uniform buttoned and tucked stood up. "If he wants a shot at both of us, Liz, let's give it to him–"

A shot erupted from the barrel of Tobias' .45, clipping the hip of the blonde Psychic. She collapsed soundlessly to her knees, the bullet burying itself into the training room floor. The sudden shock of the violent act rendered her speechless. Every eye jumped to her, all but the purple-haired Leash, who had been tackled off of her feet and barely managed to get her arms in front of her face before Tobias was raining laser accurate fists and elbows. An overhead elbow strike finally rendered her arms useless and they collapsed over her head. She felt the warm steel barrel pressing against her forehead.

"Dead."

The one word proclamation rang like a siren for the space of a moment. Nobody had moved except Agni who had raced forward and then stopped when the violence had subsided. She was heaving anxious breaths that were accompanied by sparks and wisps of smoke.

"Are you out of your damn mind?! You don't use a gun to–"

"To what?" Tobias said as he stood and offered his hand to the bruised and trembling Leash. "To teach? You asked me to show them how they were vulnerable. That's what I'm doing."

He turned his attention to the wounded Psychic. "That shot should have missed the bone. Can you stand?"

The Psychic shook her head in mute shock and then slowly nodded before standing.

"Kill a Psychic and the Leash dies. That's the lesson," Tobias explained. "All of you walking hand in hand, so eager and confident in your paired strength that you don't realize you are each other's only weak spot. Threaten a Psychic and the Leash panics. Engage a Leash and the Psychic retreats."

Tobias hoisted Liz to her feet and then holstered his weapon. Agni stood motionless, still in shock at the blatant act of violence.

"You - you tricked me into showing you who my Psychic was," the Leash spoke, still recovering and now furious with herself.

"By challenging both of you, I got your Psychic to reveal herself. You flaunted your weakness, and I exploited it," Tobias spoke coolly. "You hesitate. I don't. Now, do I have the attention of the class?"

Now that he had a captive - albeit frightened - audience, Tobias began his lessons. He instructed the students to move some of the weights in the training area and put them in a circle with a five meter diameter. Then had all the students stand in a circle by their respective pile of weights.

When the room was in order Tobias began to give instructions "Welcome to the bullring. Leashes you will be expected to fend off attacks from all sides–"

A muscular Leash wearing a uniform several sizes too small interrupted him. "We do this kind of training already. I thought this was supposed to be something new."

Tobias paused then turned and smirked at the musclebound fool. "Thank you for volunteering. What was your name?"

"Marcus," replied the dense Leash.

"Please come to the center of the ring, Marcus."

The Leash approached the center of the bullring while Tobias exited at the side, providing directions. "What's about to happen is that the other Leashes will throw these various weights at you, and your job is to stop them. At the same time, all of the Psychics present will attempt to invade your mind. You have to focus through the distraction."

Marcus cocked an eyebrow and revealed a half smirk.

"And begin!"

The Leashes wasted no time hurling the various weights and shot puts at Marcus. All of the Psychics were focused intensely, attempting to infiltrate the Leash's thoughts while he was expertly defending and deflecting the blows. Knees, elbows, forearms, and palms elegantly deflected all of the incoming projectiles. A well trained eye would be able to see his brow furrow and his eyes flinch occasionally as he concentrated through the physical onslaught to deflect the mental attack. In truth, he handled himself with applause.

Agni allowed herself a moment of smug pride. These young Leashes were doing an outstanding job. They had taken their training seriously and even in the face of pseudo-sadist they were handling themselves very well.

"Stop" Tobias ordered.

All of the Leashes discontinued their barrage, most of them breathing heavily.

Even the Leash, Marcus, though standing up straight and controlling his breath, was dotted with perspiration and flushed. "See. I told you. This is business as usual for us."

"I didn't say we were finished. Who is your Psychic?" A short, curvy girl with a bob haircut and thick glasses stepped forward "Would you please join your Leash in the center?"

"Now wait a minute, she's not a Leash. If I missed a block and got hit I'd be ok, but one of these weights could kill her if it hits her," protested Marcus, his substantial frame finally letting his chest heave with the exertion he had just demonstrated.

"Your Psychic is not a strength, they are a weakness. No matter how adept they are. They are still fragile and still easy to dispatch. So one of two things has to happen. You either learn to defend them, or they learn to defend themselves independent of you." Tobias' gaze was hard and cold.

Agni felt a surge of anger. *How dare he call me fragile.* But as she looked around, she could see it on all of their faces, they were afraid.

Marcus felt as if his mouth filled with ash as he tried to swallow.

"Leashes, on my mark, attempt to kill his Psychic. Psychics on my mark attempt to invade their minds. Do you all understand?" All of the Psychics and Leashes stared at each other, hesitant and nervous.

"Do as he says," Agni spoke, her voice low, nearly a whisper, like a thought that had snuck its way past her teeth to make itself known.

"And GO!"

The Leashes reinitialized their assault. The previously well composed Marcus was now in full panic-stricken defense mode. Weights crashed into his ribs and joints as he whirled frantically, attempting to protect his Psychic from harm. To her credit, the Psychic was in full unblinking concentration attempting to stop the mental attack that her partner was under. But one Psychic against seven isn't good odds, even for a powerful telepath.

Finally, in the midst of the endless assault, a Psychic must have broken through his mental barrier and was throwing up one image after another. Marcus resisted to the best of his ability. But after a particularly well placed weight smashed into the bridge of his nose, he collapsed on top of his Psychic, using his size and weight to protect her.

"Stop." Tobias's instruction was flat and final.

The Leashes dropped whatever weights they were holding with hard thuds; many of them collapsed to the mat, heaving deep exhausted breaths. Tobias calmly walked to the center of the ring, up to the whimpering Leash and put his index finger to the back of his head.

"Bang. Now you're both dead. This is the fatal flaw of the Psychic Leash pairing. Kill one and two die."

None of the Psychics or Leashes could look up. An impossible to cover vulnerability had been revealed. A room full of people that an hour ago had thought themselves nearly invincible, gods amongst men, sat helplessly staring at each other for an answer to their weakness.

"Any questions?" Tobias asked, fully expecting this to be his very last moment as an instructor. Assuming the harshness of his method would have earned him a sharp veto from anyone who was bearing witness. Maybe they'd kill him, or maybe, just maybe, they'd give him his freedom.

"What time do you want them here tomorrow?" Agni spoke, her voice burning clear and resolute.

Tobias had to force his annoyance down. "Bright and early. Show up ready to work. Today was the warm up. Tomorrow we find out what you're made of."

CHAPTER 1.7

The Nature of the Merge

"A Leash must be devoid of some portion of their latent Psychic abilities, this allows a space for a Psychic to implant their own consciousness. This will lead to feelings of deep connection between Psychic and Leash but not of an intellectual kind. They will remain able to hide thoughts from each other but not feelings. But they will share emotions and traumas."

Dian's eyes fluttered open. Across from her was the slender figure of Melania, her jet black hair framing her alabaster features. While she was sleeping Melania looked older than she did when she was awake, a woman in her forties with the Psychic ability to introduce images would never appear a day over 20 to anyone who was looking. It was something Dian didn't understand.

She was beautiful, and her slight age lines showed her history. The crinkles around her eyes revealed her years of experience. Dian had only seen Melania on assignment once or twice, but she was truly a soldier to be envied. Laugh lines around her mouth curved into her perfect pink lips. Dian reached over and brushed a stray hair away from Melania's face. She watched in fascination as her wrinkles smoothed and her hair darkened. Even as her eyes remained closed, Dian knew she was awake.

Melania's eyes fluttered open. "Hello there, pet. Rest well?"

Dian nodded, afraid that the sound of her voice would shatter the intimacy.

Melania slid in closer until her nose nearly touched Dian's. "Can't speak, pet?"

Dian felt her cheeks and ears burn and her breath catch in her lungs as Melania moved in to kiss her. A moment before their lips made contact there were three sharp knocks on the door.

"Dian," came from the deep earthy voice of Syn.

Why hadn't she felt him approaching? The Lightning Psychic sprang out of bed, her wild red hair and bed clothes a tousled mess. She went about flinging her clothes here and there and trying to hurriedly get dressed.

"Dammit, I forgot we had to go report in. We got back so late last night we didn't get a chance. Gregory is gonna kill me."

"Come in, Pops," the frantic Dian shouted.

The doorknob turned and Syn entered wearing his Academy uniform. He never wore it anywhere except when making official reports to the Academy, but he had felt, much like he did in the military, that wearing his uniform helped put the newer recruits at ease. His smart, well pressed uniform was offset by his bushy salt and pepper beard and his dreadlocked black hair.

The Hunter Leash entered the room and immediately averted his eyes as Melania rose from the bed, pulling the sheet with her to wrap herself in.

"Ms. Melania," Syn greeted her in his politest fashion.

"Hunter," Melania replied, her honeyed tone hardened slightly.

Syn was a man with little fear, and a nearly incorruptible moral code. The kind of man Melania hated most.

"OK, we have a meeting to get to, right? Let's go!" Dian sputtered as she tumbled out of her closet wearing her Academy jacket over a stained shirt and loose fitting canvas pants. Syn smirked, Melania glowered.

Dian skipped her way over to Melania, propped up on her tiptoes, and kissed the much taller woman's cheek which earned her an affectionate hum. "I'll be back later, Mel. Will you be here?"

Melania was staring hard at Syn as if he was some feral beast that was stealing her meal "I'm afraid I'm not sure. I have an engagement today."

Her flat tone caused Dian's cheerful face to shrink. "Oh, ok. When you get back then?" she asked tentatively. Melania turned her attention to the windblown redhead and then suddenly Dian caught a wisp of flowers and could feel sunshine warming her skin.

"Of course."

Syn and Dian made their way out of the dormitory suites and into the main circle of the Academy's first floor.

"Pops, I have a question."

Syn grunted his affirmation.

"Am I pretty?"

Syn thought to himself for a minute.

"Silence isn't very reassuring, Pops."

Syn chuckled. "I was thinking. Pretty means a lot of things. Pretty to me may not be pretty to someone else."

Dian shrunk, her eyes on the ground contemplating her scuffed and dirty boots. "So no then?"

Syn shook his head. They had made their way to the front of the cafeteria, the smell of fresh baked bread and fried meat filling the air. He fumbled for an explanation.

"When I was a boy, and after my mother had died, my dad would go on hunting trips for food and I would have to stay at the house and fend for myself. When he left he would always say the same thing to me: 'Son, I'll be back before the first autumn storms start'. So I would work at the house. Weed the garden and grind flour out of grains and take care of myself. Every night I would go outside and watch the horizon for the storms to roll in. They always came in waves. First was the changing of the wind. When it changed I knew I had to harvest all the food I could from our gardens and store it, before it rotted or animals got to it. Then came the smell that signaled the world was getting ready to change again. Then right before the rains came, there were purple sunsets and bolts of lightning. And I knew my father would be home soon. Some people think the sunrise is beautiful or the ocean is beautiful. But to me, nothing has ever been more beautiful than lightning leading a storm."

As they stepped into the elevator to head to the third floor, Dian grabbed the sleeve of Syn's Academy uniform and laid her head on his bicep. "Thanks, Pops."

The Elevator door dinged open and they walked into the half circle common room of the admin offices. "You're going to have to deliver our report to Zander, I have to meet with the council."

Dian looked horrified at the prospect. "WHAT?! By myself? But he's so scary!"

Syn allowed a smile to curl his broad face. He had personally witnessed Dian fling bolts of lightning at an entire military base, short out their power, electrocute pipelines causing them to burst inside buildings, and, in one desperate situation on a particularly stormy night, had nearly killed both of them by turning the sky itself into a falling minefield. All of that and was still scared to talk with their superior about a simple report.

"I'm running low. I have to go in and have a Wash performed. You'll be just fine."

Dian pouted as she trudged off toward Zander's office. Syn turned his attention to the door closest to the elevator. He knocked three times before the door was opened by a young, fully armed Soldier Team. When they saw Syn they both snapped to attention.

He leaned his head down into the monitor strapped to his wrist. "Leash Syn, checking in."

"How can we help you, sir?"

Syn nodded politely to the young Soldier who had addressed him. "I need to complete a Wash. May I come in?"

The door swung open wide, followed by a second, much heavier door. Syn entered the dark and circular room full of large, plush, partially-reclined seats. In each seat was a Psychic, or what was left of one.

This was the Council: Psychics who had lost their Leashes and experienced mind death. They were wretched creatures - always panicking, always fragile, confused and afraid. In Syn's mind they were wounded animals that were better off put down, but the Academy kept them alive because of the secondary side effect of mind death.

When a Leash dies, the remnants of all their Psychic energy is emptied into the Psychic and makes them exponentially more powerful. All strength with no direction. The seats they were in had specialized helmets on top of them to slow their Psychic activity and place them in a type of waking comatose. It stunted their Psychic abilities, allowing their fragile minds rest, until they were needed for the Wash.

Syn walked into the middle of the room and closed his eyes. The young Leash who had let him in the room approached a panel on the wall and flipped a switch. His Psychic stood on the other side of the door making sure the exit was air tight and secure. Several mechanical whirs issued from the chairs where the Council members were resting, then it began. The whimpering of the council followed by wails and tears as their broken minds began to wake and remember their own nonexistence. creatures surviving in a state of constant birth and death, unable to hold a thought for more than a moment before it escaped them again back into the ether.

"We ... hurt. Why do you wake ... us?" One of the Psychics moaned painfully.

Syn swallowed his pity; there was nothing he could do for them. "I require a Wash, please."

He spoke softly over the collective groaning of the Council. In the midst of their wails and sobbing, Syn felt the surge start. their unrestrained Psychic energy filling the room to the brim. He could feel his skin drinking in all the power that was filling the air around him. His heavy frame felt light as a feather, and the void that held place in the body of every Leash, their vacant pool of where their Psychic energy once rested, went from holding the last remaining trickles of power to a tidal surge of energy. An ocean of strength flowed into him. Syn had to actively try and pull himself out of his trance. The raw pleasure that was generated by the Wash could be overwhelming. After several moments Syn could feel his capacity met and the Psychic energy began to ricochet off of him. He had to fight hard to pull away and formulate words.

"I'm–I'm through." Syn heard his own hazy voice as if it were thousands of kilometers away.

The young soldier Leash flipped the switch, and with a great deal of effort, the machines that held the Council whirred for a moment before the sounds of wails and whimpers slowly died.

Syn stood heaving and panting, his strength restored. "You never get used to it, I guess," the Hunters Leash said dreamily.

"That's why they rotate our shifts every two weeks." chirped the Soldier Leash in an almost overly cheery way.

Syn was reminded of what they called "Wash sickness" for Leashes who had to work on council duty for too long. They would begin to lose themselves and become addicted. It wasn't a job anyone wanted, but once they had it, they had difficulty leaving it.

Dian tapped gingerly on Zander's door, almost hoping he wouldn't answer. She had to mask her disappointment when Gregory opened the door. Although he was a kind man, he was still the Head of Personnel for the Academy, and any one person that held such authority, no matter how kind, made the Lightning Psychic suspicious.

"Well, hello Dian. Here to make a report?"

The red head stood up as straight as she could, suddenly very aware of her sloppy uniform. "Yessir. I'm here to report on our trip to the Kimmora region, sir." She felt herself blurt in an almost shout. She lowered her eyes and stared hard at her shoes, glaring inwardly at herself.

Gregory laughed warmly. "Well, you'd better get in here then and rescue me from being given more work myself."

Dian slinked past the tall, dark-skinned Academy head. Zander sat behind his desk looking razor edged as always, staring so hard at his computer screen she wondered if he was interrogating it.

"Dian, report?" Zander asked without looking away from his screen.

He was always a little easier to deal with than Mr. Gregory, he said less and was more direct in his questioning. Some people thought of him as rude, but he reminded Dian of Syn. Dian reached into her shirt and pulled out a small chip and handed it awkwardly across Zander's oversized desk. Zander picked up the small chip and immediately loaded it into his computer.

"Was the target neutralized?" Zander asked as he read the report which answered exactly that question.

"Yes'r. Two power plants, a water filtration facility, and seven food storage bunkers," spoke the nervous redhead.

"Any confirmable soft targets?" Zander asked.

"No sir. We burned all the guards that Syn had to shoot. Looks like a freak lightning storm did all that damage," she remarked somewhat proudly. They had been very thorough, between the two of them they had to burn no less than a dozen bodies. And Syn was meticulous at policing his casings and hiding their campsites.

"Obviously you missed something." Zander adjusted his glasses before he began typing furiously on his computer.

After several moments of incredibly tense silence, he finally spoke. "We intercepted an intelligence report which placed two operatives with custom weapons five kilometers from the attack site. Poaching. How is hunting in Kimorra this time of year?"

Dian was speechless. There weren't any survivors, much less one she wouldn't have sensed.

"Sir. I–"

"I personally think we were sold out by the client," came Zander's exasperated response. "I think we were hired for a job, and then the Academy's involvement was revealed to the target in order to distract from the client themselves. Which means we're about to have an in-house contract open up. Feel like some payback?"

Dian cycled about eight emotions in a nanosecond, confusion at his words, concern at his evidence, anger at the revelation, and now driven by the prospect of frying some assholes who were trying to sell her out.

"Bet your ass, boss."

"Good. You leave immediately." Zander replied matter-of-factly.

"Zander, they've been gone on assignment for over a week. Perhaps we have another team that could take their place on this particular assignment?" Gregory spoke up. Zander gave him a look; it wasn't an angry look, but more like the way one spouse looks at their partner when they've had too much to drink at the party and they start talking about their sex life.

"No, sir. Pops and I will handle it. Nobody sells me out. Just tell us who we're killing."

Zander looked approvingly at the fiery young woman. "Good. You have two days to prep. Get ready to leave."

Dian stood and walked briskly out of the room, fuming. "Wait 'til Pops hears about this. I'll BBQ these assholes. Dammit!" Dian flicked her wrist and the door to Zander's office slammed so hard it rattled its frame.

"I don't appreciate being undermined, Gregory. I don't interfere with your politics; I'd appreciate it if you didn't interfere with my troops." Zander's icy tone stamped his point on the atmosphere of the room.

"They aren't weapons, Zander. They are people. You can't run them to death. They need the opportunity to be normal as often as they can," Gregory said compassionately, his warm deep voice softening even the most steely disposition.

"Weapons are precisely what *we* are, Gregory. From the minute they taught you to lift a truck with your mind. Or sent me through the Wash and gave me the power to fold steel like paper. Weapons are what we were instructed to be. So weapons are what we became."

Zander finished whatever it was he was typing on his computer and turned to face his partner. "And for a weapon, might I add that you're getting a little doughy around the middle. I thought you were going to start working out?"

"You're only angry because when the cafeteria makes donuts they always let me have some from the first batch, and you have to get whatever cold stale mess is left over."

"Get out of my office." Zander said with half of a smirk.

Gregory chuckled. "Can't. All my stuff's in here."

Aspis swiveled in her gun nest, watching Xiphos walk around the convoy. He quickly and efficiently examined each of the guards, checking for injuries and making sure that the four men who had been in the flipped vehicle were none the worse for wear. It had been more than a little amusing to watch their faces as Xiphos had lifted the 3,500 kg vehicle and set it right side up so the damaged tire could be replaced.

She climbed out of the gunner's hatch, onto the roof, and faced off in the direction that the ambushers had initiated their attack. Xiphos crawled up next to Aspis and sat down back to back, leaning his head against her shoulder. He was heavy, it would take only moments for his weight to be uncomfortable, but she bore it as long as needed, understanding her partner's weariness.

"I feel like I haven't slept in a week," he said, his voice raspy with exhaustion.

Aspis lit a smoke and allowed her mind to go silent for a moment, her forced calm seeped into him and made his weary mind peaceful.

"What the hell happened to me?" he finally said, exhaling simultaneously as Aspis conjured a lung full of smoke into the black evening. She pulled a small box out of her back pocket and held it in front of herself.

"A weapon, collected from one of the assailants. Looks to be some kind of handheld pulse weapon, although what it's pulsing I couldn't begin to say," she said.

Xiphos sat up, trying to blink the drowsiness away. "Aspis, I don't know that I'm gonna be much good for the rest of this trip. Whatever they did to me sapped me. It's gonna take most of what I've got left just to keep my body moving."

Aspis had suspected this and had been debating on informing the client, but she knew it could cost them a contract. "Wonder how Zander would take it if we walked back up to the Academy before the assignment was finished?" she asked absently.

Xiphos laughed. "He'd eat us."

Aspis scoffed. "We do need to get this, back to the Academy for examination. How did a gang of desert hooligans get their hands on this kind of tech?"

Xiphos turned his head and examined his partner; she looked wild. Her hair unkempt, and her uniform dirty. The fire red cherry on her cigarette illuminated the small space near her face. "Why couldn't you sense them?" asked Xiphos.

It wasn't an accusation, but more of a professional curiosity. He knew that Aspis had been doing scans and unless every one of their assailants had been extensively trained, there was no way that she wouldn't have been aware of their presence.

"That one I can answer," she said as she tossed a small device to Xiphos. It was curved and flexible and appeared as if it fit around an ear.

"Psychic dampeners. They aren't a new concept, but I've never encountered a model *this* sophisticated," she said through a savage smile. "Most of them I've seen are beta dampeners; they send out a steady signal that can muddle what we hear but not shut it out, like the instructors use to train the Mumblers. In this case those would have given them away quickly. But these seem to adapt with each signal a human mind puts out. It's like it takes the waves naturally produced by the brain and replicates them in reverse, creating a negative output. Not just nothing, less than nothing."

Xiphos would have been interested if he hadn't been so tired. "Well, it didn't keep any of them alive. Did we do a field exam of the bodies?"

Aspis flicked her ash. "You mean of the pieces you left that were big enough to examine? Yeah. No uniforms, no distinguishing markings, no weapons of specific origin. Just assassins. Well armed, well informed, but poorly trained assassins."

Xiphos sighed deep and heavy. "I'm gonna go check on the client. Nobody has heard a word from him since all this happened. Probably scared to get out of his transport. Gotta go do my due diligence, huh?" He slid clumsily off of the truck, the shift in weight making the vehicle rock, and began trudging to the front of the caravan.

Aspis was left to contemplate the cigarette in her hand. *None of this makes sense. Where would a bunch of amateurs get this kind of equipment? Who would put this kind of technology in the hands of...well anyone?* She flicked her cigarette away. *To hell with it. My head hurts.*

Xiphos trudged his way to the escort car, too tired and drained to be truly concerned about the client, but duty was duty. He went around to the driver's side and tapped on the window with his knuckles.

After a moment the door opened, and the driver got out. She was a small framed athletic woman with short, dark brown hair and honey colored eyes. He wasn't used to seeing fair skinned people this far north, and since they had been denied dossiers on the security team, her appearance came as a surprise.

"Ty v poryadke?" Xiphos asked the young woman, trying his best to sound concerned.

She nodded nervously, he assumed she was still shaken from the combat that had taken place earlier. "D-da, spasibo," she confirmed, her accent less smooth and more staccato than any Northerner he had ever met.

Must be a refugee. But on a security force? Xiphos felt his fingers twitch and tried to curl into a fist before he caught himself and released his hand. *Overthinking.*

"Take a break, I'm gonna speak to your boss," Xiphos said.

The girl nodded and started walking toward a group of other guards tapping the pack of cigarettes she had stowed away in her uniform pocket. Xiphos knocked on the back driver's side window, after several seconds he knocked again. No response. He knocked again.

"Ser?" Xiphos tested the handle of the door, it popped open and he swung the door wide. Inside was a young man, his rich looking red brown skin and black hair warm against his wrist length white silk shirt. His head hung limply forward as if he was sleeping, a small pool of crimson staining the white silk of his shirt, Xiphos reached forward and tilted the boy's head back. Above and behind his right eye was a small hole from which the steady stream of blood had been issuing.

Aspis, don't react, Xiphos mentally reached out to his partner. *The client is dead.* He felt her presence fill his mind. No alarm, no fear, just calculation.

How? When? She fired her questions rapidly, all the while her strategic mind running through their available information.

Single gunshot from the look of it. I think we've been set up. Everything is off. Which means the next step is to eliminate us. How do we proceed? Xiphos was trying to rapidly do a mental inventory of how many guards there were near him.

I'm coming to you, just keep acting like everything is fine. Aspis instructed.

"Stop." Xiphos heard the voice from behind him, too far away to be directed at him. He ducked his head out of the car and looked up.

Aspis was between her vehicle and the escort car, both hands raised. Two of the guards were aiming their weapons at Aspis. Xiphos reached into his stores of Psychic energy to find it almost depleted.

If I rush them, I may be able to take them in a blitz, but it would probably kill me, and then Aspis. He tried to keep his thoughts composed and think of a strategy while Aspis was slowly being surrounded by the guards. The honey-eyed driver was barking orders at the remaining guards, her shaken demeanor absent and replaced with fierce competence of a squad leader.

"If the Leash moves, kill the Psychic." Xiphos planted his feet as he heard the driver give the command.

They are well informed. Do you have a plan? Xiphos asked Aspis, utilizing their shared connection.

They don't seem to want to take us alive. How quickly can you get to me? was her stony response.

30 meters – two seconds, give or take."

The honey-eyed soldier raised her chin and aimed her weapon carefully. "They executed the minister's son, fire at will!"

Clink. Clink. Clink.

"Hold your fire. HOLD..." the honey-eyed woman ordered the men at her command. Her focus was steady, but her eyes were wide. Three grenades were floating midair around the semicircle of gunmen, Aspis had her eyes closed in concentration.

Xiphos started moving toward Aspis as quickly and smoothly as he could. *Why didn't she just make a shield?* he thought frustratedly, but he knew that making a shield that covered almost a full circle was basically impossible. It would require too much focus and too many calculations, for even the world's most focused Psychic.

"Move and I release all the triggers." Xiphos could hear the deep warble in Aspis's voice.

"She's bluffing, back away..."

Four additional pins sounded.

The seven grenades floated up, their pins pulled, triggers being forcefully depressed. Xiphos was now close enough to see the intense perspiration on Aspis's face.

"I'll kill all of you. Don't move." Aspis forced the wrath in her voice to show over the mental exertion.

Xiphos gently and slowly scooped her body up, her face wrinkled in concentration and he began to walk quickly as he could to the truck with the mounted 50 cal. He sat Aspis down in the driver seat, her breathing was now ragged and uneven, the gunmen were all inching away from the floating mines their weapons raised but far from well-aimed as their concentration was focused solely on the floating grenades that were, in some cases, millimeters from their heads.

Xiphos climbed into the passenger seat as Aspis heaved her exhale and all of the grenade triggers released at once. Chaos ensued as the riflemen fell over themselves, running in every direction to get away from the impending blast. Aspis shakily started the truck and threw it into gear, the back wheels spun wildly kicking up sand and stone as she whipped the vehicle around.

More than a half dozen simultaneous explosions occurred at once, followed by human screaming and hail of gunfire that bounced off the armor plating of the vehicle they were driving as fast as they could in the opposite direction.

"I guess you got your wish, Xiphos. We're going home."

CHAPTER 1.8

Mind Death

"Mind death is the experience that occurs when a Psychic loses their Leash or a Leash loses their Psychic. If a Psychic dies, the piece of their mind that is used to fill the Psychic void in a Leash dies as well, leaving the Leash emotionless and hollow. If a Leash is killed, the part of the Psychic's mind that was used to create the merge leaves the Psychic alive, but they will experience the world instantaneously while they experience their own death. The human mind isn't made to exist in either state of being, the result we refer to as mind death. It is also the reason that Psychics and Leashes who commit crimes cannot be executed, only imprisoned."

A ngel wiggled his toes, using the motion to distract his mind and steady his balance. His palms were pressed flat into the floor, his legs arched in a fully erect handstand. Perspiration ran down his slick, shaved head to pool between his tattooed fingers. His elbows began to bend as he lowered himself to the floor, his legs flexing and waving slightly to increase his balance. His nose touched the ground then his muscles contracted and he began to make his ascent again raising his body back up until his arms were straight pillars again.

"3,679. 3,680," Angel stopped counting as he felt something familiar walking down the hallway. A fragrance at the edge of his perception, like crushed flowers in a vase on the other side of a room. He lowered himself to the ground and laid flat on his cell floor.

"Angel, my love, won't you stand up for me?"

Angel opened his eyes and made eye contact with his Psychic. "Melania."

The black haired beauty glided her way across the hard concrete floor. Right behind her was a slim-framed man, bespectacled and nervous looking. His rifle held tight against his chest. Probably a Mumbler, sent to oversee the conversation between Melania and Angel.

He stood up, facing the glass. Melania was the only living creature that commanded Angel's respect. Even if he had some affection for Syn, it wasn't the adoration he held for his Psychic.

"Did you bring me a snack, or is the boy a precaution? Have you come to fear me?" He addressed his Psychic, but his eyes never left the guard.

Melania glanced passively at the young Leash who had stopped several meters behind her and was facing the opposite direction. "He won't bother us. I needed to see you. I've been so worried about you," her voice caught slightly, something that none but those who knew her best would have detected. It was true she had missed him; despite his homicidal tendencies, Angel and Melania had served together for nearly five years during the Psychic War and had been paired for many years before that. Their connection was deep and old.

"They're starving me in here," Angel groaned, pressing his face to the cool wall of his cell.

"Don't whine, brave boy. You're stronger than that," Melania purred, her face inches from the transparent cell wall. She released slow steady tendrils of Psychic energy from her body that reached out for Angel. They shrank and evaporated as they touched the tempered glass that interrupted the frequency of her substantial Psychic energy. She gritted her teeth in annoyance.

"How much longer–"

"Hush, Angel. You must be patient. Gregory and Zander will come to their senses soon, and you won't be rotting away in here anymore. I'll have you out soon. Just trust that I'm doing what's best for all of us."

Angel backed away from the wall, his lip curled upward in a contemptuous sneer. "You mean best for you and your new little pet? Even through my prison walls I can smell her influence on you. You're getting soft, Goddess of Nightmares."

Melania felt a surge of rage Wash over her, but she dismissed it quickly. "You won't speak of her again, Angel. She is all that has distracted me substantially since your imprisonment, and she will be treated with the same consideration."

Angel softened his fanged smile. "Don't worry. I don't plan on eating your pet. My confinement has made me disagreeable."

Melania pressed her hand to the wall. "As it would anyone," she hummed.

He looked into her sympathetic face, and for a moment his voice wavered with vulnerability. "My Wash is dissipating. I'm starting to feel the cracks in my bones and the shortness of breath."

Melania cooed at him through his prison wall. "We must get you a Wash then. If you get weak, then so do I."

The guard who was with them cleared his throat. "Time is up, Ms. Melania. Please finish–"

Melania flicked her wrist. The guard went rigid, crumpling to the ground. Melania considered the guard for a moment. Had she over-done it?

"Killing the boy for rushing you? You always were impatient," Angel mocked softly while he stared unblinking at the human pile on the floor.

"Not dead. Just a little push in the right place and he's sleeping like a baby," she confirmed before turning her attention back to Angel. "Please be good, dear Angel. It will be difficult to get you out of here if you keep making them all afraid."

Angel didn't look away from the crumpled mass on the floor. "If they didn't want to be afraid of us, they shouldn't have made us monsters."

He leaned forward and pressed his cheek to the glass. Melania pressed her palm flat against the place where his cheek would have been had there not been a wall in between them, willing the warmth of her skin through the impermeable shield.

"I couldn't agree more."   .

The glow of the computer screen was all of the illumination the small room had to offer. The Specialist slid his round framed spectacles up his nose as he typed his report.

Expected return delayed due to unforeseen circumstances.

He thought for a moment. He never liked sending an employer bad news.

Everything's in the plan, he thought as he deleted his last few lines. Instead, he typed *New opportunities presented themselves. Will be delaying return in order to explore every possible opportunity.*

Finishing his report, he clicked submit and sat back in his chair, running his fingers under his glasses in order to rub the fatigue from his eyes. He stared at the ceiling, wanting to sleep, but knowing he had more work to do. He wouldn't get this type of opportunity once he was around Blaine again and his constant prattling and incessance.

He sat back up and continued typing at the computer. As the minutes ticked by, search window after search window opened and closed as he reviewed reports, personnel files, and ongoing tasks. Finally he found what he was looking for.

Level Four deployment status filled the top of the monitor as a restricted access banner dominated the center of it. He reached into his shirt sleeve and removed a small remote plug, inserted it into the side of his computer and in a few seconds the screen filled with garbage information characters in various languages and scripts. He knew that the device was listening for ticks in the system, information that would respond to the overabundance of electronic stimuli in a specific way. After several moments the password filled itself in. After a few seconds the screen changed and opened to a list of paired code names and statuses.

Shield Psychic Marie (Aspis) and Sword Leash Elijah (Xiphos): Deployed

Kinetic Psychic Molly (Bia) and Mountain Leash Jeremy (Cratus): Deployed

Collapse Psychic Amanda (Anubis) and Silence Leash Katherine (Bathala): Deployed

Decay Psychic Luke and Soldier Leash Catha: Stationed

Storm Psychic Vanessa (Dian) and Hunter Leash Roger (Syn): Deployment pending

Pyre Psychic Krisha (Agni) and Tornado Leash Amil (Rudra): On standby, Academy.

Nightmare Psychic Melania and Shred Leash Angel: On standby, Addendum lockdown.

Energy Sync Alyssia: Assigned to Education

Each one had a series of dates and times, but nothing so specific to assume when they would all be returning or when their next deployments would be. Even with all of the encryptions hacked, the Academy still guarded their most dangerous secrets very closely.

He did a rapid search for a medical report.

Tobias Marshall, height 175 cm, weight 81 kg, H/E Blonde/Green.

Physician's Notes: Patient stable. I'm not sure what will occur with his neural map after he wakes up. He lost 38% of his blood. Stopped breathing numerous times. He shouldn't have survived; moreover, he couldn't have survived. Yet all major organs have been repaired and are functioning normally. I don't know how much human will be left of him when/if he wakes up. Only time will tell.

Additional Notes: Patient's body covered in scars and injuries, bullet holes, and what appear to be scratches or deep gashes all over. Skeletal exam indicates he's had dozens of broken bones. Psychic scan shows him to be devoid of passive Psychic energy, which we recognize as impossible, but the traces must be so minute that we aren't able to sense them. Tobias Marshall is an anomaly. Further tests required.

He mumbled to himself. As he looked down the rest of the names and statuses, he contemplated the possibilities before him.

"The window is narrow, almost non-existent."

He closed the computer window, making sure to cover his footprint and delete his time stamp so it wouldn't show that he had even accessed the information. He looked at the clock on his monitor that read just after 0200. He had all the information he needed to complete his task, now all he had to do was wait. He leaned back and smiled to himself.

"Soon, Mr. Marshall. Soon."

"Say ahhh," instructed the slightly more erratic than usual Dr. Luke to Catha.

The stone faced older Leash complied. He shined his light into the back of her throat as he placed two fingers against her carotid artery and closed his eyes to count for a pulse.

"I am well?" Catha asked in her halting manner.

"Shh, my love. I'm counting, and it's hard enough to concentrate with your pretty face right in front of me."

Catha twitched slightly. "I am old," she stated flatly.

"And I am skinny," said Luke as he pressed his stethoscope to Catha's chest, an action that made her breathe a little more deeply than usual. "What's that got to do with how I feel about you?" he said as he finished his exam and kissed her cheek.

"Excuse me, Doctor."

They heard the deep rich voice coming from the doorway to the infirmary. Luke finished his notes and gestured to the woman on the exam table. Catha quickly buttoned up the shirt of her uniform as Luke walked out of the examination room to see the tall and sturdy Syn standing in the doorway.

"Dian and I are heading out soon and I wanted to gather some provisions before we got back on the road," the Hunter Leash explained.

"So soon? You two just got back. I haven't even had a chance to examine you yet. Dian had small Melanoma indicators last time I gave her a checkup. I still have to check for an additional spot," argued the energetic doctor while he pulled the large burly man into the room and sat him down in the nearest chair.

"We're both fine, Doc. I just need some sup–" Syn started, but as his mouth opened, Luke stuck a depressor into his mouth and looked at his throat, then moved his free hand up and spread Syn's eyelids to examine his pupils.

"Oh, just fine, huh? And you know this because of all your medical experience, do you?" Luke fussed a little more, but he knew the Hunter Leash was right, he could tell by the scent on the air that Syn had recently experienced the Wash. Psychic energy swam through Syn's blood like wildfire. His body was in perfect condition, and it made the doctor a bit irritable.

"What about Dian? She needs to come in to see me as well. Unlike you, she doesn't have a well of Psychic energy putting her bones back together every time she gets hurt," stated Luke with unconcealed irritation.

"I wouldn't be much of a Leash if my Psychic got hurt to the point of needing a doctor, now would I? Besides you know Dian hates needles, and she wouldn't stand for an examination anyway."

Luke tsked disapprovingly. "The nature of her manifest has her in constant contact with ionized air which is known for causing skin cancer. The last time she came in I had to remove several small spots. If untreated it could mean–"

"I'll look after her, Doc. I always keep a field knife sharp enough to cut out any spots that might pop up anyway. And like I said, I doubt she'd sit still for an exam."

"Tie her down?" Catha interjected with a smile as she walked out of the examination room. This made both Syn and Luke laugh.

"You're welcome to try, Ms. Catha. Just let me know when you try so I can make sure to be far away from the Academy."

Luke sat back in his chair and sized Syn up seriously. For a moment his hyperactive personality quieted, and he asked a serious question. "Where are you two going on such short notice after just arriving back at Academy, Syn? What could possibly be so important that another team or teams couldn't handle it."

Syn stood up, his tall muscular frame imposing no matter how well you knew his gentle nature to be. "Evidently the client from the previous assignment would like plausible deniability for hiring us to take out their competitor. So they leaked photos to the target of Dian and myself carrying out the contract and told them that the Academy was who took out the contract on them. They have violated their contract, so Dian and I are going to clean up the mess."

He shrugged one of his meaty shoulders in a gesture of indifference. "Seems foolish to me; they should have known it would get back to us. Either way the result is going to be the same."

Luke furrowed his brow and became lost deep in thought. "That doesn't make any sense," he said softly. "No region, even the small or disorganized ones are stupid enough to try and sell out the Academy."

Syn raised one eyebrow and let a ghost of a smile grace his lips. "I think you greatly underestimate human stupidity, my young friend."

Luke snapped out of his thoughtful trance. "You might be right. You'd have to have a death wish to turncoat the Academy."

Catha ran her fingers from the small of Luke's back to between his shoulder blades, a quick, intimate gesture, but she saw his shoulders relax and his body language softened.

"Peace, Luke?" she spoke quietly.

Syn took the two of them in for a moment. The young doctor had come to them only three years ago. He had an impressive record as a battlefield medic, nearly zero fatalities on his record. He had been with a small mercenary force called RANCOR and had avoided being registered by taking on professions that allowed him to hide his abilities. But he had been required to turn himself over to the Academy when he reattached a friend's leg that had been blown off by a landmine.

Syn had been a combat instructor for the Academy at the time, teaching Psychics and Leashes small arms combat. He remembered the way Luke had injected himself into every aspect of Academy life. He was popular, helpful, and kind. He and Catha had arrived at the same time, her halting manner already intact, but had steadily gotten worse over the last three years.

It had never made any sense to Syn why such a young Psychic would be paired with such a wizened Leash, her advanced age meant that the Wash sickness would take her much sooner than others. But next to Syn, Catha was the foremost weapons expert at the Academy and often helped with firearm instruction when Syn and Dian were out on assignments.

"So the supplies you needed?" said Luke, breaking Syn's concentration. His thoughts had run away with him again.

"Ms. Alyssia, I don't understand? There wasn't always an Academy?" asked one of her nine year olds, a gifted Tickler with freckles and sand colored hair.

"Actually the Academy is fairly new," she explained patiently. "It's only been around about 60 years. The Father founded the Academy a few years after the Psychic Registry began. He wanted a safe place for all the Psychics to be able to live without being discriminated against by the world at large. So while we couldn't stop the Psychic Registry, we did have a safe place to live that was run by other Psychics."

"Why do we call our founder The Father? It's kind of a weird name," asked a young blonde girl with an oversized blue bow in her hair.

"It's a title of respect. He never submitted himself for the Psychic Registry and was too strong to be forced to register, his strength and self-reliance are both things that we pride ourselves on here. Even his tombstone reads *Destiny by our own hand*. Out of respect, we keep his name hidden and safe. He was, after all, the first recorded Level Four Psychic."

"What was his manifest, Ms. Alyssia? Could he breathe fire like Lady Agni?"

"I'm not sure. I guess it could be anything you wanted it to be." Some of the kids cheered while others groaned.

"That's not cool!"

"I wanna breathe fire!"

"Could he heal or anything?"

"I named my fish after Rudra."

Alyssia adored their infectious enthusiasm. "Alright, class. Take a few minutes at your tables and discuss what you would want your manifest to be if you reached Level Four, use your talking chips so everyone gets a turn."

The students began talking with each other excitedly about the abilities they had seen from their elder Psychics and some that they made up themselves.

"Al, got a minute?" Alyssia knew it was Dian before she turned around. The Psychic energy that surrounded the fiery red head was heavy and flowing like creme or a nimbus cloud in the distance. Alyssia liked Dian, they were about the same age and Dian had a certain freedom that Alyssia envied a great deal.

"What's up, Dian?" Dian was wearing most of her uniform but it was sloppily put together, she had on her uniform pants and her jacket, but her shirt and vest were missing. Under her Academy jacket was a stained white shirt that was several sizes too big tucked into her uniform pants. Her hair looked clean but unbrushed, and she was wearing heavy hiking boots instead of her Academy issue set. She was disheveled and adorable.

By contrast Alyssia was wearing her full Academy uniform, her instructor bars neatly attached to her shoulder, and her platinum blonde hair freely flowing around her face. But somehow being so well put together next to her friend's shabby confidence made her feel self-conscious.

"I heard about the incident in the infirmary. Some guy hurt you? Are you ok?" Dian asked whenever Alyssia got close enough to her for Dian to speak and not alert the students.

Alyssia stifled for a moment and resisted the urge to touch her own neck. "It was a misunderstanding. Dr. Luke asked us to do an experiment that sort of backfired. Everything's ok now."

Dian looked unconvinced. "You should have killed him."

Alyssia fought the urge to laugh. That was Dian's solution for nearly everything. "Next time. Didn't you just get back from assignment? Why do you look like you're about to leave again?"

Dian looked over her shoulder as if she expected someone to be right behind her "Yea. Something went sideways on our last assignment." Alyssia saw her friend's furrowed brow and could feel the change in her energy.

"What's bugging you about it?" Alyssia asked, trying to read more information between Dian's knit eyebrows.

"How many assignments have Syn and I been on? How many facilities have we destroyed? How many people have we killed? We've NEVER had our cover blown," Dian said with skepticism. "Even when I'm a little out of hand, Syn is an expert at covering our tracks. It just seems off."

Alyssia regarded her friend with concern. Dian raised her eyes to meet Alyssia's. "Sorry. This isn't your problem. I actually came to ask if you could cover for me in a few days. I volunteered to help with some kind of training session the higher ups came up with. Something about additional combat training for a group of Mumblers and Ticklers. They said they just needed me to referee. Anyway, could I talk you into doing it for me?"

Alyssia smiled. "Oh, I get it. You weren't worried about me, you just don't want to have to work. That's fine, I guess. What are friends for if you can't push your chores off on them?"

Dian laughed. "You're a lifesaver. Two days from now, after school hours, of course, down in the training room. Agni is gonna be there, I think." Dian's eyes flickered involuntarily.

Alyssia liked Agni and Dian, but they had never gotten along with each other. There didn't seem to be a direct reason, and Alyssia had always just chalked it up to their manifest abilities being so similar.

"When do you leave, Dian?"

Dian looked behind Alyssia at the kids in class. They were small, they were fragile, they were ignorant and beautiful. Dian envied them, hated them, and loved them.

"We're leaving now. Take care of those babies. They need to be kept as far from all this crap as we can keep them."

Alyssia smiled. She wanted to hug Dian, but wasn't brave enough to try. Dian felt the uneasy tension of words unsaid, but smirked and turned away waving passively "By the way, a man's only supposed to grab you by the throat if you ask him to. Otherwise you're supposed to kill him. Don't let it happen again."

Alyssia's cheeks and ears burned red with embarrassment. She had toyed with the notion that she was attracted to Tobias, but the thought didn't seem to stick. She wasn't attracted to him. She was intrigued by him. He didn't make any sense, the way he could go from a violent monster to an open book. How he could seem totally innocent and curious then when asked about the people he'd killed became this impossibly deep well of hate.

"Miss Alyssia, Jamison said he wants his manifest to be candy. Will you tell him that doesn't make sense?"

Alyssia turned to her students and smiled. *I wish my manifest was candy*, she thought more than a little sadly to herself.

CHaPTer 1.9

Primary Purpose

"The Leash Protocol was adopted in order to appease the general public before the beginning of the Psychic War, also known as the Twenty Year War. In order for The Father to create the Academy, he had to meet certain stipulations that were required by world leaders.

1: Psychics had to have a designation that they could be recognized by.

2: Psychics must be taught that if their abilities were going to be used, they had to be used for the betterment of mankind.

3. Psychics are required to forfeit citizenship of their respective countries and become citizens of the Academy.

4. A contingency plan must be put in place to tether the Psychics so that they are dependent on the Academy.

5. The Academy must be self-sufficient and must - in all cases - provide for its own needs. No country or region will be required to pay taxes or provide military support to the Academy."

Xiphos heaved a sigh of relief as the Wash permeated every molecule of his body.

The trip back to the Academy had been brutal as he struggled desperately to try and keep his tiny flame of Psychic energy burning so that his body wouldn't fall apart and in on itself. They had made it, but just barely.

The whimpers of the council had finally gone quiet, or perhaps he was so rapt with the feeling of his body returning to its natural state that he simply had blocked them out. He felt his bones mending and his organs returning to their full function.

We have to come up with some kind of alternative to this. That was way too close, he thought as he flexed his muscles and felt the strength and limberness return to them.

His Wash concluded and he exited the chamber as the members of the council were placed back into their neural sleep. Their existence bothered Xiphos, but he reminded himself that they themselves were barely aware of their own existence, so maybe it didn't matter.

The Leash who had stood guard over the Wash seemed dazed and a bit woozy.

"You Level Four guys sure do need a lot of juice," he laughed sheepishly, drunk on the residual Psychic energy. "When you guys Wash, it's hard to function for a little while afterwards."

Xiphos felt a twinge of annoyance, like he had just been accused of eating all the food in a pantry, but he dismissed it quickly. It wasn't his fault he had been paired with Aspis. It wasn't his fault he had taken to his Merger so effectively. And it damn sure wasn't his fault he was sent on missions that required the greatest amount of expenditures to him personally.

He knew that he himself was a bit power drunk at that moment and that his annoyance would pass. The kid was right, it did take a lot to get his body back into working order after a big assignment. He walked across to the large wooden door on the other side of the hall. He tapped twice and waited for the command to enter.

"Come in."

He turned the knob and pushed, the door resisting a little before opening.

"I think your door frame might be bent, Boss," said Xiphos absently.

Zander made an annoyed noise and then turned his attention back to Aspis who was sitting rigid in the other office chair. "So the client was..."

"Dead, sir. Single gunshot from what Xiphos could assess quickly at the scene," answered Aspis stiffly.

Zander put his head in his hands. "So let me see if I understand everything that happened. You were attacked by a well-armed, poorly trained merc group. You dispatched them. Then when you went to check on the client you found that he had mercenaries working for him and he was already dead. And that the gunshot looked fresh enough that there is no way he was dead at the beginning of the assignment."

Xiphos, never one for formal stances and salutes, leaned lazily on his back leg against the back wall. "The blood on the guy's shirt was still wet, but all of that is on my neural link, sir."

Zander sat up in his seat, his brow furrowed with concentration. "We're getting a lot of interesting happenings on assignments lately. Agni and Rudra, Syn and Dian, and now you two. Anything else happens I'll assume someone's out to get me," he said as he took his glasses off and rubbed his eyes.

Aspis shot Xiphos a worried glance. Xiphos knew what was about to come next and was genuinely concerned about the reaction.

"About the ambush, sir. There are some other details we feel like you need to know," Aspis said with hesitation.

Zander put his glasses back on and began typing at his computer again. "Wonderful. What other delights do you have in store for me?"

Aspis reached into her pocket and placed the small black box on Zander's desk alongside the neural dampeners that the mercenaries had used when they attacked them. "These were in our assailants' possession. The dampeners seemed pretty standard issue equipment except for the way they dampen. Instead of creating dead space, it's like they match and respond to frequencies. I couldn't even hear their silence, sir."

Zander stopped typing for a moment and picked up the dampener. It was small and unassuming. He turned his attention to the black box. "And this one?"

"It seems to be some kind of weapon, sir. When it was activated it ... " Aspis hesitated, looking at Xiphos apologetically. " ... it hurt Xiphos."

Xiphos looked back at his partner reassuringly. There was no need for an apology, the information needed to be relayed.

"Explain?" Zander asked Xiphos.

"Sir, it was a sound. High pitched. Almost not a sound, but more like a high frequency vibration. It made it feel like my blood was on fire. Like I was burning from the inside out. It was painful and left me ... " Xiphos paused as he searched for the correct word. "...drained. It left me drained, sir."

Xiphos hoped his report was professional sounding because in his own head it sounded like excuses.

"Did it affect you, Aspis?" Zander asked the Shield Psychic.

Her head snapped toward him. She hadn't been aware that she was staring sympathetically at Xiphos. She wasn't used to seeing her partner and best friend look so defeated. "No effect, sir. I couldn't hear it, and I felt nothing out of the ordinary."

Zander put his elbows on his desk and laced his fingers together. "Alright. Thank you both. Aspis, I'll need you to file a full paper report on the events. Xiphos, do you consent to have her file your portion of it as well?"

Xiphos nodded before adding, "That's fine, sir, but I don't mind filling out my own paperwork–"

Zander cut him off. "That won't be necessary. Aspis will be fine to fill out your portion while you're in lock up."

Xiphos and Aspis both went rigid.

"What?!" Aspis spat as she rose to her feet. "What do you mean he's going into lockup? You're punishing him for getting ambushed? Then there's no reason for me not to go with him. If you're going to punish one of us, you need to punish us both!"

Aspis, shut up. Xiphos's soothing voice vibrated in her mind. She snapped her head to look at him then back at Zander who was now leaning forward in his seat contemplating the young woman very seriously.

"Psychic Aspis, your partner left your caravan detail undefended—"

"To scout ahead!" Aspis shouted. She felt Xiphos's hand on her shoulder, not realizing in her anger he had walked up to her.

"Undefended," Zander continued calmly. "He wasn't present at the beginning of the ambush. He arrived late to the defense after the first salvo of rockets were launched, according to your own report. He then failed to dispatch the assailants because he was injured by a weapon that was evidently tailored to harm ONLY him. Then, he was the first and only witness to see the client was dead. Now, how much of this sounds suspicious to you?"

"But Xiphos would never—" Aspis felt herself on the verge of tears.

"Of course you and I know that, but do you expect a client, one who paid your incredibly substantial fee, to believe it?" Zander interrupted her. "I certainly would not. Not to mention, you killed any of the other witnesses who could have been interrogated, and I don't imagine any of them that survived will be very willing to cooperate with us after you blew them all halfway to hell."

"I didn't have a choice," Aspis choked weakly. She knew Zander was right. Every logical part of her brain knew that everything he said was absolutely right, but she still couldn't stand the idea of Xiphos being locked up like a criminal. Like Angel.

"That's not how the client will see it. So until we get both of your neural links mapped and can piece together what actually happened so that we have reasonable and accurate information to give to the client, we will place Xiphos in lockdown in order to appease the client. This way we don't harm our relationship with them, we maintain our integrity, and Xiphos will be safe from further reprisal until we get this mess all sorted out. As soon as we have some kind of solid documentation and proof that the Academy wasn't responsible for this attack, we will release Xiphos from holding."

Aspis tried to straighten herself up, but she was still upset.

"It makes perfect sense, Aspis," Xiphos told his partner reassuringly. "It won't be long, and you can come visit me anytime you'd like. I'll be out in no time. You'll see." He turned to face Zander. "Do you plan to arrest me, sir? Should I get a guard?"

Zander shook his head. "No, Xiphos. Go back to your quarters and shower and pack a rack bag. Turn yourself into holding no later than tomorrow 0600. Understand?"

Xiphos stood up straight for the first time since he had entered the office, gave a snappy salute. "Yes, sir." He turned on a heel and marched out, closing the door softly.

Aspis felt like she had ash in her mouth.

"I expect your report on my desk by 0800 tomorrow, Psychic Aspis. Understood?"

She blinked slowly and opened her mouth several times before the words came out. "Yes, sir."

I'm going to KILL Dian when she gets back, Alyssia fumed to herself.

If Dian had told her that the training session she was supposed to oversee was combat training led by Tobias Marshall, she would have made her friend find someone else to do it. At least that's what she told herself.

When she had gone to get more details about the assignment the day before from Agni, the Pyre Psychic had mentioned the parameters of what would be happening. Alyssia was fairly certain she had stopped breathing for several minutes. Her last encounter with Tobias had left her deeply confused and anxious.

"You'll need to go and check out weapons from inventory," Agni had said during their early morning meeting. "Two cases should be plenty. And make sure you ask for salt shot, I'm concerned this Marshall character may accidentally kill someone otherwise."

Accidently? Alyssia thought. *I'm surprised he hasn't done it on purpose already.*

Weapons inventory was, besides the kitchens, probably the cleanest and most well maintained area in all of the Academy. Leashes and Psychics who were going on assignments would make their stop here before they left to get ammunition or check out weapons. Some Leashes preferred to have their own personal weapons. Syn, for instance, owned an extensive collection of firearms and would often come and provide weapons demonstrations for Leashes and Psychics who were unfamiliar with handling guns.

Alyssia herself was a fair shot when it came to stationary targets at a 79% accuracy ratio. But the digital drills with moving targets and simulated attacks knocked that score down to a meager 18%.

She sighed deeply at the thought. *Still crack under pressure.*

There were two Leashes and Psychics present in the room, all sitting at a small table talking behind the clear plastic wall, the same material that made up the cells in the holding facility. As Alyssia approached the window, all four of them noticed her, but none made any quick movement to ask what she needed.

She was used to the treatment. She had a boogeyman reputation. It was common knowledge how many times they had tried to pair her. Even though no one had said anything, promising Leashes vanishing and a Level Four Psychic roaming around unpaired was enough reason for people to ask all the right questions. She was used to it, but it didn't make it any more fun to deal with.

"Excuse me, I'm here to pick up supplies for the session in the training room today. I was told you would have the order all ready for me."

One of the Psychics, a polite young man named Dylan stood up with a warm smile that didn't quite make it all the way to his eyes and came to the window. "Yes ma'am, Ms. Alyssia. The two cases and the salt shot, right?"

He passed a clipboard through the window for Alyssia to fill out while he went to fetch the cases for her. "Alrighty," he said with that same mirthless smile. "These are due back by end of day today or first thing in the morning. Please don't leave any live rounds in any of the weapons, even if it's salt shot."

Alyssia tried hard not to notice how the other Psychic and both the Leashes at the table were watching her, eyes all slightly narrowed, body language tense and ready. She tried to return Dylan's smile, but found it was just as mirthless as his. "Will do. Thank you very much."

His smile broadened just a little, but his eyes remained unfazed. "My pleasure, ma'am."

Alyssia took the cases and headed for the door.

I still can't believe they let that monster work with kids.

She hadn't meant to hear the thought, but it was so loud that she couldn't have avoided it. She wheeled around, her face flushed and her ears stinging. "Excuse me?" she said before she could stop herself. "All I said was 'my pleasure, ma'am'," Dylan said, his smile still perched. Whether he knew it or not, though, his right hand had drifted to his sidearm.

Alyssia felt herself take a half step forward when a hand touched the small of her back gently.

"Aly-ssia, you are well?"

Alyssia looked up into Catha's bright green eyes. "I– I am," she stammered.

Catha smiled, small and wizened, but genuine. The older Leash had a matriarchal charm that Alyssia had always loved. "We walk?" she inquired, asking permission - in her own broken way - to accompany the young Psychic.

Alyssia nodded quietly in agreement, feeling her indignation cooling. Catha turned her head to the group of Psychics and Leashes who were still sitting at the table behind the window of the inventory room. "Section A, re-polish. Section G through I, re-spring. Before dismissal," Catha commanded coolly.

Dylan's fake smile evaporated. "But ma'am, shift ends in an hour. You're talking about four hours worth of work!" All of his charm evaporated.

Catha squared her shoulders and looked at all of them with a level of hard scrutiny only she could conjure. "Polish quickly," she responded flatly.

Catha had taken one of the cases out of Alyssia's hands as they walked. Alyssia hadn't asked her to, Catha had just sort of taken it. "Aly-ssia, well?" she asked the girl.

"I am. Could you tell I was upset?" Alyssia responded bashfully.

Catha smiled for a moment before responding. "Luke angry, shakes. Aly-ssia angry, cold."

Alyssia was mortified. "You could feel all that?" she said sheepishly.

Catha stole a glance her way, then smiled. "Like you angry. Funny."

Alyssia blushed. "Funny? I'm ferocious. Not a funny bone in my body."

Catha let out a soft one-note laugh before her face became stern. "Care for self, Aly-ssia. Make friends?"

Alyssia shook her head. "You, Agni, and Dian are the only people who speak to me on purpose. I'm not good at making friends. I've got my kids, though, and they love me."

Catha stopped mid-step and turned to face the young Psychic. "Boyfriend?" she asked with a scrutinizing gaze and more than a little ferocity.

Alyssia was shocked and then overcome with laughter. "Boyfriend? Are you nuts? No way."

Catha's expression softened from a look of ferocity into a look of concern. She didn't speak for a few seconds then, with certainty, "Girl-friend". Her face broadened into a warm, genuine smile, and they both erupted with laughter as they finished walking to the training room elevator. Catha handed Alyssia back her case and smiled.

"Thank you, Madame Soldier Leash. You made my walk much more pleasant with your company," Alyssia said appreciatively.

Catha reached out and touched the young woman's cheek, an unusually affectionate motion for the normally stoic Leash. So out of character in fact that it sent chills down Alyssia's spine, but she resisted the urge to pull away.

"Aly-ssia, careful. Funny bones break."

Then she turned to march off.

Alyssia smiled at her friend, but felt a knot twist itself into her stomach as she stepped into the elevator.

When the elevator dinged, Alyssia stepped out into the massive training area. Away from the elevator several paces was the running track, marked off and separate from the rest of the exercise equipment. After crossing over the track, in neat rows were sparring circles ranging in size from three to twelve meters. In the very center of the room congregated a small group wearing athletic gear, stretching, and warming up. Standing slightly off to the side was a dark-skinned, black-haired beauty that Alyssia knew had impossible green eyes.

"Agni!" Alyssia said as she approached the Pyre Psychic. Agni greeted her with a full warm smile as Alyssia set the two cases down on the ground.

"Alyssia, glad you could make it. We're still waiting on the *instructor*." Agni said the word with no small amount of venom.

Alyssia smirked despite herself. "Has it been that bad? I know you said he was a bit ruthless."

Agni turned her head to the young platinum haired Psychic and narrowed her eyes. "He's a monster. The only advantage to having him as an instructor is that most of these pairs will have to fight monsters at some point in their time here." She looked back up at the students who were still warming up, stretching, and doing basic calisthenics. "He has shot them, beaten them, brutalized them mentally and physically. The only reason we're still conducting these exercises is because he hasn't killed anyone yet."

Alyssia looked at the recruits who all seemed to be absently warming up. "They don't look afraid, and people have died during training before ..." Alyssia clamped her own jaw shut. *What am I saying? Am I defending him? What's wrong with me?*

She glanced up to see Agni looking her over with an unreadable expression.

"You're right, people have died here in training before. Improper handling of guns, carelessness with the exercise equipment, even failed mergers..."

That one stung Alyssia more than she would admit, but she listened as Agni continued.

"But never have I seen a person with such callous disregard for the well-being of others. It's like he thinks life has no meaning," Agni said as she shook her head. "Nevertheless, his results are impossible to argue with. These recruits over the last three weeks have gone from a group of cocky, unfocused kids into something animalistic. They react so quickly now. And they fight so much harder than before. But with an instructor that makes every day a life or death situation, it's easy to see how."

At that moment the elevator dinged and both Tobias and Rudra stepped out. Rudra was dressed like his sister in their sharp black and gold Academy uniforms, their gold bars indicating them as combat specialists.

Alyssia had always been a bit envious of them. Not really the Combat Specialist title, but the gold bars looked so snappy and official. Her uniform carried a white Academy personnel stripe with a blue line through the middle indicating she was an Instructor. She fought the urge to reach up and touch her own shoulder bars.

Tobias was wearing a pair of Academy uniform pants, a pair of Academy combat boots, a skin tight, and a long sleeved black shirt that shimmered in the reflective light of the training facility. She recognized it as his smart fiber shirt that he had arrived in. His gun holsters, although empty except for one of his 45's, were strapped around his thighs. He also hadn't shaved in the past few weeks and his red blonde beard made him look even more ferocious than usual.

Alyssia gulped hard. It was the first time she had seen him since their tour together and suddenly that deep anxiety of being near a wild and dangerous animal came to the front of her mind. Where Agni and Rudra both had a similar effect on her Psychic sense of taste and made the air taste like spices, Tobias still filled her Psychic senses with an acidity that made her eyes sting. She had to pull her own energy into herself so as not to be distracted by it.

"Agni, did you hear that Xiphos and Aspis are back?" Rudra said as he approached.

The Tornado Leash walked past Alyssia as if she wasn't present. It didn't bother the Energy Sync, she would rather be ignored than draw his ire.

"No, I didn't. Are they alright?" Agni asked with concern.

"They are now, but Xiphos was pretty messed up when they got in," Rudra said. "They were ambushed and the whole mission apparently went to hell. There is going to be an investigation into it apparently. Routine procedure stuff, but they've got Xiphos in lockup until they get him cleared."

Agni's eyes went wide, and her head snapped to the far end of the training facility where the large steel doors and armed guards protected the lockup facility. "I ..." Agni mumbled, then looked at her brother, seeking permission.

"Why do you think I came down here?" Rudra said with a chuckle. "Go ahead, I'll cover this session for you. Besides, I've been curious about our newest Instructor's teaching style since I've heard so much about it."

Agni beamed. Her brother knew her so well and intimately that often they didn't even need to speak to understand one another. "Thank you," she said as she began to walk across the facility, then stopped and turned to face Rudra. "Alyssia will assist you if you need anything, Ru." Her voice carried a weight of authority that made Rudra scoff and Alyssia wince.

"Understood," said the Tornado Leash with finality.

Alyssia turned back to the Psychic and Leash pairs that were warming up and stared at them without actually seeing them. *Dian owes me big time for this. I swear if I had known I never would have —*

"Hey Al, you bring my guns?"

Alyssia's thoughts were cut off by Tobias' question. She looked up to see him staring at her, his hard green eyes like a big cat, trying to decide which part of her would be easiest to rip out with his teeth.

"Y-yes! Sorry, Mr. Mar ...I mean, Tobias," she sputtered as she picked up the cases and put them in his hands. He raised an eyebrow then set them back on the ground and opened up the cases.

He called all of the young pairs over and handed each one a gun, two magazines and a box of the salt shot per group. "We've done quite a bit to focus your reaction time and your initiative. Today we will be working on decision making skills and how to determine in a split second what's the best way for you and your partner to survive."

Tobias closed and locked the empty cases. He carried the cases and placed them in two separate points in the room, creating a triangle out of the space where the recruits stood and where the cases were. "Today's objective will be to defend your Psychic or your Leash under duress. Decide what's the most efficient way to stay alive. Because even if you're bulletproof, there is only so much punishment you can take before your body stops working properly and you run out of your Psychic energy and die."

Tobias motioned for all the recruits to clear the space. "Two brave souls," he said with an air of authority. All the young Psychics and Leashes looked at each other. This was his horrifying catch phrase, and everyone knew that whoever went first would end up getting hurt the worst.

Rudra scoffed softly. "Man, you've really gotten them all shaken up. Alright, I'll go first. Who else?"

No one stepped forward. The respect the recruits had for Rudra was immense; they knew him to be fierce, friendly and impossibly strong. but even that wasn't enough to make them volunteer.

"Don't all jump at once," Rudra said begrudgingly.

"Sir, we will volunteer. Mister Rudra shouldn't have to step up and do our jobs because we're being cowards," a rosy-cheeked female Psychic with walnut-colored hair said. Her Leash, a gangly boy with shoulder length black hair and large, kind, eyes stood up. He reminded Alyssia of a puppy, albeit a well-chiseled, super human puppy.

"Hand Tracy the gun, and cross to that gun case," Tobias indicated by pointing the barrel of his own salt shot loaded pistol. "Tracy, move to the far gun case over there."

When they were in position, Tobias completed the triangle with his own body. "Alright, kiddies. The assignment is easy. Overpower me before I kill you. Understand?"

The Psychic and Leash looked at each other and smirked. "You're sure, sir?"

Tobias didn't answer, just raised his salt loaded pistol and fired at the Psychic.

The young Leash had been anticipating this, and the moment Tobias had raised the gun he had begun sprinting to intercept. The salt shot hit his skin and stung like dozens of bee stings at once. But he knew that his Psychic was safe and that he had anticipated correctly. The salt shot kept assailing his skin, hitting from slightly different angles. He managed to straighten himself up enough to put eyes on Tobias but only for a second before a shot ricocheted off his left orbital and he was functionally half blind. Then, to his horror, a shot hit him in the side of his neck. He knew at once it had come from behind him.

"Conner, get down!" Tracy shouted.

The young Leash tried to sink to one knee, but a vice-like hand grabbed him by his trachea and pulled him upright. He knew it was Tobias and that at this range he could overpower him. He closed a fist to attack then heard Tracy scream.

Rudra was horrified and mesmerized by the five second interaction. Tobias had played them both. When he raised his weapon to fire at the Psychic, the Leash had rushed to put himself in between them. Tobias had then sidestepped so that the Leash was directly between himself and the Psychic. The Psychic had tried to raise her own weapon to fire but couldn't shoot for fear of hitting her own Leash. All the while Tobias had slowly stepped closer and closer, firing at just the right intervals to keep the Leash from being able to see his approach clearly. When the Psychic realized what was happening she even chanced a shot but hit her Leash instead. When the Psychic had finally called out to her Leash to move it was too late. Tobias had grabbed the Leash by the throat and, using him as a human shield, fired off two more shots both of which hit the Psychic and knocked her down.

Rudra was in awe. It was one thing to hear Agni talk about how dangerous this man was, it was another entirely to see him in action.

That probably would have worked on me if I'm being honest, he smirked.

Tobias walked over to the young Psychic and gave her a hand up, the speckles of blood on her athletic shirt shining wetly against the industrial lighting in the underground complex. "What was the mistake?" Tobias asked flatly as he walked back to his starting position.

"I should have tried to attack you instead of protecting her," the Leash answered.

"That's right. By rushing to get between us, you limited yourself to defense, prevented your partner from attacking, and turned yourself into a human shield for me as much as her."

"But if I hadn't gotten in between you, you would have shot her anyway," Conner protested. Tobias looked at the boy hard.

"Tracy," Tobias said flatly, the young Psychic looked up just in time to see Tobias's pistol clear its holster and point at her. She flicked her wrist and the pistol flew out of Tobias's hand, skittering along the floor several feet to the left. When she refocused back on Tobias, he had closed the distance between them and was in the middle of throwing a hard right cross aimed directly at her partner's chin. She reached out with her mind, focusing on Conner, and pulled. His body lurched back suddenly, out of reach of the incoming attack, but he managed to keep his balance.

Tobias stopped. "You don't trust your partner. You think she's inferior, but of the two of you, she's the only one who took initiative and tried to attack. She trusted you to do your job, but you didn't trust her to do hers. Today it is you, despite any extra physical capabilities, who are inferior."

The young Leash examined his shoes.

"Break into groups of four and repeat this exercise. Whoever the odd one out is, take notes. Try not to screw up and accidently kill each other," Tobias instructed.

As they began, Tobias walked around the groups before coming back over to stand beside Rudra.

"That was interesting," Rudra said with a smirk. "Tell me, Mr. Marshall, where does one go to learn to fight against Leashes and Psychics the way you do?"

Tobias was quiet for a moment, then he finally spoke. "My teacher was a Leash."

Rudra wasn't often taken aback, and his shock sent a Psychic ripple through the air that made the hair on Alyssia's arms stand on end. The deep well of Psychic energy that a Level Four Leash possessed seemed fathomless. But it was the only way they could do the impossible things that they did with any level of consistency.

"You were trained by a merged pair?" Rudra asked incredulously. "What were their names? Who were they? What level?"

Tobias shrugged one shoulder while looking over the students who were still in the midst of their exercises. "Couldn't say. And now they're both dead," was his flat reply before he walked back over to the groups of students.

Alyssia watched him walk away and fought the urge to reach out to his mind. It wasn't hard to resist for she remembered what she had encountered the last time she was inside his head and it still made her uncomfortable to think about. He was such an odd alien element to her. Something strange and out of place, like a flower growing through concrete. If, you know, flowers walked around in public heavily armed.

"Alyssia."

She was shocked to hear her name, especially considering whose voice it was.

Rudra was looking at her hard. "Luke mentioned to me that he had you try to examine Marshall's mind once. What did you find?"

Alyssia thought for a moment. *Did he read my mind?*

No, not even strong Leashes could do that. It was equally unsettling that Rudra was not only talking directly to her but had actually used her name instead of *kid* or *vampire*. "He's got the strongest mental defenses I've ever seen. From anyone. I could have dug deeper, but his body reacts pretty violently to Psychic intrusion."

One of her hands lifted slightly as she had the overwhelming desire to cover her neck, then got mad at herself for her fear.

I'm a Level Four Psychic, dammit. I could throw him across the room if I wanted to!

She let the thought simmer in her mind for a moment until the image of tossing the dangerous mercenary around like a ragdoll made her feel more at ease. It wasn't the type of thing she would do. She seldom used her Psychic abilities for anything important and never a significant enough quantity of it to be dangerous. Most people didn't even know she qualified as a Level Four. But the thought did make her smile.

The Psychics and Leashes were becoming progressively more creative, using Psychic energy for trips and pushes and pulls. One really clever Psychic just pulled the gun out of her assailant's hand while her Leash rushed them. They all learned quickly. But with an instructor who had absolutely no qualms about injuring students, it made sense that they would have to learn their lessons quickly in order to stay uninjured.

Suddenly Alyssia became aware of a chill, a presence like a deep unfathomable ocean that made the air taste like ice, accompanied by the smell of flowers.

"Hello Rudra, sweet boy. How are you?"

Rudra's cheeks flushed but his demeanor stayed cool and charming. He turned and flashed that perfect smile at the Nightmare Psychic as she approached. "Here comes trouble," he said playfully to her.

Melania moved with her typical ethereal elegance, long, strong legs carrying her perfect body with all the grace of a dancer. her black hair highlighting her fair skin and pink lips. She was truly one of the most beautiful humans to ever walk the earth. Of course, it was, at least in part, her Psychic glamor which created the illusion of impossible, superhuman beauty.

Alyssia knew she was approximately twice the age she appeared, but that didn't matter. What mattered is what you saw. Melania knew this and used it to her full advantage. "And hello to you, too, pretty thing."

Alyssia felt just the lightest tickle of Melania's Psychic nails on the small of her back through her uniform. It covered her skin in goosebumps and turned her cheeks and ears scarlet. "Hello, Miss Melania. How are you?"

Alyssia heard her own voice as far too soft and tried to harden it on her last words but it had just served to make her sound more nervous. Melania smirked at the platinum blonde-haired girl then smoothly approached and slipped her arm through Rudra's. They stood shoulder to shoulder, both tall and strong. Very suddenly, Alyssia felt like the wallflower at the dance.

"Come down to see Angel?" Rudra asked, their familiarity palpable.

Melania tsked at the dark-skinned Leash. "He needs to undergo a Wash; he's getting weaker, and I'm starting to feel the effects myself."

"Want me to talk with Gregory about scheduling a time for it? You know he will want the extra security," said Rudra just a tad too eagerly. "I'd be happy to oversee and assist if you'd like?"

Alyssia always thought it was ridiculous how people acted around Melania. Sure she was beautiful and powerful and smelled like a field of fresh cut flowers...

What was I thinking about? She felt herself swoon slightly. She realized, like every other person who got close enough to Melania, she was being soaked up by her ever present Psychic glamor. As frustrated and angry as it made Alyssia to feel the heat in her own body rise despite knowing it was an artificial attraction, she could not deny how shapely and alluring the black haired woman was.

"What is he making them do? Why are they shooting each other?" The Nightmare Psychic said with a practiced disinterest.

"Initiative exercises. Brutal ones," said Rudra. "He's demonstrating how an individual assailant can overpower a Psychic and Leash with tactical ability even if they are outclassed by raw firepower."

Melania didn't need his explanation but listened anyway while her sharp eyes took in the mock combat situations. She was, without a doubt, the most seasoned and, arguably, the most powerful Psychic at the Academy. While Syn and Catha both had military backgrounds and were both seasoned soldiers, they were Leashes. Neither of them had ever fought the way that Melania had. She had served in the Psychic War where she had earned her name as Nightmare Psychic whenever an entire battalion of troops had committed suicide because they couldn't get the imaginary spiders off of their bodies.

"And what makes this particular instructor so qualified to teach this? Aren't there other Leashes who could do this just as well?" Melania asked now sizing up Tobias while he walked around the students, giving advice and occasionally adding another layer of distraction for the teams to fight against.

"He's not a Leash or a Psychic," Alyssia heard herself say, a little surprised she'd found the nerve to talk at all.

Melania turned her icy eyes and her full attention to the young Psychic "Oh? Just a contractor then? Are we outsourcing our training now?" she chided softly.

"He's killed four pairs. The closest thing we've ever seen to a professional Psychic killer. He even won a fistfight against a Tickler Leash."

Melania released a surprised laugh. "This little man? You're describing a monster, not some scruffy soldier boy."

Rudra shook his head, his expression unchanged. "I've seen him fight. Believe it when I say, he's ice cold."

Melania let her full lips curl into a dangerous smirk. "Then I'll just have to see for myself." She raised the hand that wasn't wrapped around Rudra's bicep and waved. "Excuse me, Mr. Instructor, sir. I have a question."

Tobias raised an eyebrow in her direction then kept working with the group he was instructing.

Melania didn't like being ignored. She unwrapped herself from around the Tornado Leash and walked onto the area where the other Psychics and Leashes were working. As she passed each group, they lowered their weapons and ceased their attacks on each other. By the time she had covered half the distance to Tobias, every group had stopped working and were watching intently, the smell of flowers hung crisp in the air. Finally, Tobias couldn't ignore her approach anymore. He let out an irritated sigh as he turned to face her. "Excuse me, Mr. Instructor, sir. But I have a question."

"If you're waiting for an invitation, lady, I'm running out of patience." Tobias said, his voice like granite, cool and hard.

Melania was a bit taken aback, she was used to people falling all over themselves to accommodate her. Only a few people had ever seemed to be immune to her charms and even fewer could resist the pheromones and adrenal manipulation, but she refused to let it deter her.

"This little exercise seems to work very well against these babies, but do you think they would work against a Soldier Psychic or a Level Four?" Her question dripped with fake innocence.

"Probably not." Tobias answered flatly.

Melania's smirk widened to a full brilliant smile. "So quick to concede? You don't have more confidence in your own training techniques?"

"You asked a question, I answered it."

"No need to be nasty, it just looks like you're having so much fun." Melania focused on the young mercenary. She reached out with her mind, her needle sharp mental precision expecting a stone wall of resistance. Instead she saw a series of flashing images of two human bodies in motion almost like a slow motion dance, various positions and forms of one body moving another with pressure and leverage.

Judo, Jiu-jitsu, Savate, Muay Thai. This man is a weapon. Melania had to resist the urge to lick her lips. *A little push, perhaps. But I don't think desire will push him. Maybe rage will.*

She didn't need to know his mind, just that he was male. She pushed gently. His adrenal glands flooded his system, his testosterone spiked, and he took a deep, controlled breath through his nose. His pupils dilated slightly and his skin flushed.

"I just want to play with you," she said, making sure that her tone had just enough mocking in it to push on his primal buttons.

Tobias was having a hard time keeping his hand unclenched. Why did this woman make him so mad? Why did he want to tear her in half? He didn't let words and mocking affect him like this, but all he could think about was snapping her thin neck.

The words came out before he could stop them. "Fine. You want to fight? We can fight. Where is your Leash?"

Melania faked a hurt expression. "I'm not good enough for you? Do you need someone else to play with as well?"

She pushed a little harder and Tobias felt his skin vibrate and his head swim.

Who in the hell does she think she is? His logic tried to regain control, but his anger was beyond his ability to restrain.

"Whatever. Take the starting position," Tobias half-snarled while he pulled the magazine out of his training pistol and checked to see how many shots it had left in it.

Melania knew she had him off balance, so instead of backing away, she leaned in, her lips centimeters from his ear. "What's the matter, big man? Scared of having me this close?"

Melania gave one last chemical push and Tobias unhinged. The barrel of the pistol slammed into the center of Melania's chest. She hadn't been expecting it. She stumbled backwards, the wind gone from her lungs. Tobias leveled his pistol at her head, the weapon stabilized in two hands, his furious eyes burning.

She moved her wrist abruptly and Tobias's feet flew out from underneath him. He slammed onto his side, rolling to face her and reset his focus. Melania's focus had returned, and the pain in her chest set her anger ablaze. She threw the gun from his hand with a quick flick of her wrist sending it sailing to the other side of the training area, but the energy it had taken for her to remove the weapon from him gave him the opening to lunge toward her.

Before Melania had finished the movement, Tobias had risen to his feet and closed the distance between them. He lashed out with both hands in a vicious combination of strikes. Melania struggled for breath as she slipped past his rage-induced punches until her lungs filled with enough air to quench the burning in her chest and she pushed.

Tobias felt a wall of Psychic energy slam into him. It sent him flying through the air landing hard on his back. The air was blasted from his lungs and he was fairly certain he had cracked a couple of ribs, but the anger dulled the pain in his chest and the screaming in his lungs only fueled the rage. He managed to roll onto his knees and drew his gun from his thigh holster, one that definitely wasn't loaded with salt shot, and took aim.

Melania stood up straight, her chest no longer screaming and her vision no longer blurred and she dug into her deep well of Psychic energy.

The room pulsed. It was like all the light in the universe had gone out. Tobias was engulfed in a blackness so complete that it absorbed all light and sound. His senses returned in slow waves.

This is her manifest. She's a Level Four Psychic. Stupid boy.

He blinked several times and tried to breathe, but even though he felt the air entering and leaving his lungs, he couldn't hear himself breathing. Then a wall of pressure slammed on top of him, crushing him to the ground. He felt every moment of the pain as if it was stretched out. Every moment sent a new ripple of agony through his body. He couldn't lift his arms, and his breath was rapidly running out.

Several kilometers outside the Academy, the sensors in a makeshift base started screaming and all of the scanners on every piece of equipment that TITAN had available went black then flashed back up with groups of readings that were impossible.

Some of them registered that the Academy occupants had gone from several thousand to several million. The pinpoints of light looked like a bomb had gone off.

Some of them registered that a nuclear bomb had just gone off and there was no life left in the surrounding areas. A furious Captain Blaine could be heard for the next several minutes bellowing, asking what was going on, as if that would solve all the issues faster.

"Sir, we don't know. The level of Psychic radiation just shot through the roof. It looks like an atomic bomb went off inside."

Blaine stared stupidly at the computer screens wanting so badly to understand the facts and figures in front of him. He didn't.

Instead, he resorted to the same old tactic: when you don't know something that clearly no one else knows either, act as if you do and then call them stupid for not. "Heathens are probably in there murdering each other. I've always said this organization was full of degenerates. Get your sensors fixed. I want a full report ASAP."

"Sir." Several unenthused voices responded.

From his cell Angel felt what could only be described as a euphoric wave of energy. He knew when his Psychic was giving a demonstration of her full ability and he was drunk on it. Even through his cell walls he could feel her particular brand of hatred soaking through, and it was intoxicating. He pressed his body to the wall of his cell and roared deep in his throat. The bespectacled Leash standing at the door pretended not to notice that the Shred Leash was beginning another one of his grotesque rituals.

Alyssia was watching the interaction between Tobias and Melania with so much anxiety that her neck was rapidly growing stiff. The other Psychics and Leashes were giving them space, the nervousness and anticipation was heavy in the air.

Melania was goading Tobias, and the normally steely mercenary was showing signs of temper. The air was changing. Melania's aura was growing like a perfumed wave of ice and death. Alyssia felt it starting to impose on her own Psychic space.

Feed, the small voice in her head suddenly said.

NO! No, no, no, no, she shrieked mentally. The animal she normally kept so well caged was being yanked out of its hiding place by the dense Psychic aura of the Nightmare Psychic.

"Ugh." Alyssia heard Melania choke out.

Alyssia looked up, Tobias had jammed the barrel of his gun into Melania's chest and she had stumbled backwards. He raised the gun to fire, and Melania ripped the weapon from his hands with her mind and threw it across the room. He rushed and she sent him sprawling. He drew one of his own weapons and aimed.

Melania erupted. An impossible wave of Psychic energy flooded around them. All of their senses were Psychically muted. They couldn't see or hear, and feelings came in slow waves. Only Alyssia wasn't blind. She could taste every Psychic and Leash in the room. She could taste Tobias and his rage. There was no pain, but an otherworldly pressure bore down on her.

Feed.

She's going to kill Tobias.

Feed.

It might kill all of us.

FEED.

The floodgates opened and Alyssia ripped the massive pulses of Psychic energy out of the air. Her skin drank in the darkness and the animal inside her groaned with pleasure then she realized that there was no animal and it was her mouth that had made the sound.

The light in the room began to fade back. The arid sensation of the room touched her skin as Alyssia regained her faculties. Tobias was face down on the floor, his breathing was shallow. Melania's normally porcelain skin looked gray and ashen, her eyes had noticeable wrinkles around the edges and her hair had streaks of gray. She was down on one knee breathing in long slow ragged breaths.

All of the Psychics and Leashes who had been watching were in different states of collapse and panic. Some crying, some covering themselves with their hands, all a mess of emotion and self-defense.

Even Rudra was down on one knee. One eye closed, the other looking at Alyssia intensely.

Tobias propped himself up slowly, rose to his feet, and crossed to Melania. He stuck out his hand. Alyssia watched as the Nightmare Psychic's hair lost its gray streaks and her skin smoothed to its perfect alabaster again.

She took Tobias' hand and rose to her feet. They looked at each other quietly for a moment.

"Thank you for letting me participate in your training exercise, Mr. Marshall." Melania turned and faced Rudra and the teams of Mumblers. "Sorry for interrupting your training session. But I imagine your breaktime is over."

She tried to manage one of her typical hyper confident smiles but to anyone who cared to look, it was half-hearted at best. Tobias walked wordlessly back over to the group of Mumblers as Melania walked toward the elevator door to the training facility.

"Class dismissed. Tomorrow. Same time." Tobias said flatly.

All of the Mumblers gathered themselves up and walked away. What had just happened was horrifying, lightning fast, and completely overwhelming. Not one of them would soon forget what had just happened. And none of them would ever underestimate the power of a Level Four Psychic again.

Alyssia looked up at each one of them. None of them spared her much attention. They all looked entirely too exhausted to even be afraid. But when she locked eyes with Melania, what she saw disturbed her deeply. The Nightmare Psychic, who had butchered whole battalions, the walking wave of black death that could make men so frightened that they'd rather kill themselves than attempt to fight through their fears, the woman who just moments ago with a flick of her wrist had nearly killed an entire room of Psychics, Leashes and one very dangerous mercenary, looked afraid.

CHAPTER 1.10
Understanding Our Heritage

"The Father created a perfect system for the freedom and growth of Psychics. Creating the Leash Protocol followed all of the parameters laid down by the Pacification Pact, and any and all peace treaties laid down by their respective regions. But with all of the benefits that the Father procured, there is one inevitable truth. If a Psychic ever defies the treaties and agreements laid down by the Academy, that Psychic must be corrected by any means necessary. If no correction can be reached, it becomes the unfortunate job of the Psychic's Leash to eliminate their Psychic. While this is unsavory and undesirable, it is the ultimate responsibility of the Leash and the ugliest unavoidable truth of the Leash Protocol."

On the small island of Roisin Dubh in the North Central Ocean, on a rocky outcrop overlooking a small discreet military facility, Syn took a full deep breath and let it halfway out.

The outpost had long since been repurposed as a base of operations for diplomats in that region and as a research facility trying to improve water purification and energy storage. On their way into the island, Syn and Dian had seen a half a dozen large buoys that were being used as collection hubs for wave energy. The towering wind turbines and solar panels were positioned around the base at locations where they would be most useful. There was even a grain vat full of hops and barley that had been repurposed after they had been distilled.

For a brief moment, Syn regretted the mission they were about to carry out. It seemed a shame to cause harm to a facility that was well on its way to changing the world for the better.

Syn refocused. If they didn't want to get shot at, they shouldn't have tried to double cross the Academy.

Several hundred meters down the rocky outcrop, Dian stood in the cover of trees. She had been standing still as stone for several minutes. The work she was doing was delicate and dangerous. Her manifest was that she could ionize air, separating electrons from positively charged ions. With a mass pulse of Psychic energy, she could make high density electric fields that could send bolts of electricity surging along a given path.

But what she was doing right now wasn't fighting one person, and it wasn't sending a bolt into a metal building. What she was doing now was precision work, and she wasn't great at it. She was concentrating ions in a number of small clouds surrounding the compound. If the clouds were too far apart, they couldn't create a big enough bolt when she discharged her Psychic wave, and if they were too close, they would set themselves off before she was ready. It was a balancing act of power and control.

Syn dropped and unrolled his pack. He pulled out his heavy compound bow and tightened the mechanism and gave the string a practiced pull. He smirked. A compound bow with a 226 kg pull would shoot nearly a kilometer.

Syn knocked an arrow and stood up straight. He channeled his Psychic energy into his eyes and skin, checking the airflow, smelling the breeze. His enhanced vision saw one of the guard towers clearly, as well as the sentry posted there. Syn drew back the arrow, mentally marked his target then raised the point of the arrow up and to the left to account for the distance and the breeze. He released his breath.

snap.

The arrow shot loose, and 10 seconds later the sentry fell to his knees, black fletching protruding from his neck.

Syn was off and running. He circled the outcropping, aimed at the next tower, and fired again. He hit his mark perfectly and a second sentry fell. He then dashed his way to a third position and aimed at the last tower. Aim, draw, fire. The arrow flew true, but the breeze changed directions at the last second and instead of sticking in the last guard's chest it slammed into the top of his thigh and the meter long shaft drove into his leg up to the fletching. The guard looked down and opened his mouth to scream, at which point a second arrow promptly slammed into the bottom of his chin and up into his brain.

Three down, Syn spoke to Dian in the way only she could hear.

Good shooting, Pops. Give me just a few more minutes.

Syn jogged back to his pack, unhooked and stored his compound bow. He then pulled out his 950 Judge. The weapon was quickly assembled, and Syn was lying prone on the ground. He set his scope on the water tower that was used as an external cooling apparatus for the whole facility.

Dian, my target is live. Are you ready? Syn's warm mental vibration pressed against her consciousness.

Count to three, she replied.

Exactly three seconds later, a shot rang out that sounded like a clap of thunder. A hole the size of a grapefruit appeared in the water purification tower, followed by the sound of a large mechanical failure and wrenching metal. The tower began spewing hundreds of gallons of water from the two holes created by the high caliber round that Syn's well placed shot had created.

It took moments for the alarms all over the base to sound. Several scientists and base employees were filling the ground when two more shots rang out. Both shots slammed into the long thin tower of one of the wind turbines, the second of which was a tracer round that burned bright red as it streaked across the sky. It cracked and swayed then began to fall. As it crashed to the ground, less than 100 meters from the outside of the base, the yard continued to fill with bleary eyed scientists, engineers, and security personnel. Blinking out of their labs and into the afternoon sun.

Dian, do you need more time? Syn's warm voice spoke into her mind, and she could almost hear him chambering another round.

No Pops, here comes the storm.

Dian dug deep, her well of Psychic energy becoming a storm cloud in the air, thick and electric. The ionized air grew hot. Several of the scientists felt their hair stand on end before Dian released the bolt she had been holding.

She pushed her Psychic energy hard. The ions and the electrons in the air were forced apart simultaneously and the clouds of ionized air that Dian had been slowly building, in the space of a moment, all aligned and a flash of white electricity raced along the ground and the air around them. More than two dozen people were instantly killed, and many more were flung all across the ground and into buildings. Any security personnel who were still standing were diving for cover. None of them had the time to suspect it was a Psychic behind the attack.

In fact none of them knew they were under attack until one more shot rang out from the hillside, and every person who wasn't dead, injured, or Dian, turned to face the rocky cliffside. Syn's final shot smashed into the natural gas line that was running along the ground near the center of the facility. The armor piercing tungsten round wrapped in a copper full metal jacket, sparked on impact and almost instantly every building on the island issued small scale explosions. Fires started to fill buildings, doors were kicked open and what few staff members on the island had not evacuated yet were quickly running into the yard.

On my way down. Be with you shortly, Syn thought to Dian as he slung his Judge over his shoulder and picked up his 6:1k, beginning his quick focused climb down the rocky encampment.

Dian had heard his thought but didn't have time to respond, she lifted one of the sheets of steel that had been blown off the side of one of the buildings and flung it at a group of guards who were rapidly heading toward the direction of the gunshot. They were crushed under the weight of the heavy metal plate. She then ionized a stream of air in front of her and high voltage flashes of electricity crackled and burned their way through one person after another.

Dian hated this part, taking life wasn't something she ever took pleasure in. But she was so good at it and reveled in her capacity to dole out death en masse, she would set about it almost instinctively. Afterward, however, she always felt a deep uneasiness.

She was hoping that the guilt would be softened by the fact that whoever had tried to make her and Syn look bad really needed to die.

Dian felt herself waning. The concentration it had taken to slowly and meticulously ionize the air in specific quantities had made her weary, but she could feel that Syn wasn't quite close enough yet to cover her. She took a deep breath and pushed hard against one of the steel walls that were laying on the ground and pulled it to herself. She ionized the air around her and ran a small but powerful electric charge through the metal magnetizing it.

Right on time. The guards on the grounds that were left had finally gotten their bearings and had unholstered their weapons. Several of them turned and opened fire on Dian, right as the steel plate covered her body. The result was that all of the bullets passed harmlessly around her magnetized shield and flew into the walls of the surrounding buildings. She knew that even if the bullets didn't have steel cores the size of her shield and the force it was producing would easily deter the bullets.

Dian, drop the shield in five seconds.

She smirked and began counting backwards from five.

Syn's rifle took careful aim and at the end of his five count, he opened fire. The half dozen guards who were fast approaching Dian's makeshift shield were dead before the first one hit the ground.

Dian exhaled for what felt like the first time in minutes, her formerly magnetized shield fell to the ground in front of her. They stood there a moment both catching their breath and examining the scene around them. Syn was looking for additional targets that might try to ambush them and Dian was marveling at the efficiency with which she and her partner had dispatched an entire encampment of people in just a few moments. The only sounds that remained were those of the water purification tower still spewing forth hundreds of gallons a minute and the internal fire suppression systems inside the buildings.

"Guess we'd better do recon now to see if anyone else is around," Dian finally said after several moments of silence.

Syn lifted up the back of his long coat and pulled out a pistol. It wasn't sleek and modern like most mercenaries carried, and it lacked the recoil gyroscope that modern firearms possessed. But it was light, and Dian knew it held sixteen, .45 bullets.

"There's already one in the pipe," Syn said sharply as his eyes turned back to surveying the scene around them.

Seventeen .45 bullets then.

They began to search the compound building by building, searching both for survivors and for evidence that they had been double crossed. The relationship that the Academy had with the regions was one of recognition and silence.

For open warfare, mercenaries were used to fighting each other. No region was allowed to have a formal standing military in accordance with the peace agreement signed 20 years before and even though every region at some point had hired the Academy for their service, they also pretended that they never had. So when an entire platoon of mercenaries erupted into flames, or a security team was ripped to pieces by some impossibly strong animal, the regions did their best to either hide it or explain it away. It was still one of the things that made this assignment so confusing to Dian.

Who in their right mind would track and record us to hide their own involvement, knowing what it could bring down on them?

Building by building they searched. The only survivor they found wasn't long for the world, an elderly male scientist who looked as if he'd been badly burned by the initial gas explosion. He was gasping for air, but a quick wave of compressed telekinesis crushed the remaining air from his lungs and allowed him to die without any additional pain.

The last building they reached seemed to have been the least damaged in their assault. It was at the back left corner of the compound and was as boxy and industrial looking as the rest of them. But it did bear several distinct differences. First it showed no signs of their battle, no burn marks or bullet holes. Secondly, unlike every other door on the facility, this one was locked and had an electronic locking system and biometric pad.

"Want me to try and bypass it?" Dian turned and asked her grisly gun toting partner.

Syn checked the outline of the door. "It looks heavy but not rigged." He put his hand on the door and pushed until the metal frame groaned under his fingers, but the door didn't give way.

Dian pressed her hand to the keypad and tried her best to cause the electricity to surge. "It must have had redundant fail safes to keep it from being short circuited."

"Give me a minute." Syn walked off and shortly after came back dragging the body of one of the scientists. "His name tag said Project Manager. Maybe he'll have access."

Dian shook her head, Syn was nothing if not efficient. They swiped his name badge through the scanner; it beeped and accepted, then when prompted they placed his hand on the scan pad. Syn had to lift his whole body up to do so, he had considered just ripping the arm off but was worried that it may offend Dian's sensibilities. She wasn't comfortable watching him slaughter their dinner; watching him dismember a human so he wouldn't have to work so hard probably would have crossed some line of decency.

The lights in the facility were still on. Backup generators kept the electrical equipment humming. Most of the rooms had computer servers or large batteries to store the energy generated by the numerous apparatus on the island. They didn't find any survivors in their search.

"I guess that means we killed everyone," Dian said, making no attempt to hide the pain in her tone.

Syn didn't ignore it, but he also didn't know how to respond. Instead of speaking, he placed one of his large dark hands on her shoulder. It made her stand up a little straighter.

"Come on, Pops. Let's see if I can break into one of these computers."

They worked their way back to one of the computer rooms and Dian took a seat. Syn was a patient man, but he didn't like feeling useless. He stood in uncomfortable silence listening to Dian type and swear softly under her voice. Dian sorted through page after page of information, uploading anything that looked valuable. As she was perusing what looked like a series of energy receipts, she found an encrypted file.

"Finally. God that was so tedious. Syn, I think I found an Academy-related file."

A moment later the encrypted file opened, and Dian was reading what she had accurately predicted was a report on the assignment to which they had previously been dispatched.

"That's wrong," she said, shaking her head in confusion.

Syn looked over Dian's shoulder. "What is?"

"The file here says ... nothing." She leaned out of the way so he could read the screen.

The assignment we hired the Academy for was a success, and the payment was processed. The assignment was accomplished appropriately. Incentive stands to work with the Academy in the future. The details of the assignment will be included in the lock file for ...

Dian turned to face her Leash. "There's nothing..."

Syn felt the change before he saw it on her face. Her face still looked confused when the heat began to fill behind his eyes.

"Dian."

"Why is there nothing, Syn? No orders. No plan. No trace of us being recorded. No instance of– of difference. No prep for us to arrive and attack. No plans for a trap. Why didn't they know we were coming, Pops?"

"Dian, we don't know anything yet," Syn said, trying to make his voice sound reassuring. He could feel the anger rippling off of Dian's body, and the questions that were flooding her mind filled him as well. She was right. Why hadn't they expected them? Why had killing an entire base been so simple?

"Why were we sent to kill these people? There was no kill order against us. I found the original assignment marked complete? If there wasn't a setup, why are we here?"

Syn stood in silence for several moments. "We–we don't know anything yet, Dian. There are too many questions that need to be answered. Maybe they just covered their tracks so well that we aren't able to find anything on them watching us."

"And if not? What if they weren't the ones following us, Pops? What if the information was bad? Only someone who knew where we were going could have possibly followed us, Syn, and if it wasn't these guys then it had to be someone from the Academy. It had to be someone who knew!"

The lights in the room began to flicker.

"Dian–"

"Did they sell us out? Send us here to clean up their mess? What!?"

"The Academy knows that even with more manpower this base couldn't have–"

"Why? Why isn't there any record of them following us? Why?!"

The heat in the room rose and Syn could feel the Psychic energy beginning to pulse and circulate.

"DIAN!" Syn raised his voice, and Dian seemed to snap back to him. "We don't know anything yet. Let's head back to the Academy. I'm sure we can get our answers there. There's a perfectly reasonable explanation. Just please try to calm down."

His voice had become warm and soothing. Dian seemed to visibly calm down, and the dense Psychic cloud in the room began to ebb.

"Yea, Pops. You're right. We need to go back. I need some answers."

The classroom rang with the sound of children singing "Happy Birthday" in every musical key at once.

Gregory was seated in a chair too small for his sizable frame. A cone shaped hat was perched crookedly on the side of his head, his broad framed glasses shielding his smiling eyes while the kids in class continued to sing until the song had concluded.

Alyssia could feel his Psychic presence in the air. It reminded her of a box of crunchy shortbread cookies that Catha had brought from one of her assignments. She and some of the older kids were busying themselves with cutting the cake and delivering it to the students and an especially large portion for Gregory.

The older students were trying to hang up the hand painted mural that all the classes had worked on, and attempting to do so with as much grace as possible which was made all the more difficult because they knew they were being watched. It really was quite impressive, all of the classes had worked really hard on it under Alyssia's watchful eye. She was a very proud teacher.

When everybody had been served, Alyssia was finally able to turn her attention back to the Academy head who was in the middle of reviewing several drawings and paintings that had been done by the smaller children. He listened attentively to each description and would ask questions to each child about their pictures, giving them a chance to elaborate and explain the work that they had done. Alyssia really admired him; he was the kind of teacher she hoped to be one day.

The festivities continued for the better part of an hour. Alyssia was getting ready to wind down and begin cleaning when there was a change in the room, a familiar pulse that made the air taste like spice. She turned to look at the doorway to the class and saw Rudra's dark hair, green eyes, and his normally charming smile pressed into a hard line.

"Director, I'm sorry to interrupt, but may I speak with you for a moment?"

Rudra asked a great deal more formally than almost any of his other interactions.

Gregory finished speaking to the student, and with a warm smile he excused himself from the room. He stood with his back to the room and their tones were hushed enough that Alyssia couldn't hear anything they were saying. And as badly as she wanted to know what was being discussed, she had left teenagers in charge of distributing ice cream.

"Sir, it may need to happen sooner rather than later," Rudra spoke in hushed tones.

Gregory's face was unreadable, always a thoughtful and considerate man. He always tried to make sure he had considered every angle.

"During the training exercise, she was almost killed, sir. I'm not sure what happened, but it seems to have affected Angel as well. If we can't get him his Wash soon, I'm afraid it may result in a partial mind death."

"Is that so?" Gregory asked in his thoughtful way "That's a pretty bold conclusion. You really think it's so serious that you needed to come all the way up here to tell me?"

Rudra wasn't sure if he looked as confused as he felt, but he did feel his face contract slightly. *What's the problem? We can't afford to have Melania out of commission, and if it wasn't for him putting that psychotic mercenary in charge of training exercises none of this would have happened.*

"Sir, I would just hate to see one of our strongest assets become a liability because she's worried about her counterpart. And I know firsthand how awful the prospect of mind death is."

Gregory examined Rudra closely. "That's a fair point. I will organize a squad to maintain Angel and bring him up for a Wash, but I will need to assemble a guard detail for it."

"I don't mind volunteering for it, sir," Rudra quickly spoke up.

"I believe you," Gregory gestured out into the hallway and they both took several steps away from the classroom door. "How are you feeling Rudra? You seem a little–" Gregory paused, considering his words carefully. "Flustered. Is there something wrong?"

Gregory pushed gently against Rudra's mind. It was a tangled mess; there was so much interference he couldn't even really find where Rudra began, and the strange foreign influence ended.

Rudra cycled defensiveness, anger, and confusion, in very rapid succession. "S-Sir?"

Gregory shook his head apologetically. "I just meant that you seem a little tired. Have you been to see Luke lately? Would you do me a favor and go see if he will give you a quick once over for me? I need to know that my best operatives are in top shape."

His voice shimmered in Rudra's ears. "Sir, I feel fine, I don't need–" But Rudra suddenly felt strangely tired, like he had been running for hours; his muscles and eyes fatigued, and concentration became difficult. "Maybe that's not such a bad idea, sir."

"Don't worry about the Wash, Rudra, I'll handle everything myself. Nothing for you to trouble yourself with."

Gregory is such a nice man, Rudra thought. *Always looking out for us. He always has such good ideas.*

"Thank you, sir," Rudra said, his voice muted and tired. As he began to head back toward the elevator, Gregory's warm expression evaporated.

He was being influenced, and only Melania is adept enough at hormone manipulation to have created effects that lasted that long. No doubt it's probably time for Angel to have his Wash renewed, but I really don't like that she's trying to manipulate other Level Four teams to influence me. I'll have to keep her and Rudra away from Angel's Wash.

He took off his glasses, pulled a small cloth out of his pocket, and polished the lenses. "Maybe Zander is right, maybe we are all weapons."

He consciously released his Psychic hold on Rudra. Gregory was not a Level Four Psychic, but he was so close to being one it almost didn't make a difference. He had always been gifted at soothing people. Before the Academy had gotten a hold of him, he was on his way to being a therapist. He still often wondered if that wasn't where his talents would still be of the most use.

"Mr. Gregory, I made you a bowl of ice cream. With lots of nuts!"

Gregory turned to see a snaggle-toothed boy with shoulder length braided hair and the most absurdly large bowl of ice-cream he had ever seen, heaped with nuts, sprinkles and chocolate sauce.

"That looks incredible, Micah."

Aspis marched past security clearance into the holding cells beside the training facility. The hallway split in two and Aspis turned right past several, mostly empty, cells. The cells had always unsettled Aspis. This prison, next to mind death, was the worst imaginable fate for a Psychic or a Leash to experience. A prison to hold the unholdable. She hitched her small pack a little higher on her shoulder and kept walking until she felt a slow warm sensation creep in between her eyes.

Xiphos, she reached out with her mind. She came to his cell, which was the same as the rest, a floor to ceiling polymer made to hold even the most powerful of Leashes. A bed, a toilet, and a small shower were the basic amenities, but Xiphos' room was allotted some additional amenities, primarily books.

Her partner was lying on his cot with a book on his chest, the spine facing toward Aspis.

"Poetry? Who are you trying to impress?"

He smiled sleepily at her.

"He does not wake at dawn to see, dread figures throng his room,

the shivering chaplain robed in white, the sheriff stern with gloom.

And the governor all in shiny black, the yellow face of doom."

"Sounds pretentious." Aspis cracked a wry smile.

"You're not wrong." yawned Xiphos. "Seemed appropriate for my current situation."

"I brought you snacks," Aspis said as she undid her pack.

The Academy was well-funded, she knew he was getting enough to eat nutritionally but high calorie protein pastes and metabolic depressants only went so far when you were used to regular food. Aspis opened the pack up and pulled out several brown paper bags. She placed them into the sliding slot that connected to the outside of the cell and pushed it in. He opened the slot and went through each bag slowly and with pleasure, savoring his small moments of something different in the face of so much the same.

"You're not gonna get in trouble for smuggling contraband down to a criminal are you?" Xiphos spoke in a sleepy blasé that made something inside of Aspis boil.

"You're not a criminal, you're a damn hero. You've saved my life so many times I don't even bother counting anymore. You and I are the people they send to protect others. And no one works more by the book than you do. It's stupid and unfair that they've locked you down here for doing exactly as you were ordered to do. You tried to keep the client safe, and if it wasn't for you I'd be dead. It's not..."

Her voice trailed off as the sensation of warmth flooded her eyes and she blinked away tears of frustration and met her best friend's eyes. He was looking at her gently, and she could feel his consciousness at the edge of hers. Like a loved one waving at you from a plane terminal. She sat down, her back against the cell wall and he did the same, the layer of the clear prison wall all that separated their bodies.

"Remember when we first met?" he asked quietly, leaning his head back against the clear poly structure.

"I couldn't stand you," Aspis responded with a dry smile that only the bricks could see. "You were so handsome and arrogant. And you were listening to that garbage music."

"Buxtehude would probably roll over in his grave if he heard you say that. But he was German, so he probably wouldn't have understood it," Xiphos gave a dry chuckle.

"What's German?" Aspis asked, not truly curious but wanting him to keep talking.

"How is it you can calculate bullet trajectory and create mathematical shields midair in seconds, but you can't remember the most basic lessons from your primary school history or civics?" He shook his head. "I swear you're completely deficient."

"What's German, Xiphos?" Xiphos heard the small break in her voice and could feel the hot lines on his own cheeks from where his partner was crying. He wanted to comfort her, but that's not who they were.

"Germany was a country before The Great War. They had good beer and great music. At least that's what my old man always said..."

CHAPTER 1.11
Use of each Psychic

"Classification of Psychics is important in understanding where a Psychic will be most useful and in the least danger. For instance, it would be irresponsible to send a Level One Psychic out to the front lines of a serious combat engagement if Level Three teams are available. By that same measure, it would be irresponsible to use a Level Three team to do an interrogation as the level of Psychic energy produced would more than likely kill whoever they were attempting to interrogate before any significant information could be acquired."

"Are you lazy, stupid, or both?!" Blaine raged at the Greenie who had just begun giving his updated report on the on-going events at the Academy. The Greenie stood, stone faced and professional. The entire battalion was used to Blaine's particular brand of belligerence at this point.

There had been no news in weeks, and the massive Psychic spike that had registered like a bomb on all of their instruments had seemed to be an isolated incident. Blaine had been camped at this outpost for nearly two months at this point and the most interesting things to happen were a massive Psychic spike and a lone military vehicle with a mounted 50 caliber rifle on the roof, being driven by a small, dark-skinned woman, who had flown past their encampment without so much as glancing at them.

"And that damnSpecialisthasn't so much as checked in for the better part of a week. Command was out of their minds to allow him anywhere near our operation or our resources."

"Sir."

"And we are no closer to getting Tobias Marshall back. Why would they even want to hold onto him?"

"Excuse me, Captain–"

"They haven't asked for any kind of ransom. Did they really just take him in?"

His stress level had been growing consistently, and TITAN Central Command and the Commandant had been asking for regular updates which, of late, had been that there was no update to give.

We should just bring in artillery, station it outside the Academy, and demand they return Marshall so that we can interrogate him and get back our damn assets, he thought. *Or else level the whole damn facility.*

"Sir–"

"WHAT?!"

"Sir, an unknown pair of individuals are approaching. They match the description of the two that left a couple of weeks ago."

Blaine bolted to the entrance of the operation room he was in and walked out into the bright midday sun. When his eyes had adjusted, he saw the two figures, several hundred meters away, moving toward them and heading toward the Academy.

He snatched a pair of binoculars from the hands of a posted guard and aimed them in their direction. One of the figures was substantially smaller than the other, a woman with flaming red hair and a heavy looking travel pack. The man beside her was larger, well built, had medium-length salt and pepper hair with a full beard and a much heavier pack.

I remember these two, they have walked by us several times. When I first arrived here these were the two that approached on their way back to the Academy.

"Anything interesting, Blaine?" Captain Montez asked. He was walking toward them, a protein bar half eaten in his hand.

"Fast approaching, two hostiles. I suggest we detain and interrogate them, and if they turn out to be members of the Academy, I suggest we hold them until the Academy agrees to release Marshall to us," Blaine spoke quickly.

While he had a reputation as a blowhard, he had in fact commanded numerous engagements that had been successful. He was a Captain dammit, and he would prove that he deserved his position. Montez was skeptical.

"Blaine, do we know how strong these two are," he questioned. "Have we received orders to detain members of the Academy? There are diplomatic ramifications; if we arrest them and they resist, we could be violating the treaty."

Montez was now all business. Blaine had been aggressive the last few weeks, but to Montez this was a long term scouting assignment, and one that suited him. He didn't want a relatively comfortable post endangered because the captain was being careless.

"If they demonstrate hostility, we have the right to detain them for a period."

Montez raised an eyebrow. "Have they demonstrated hostility?"

Blaine removed his sidearm, slid out the magazine and checked it, reinserted it and drew back the slide before replacing it in the holster.

"They're about to."

Dian was distracted and confused. Nothing made sense to her. She couldn't understand. She had shed so much blood, slept on the ground so often, been away from the people she cared about, and for what? To have the Academy turn their back on her and Syn? What had they done wrong? It couldn't be. They wouldn't–

"Dian, slow down," Syn spoke softly and calmly.

Dian had been in a rage the entirety of their journey home. She hadn't slept for more than a few moments, and she had spoken less. Syn thought that her anger would dissipate with their travel home and that he would be able to talk her into a more reasonable state, but the teenage Psychic was boiling. Her mistrust of the Academy was an ever present thought, and it was only exacerbated by the confusion of their last assignment. She was ready for war.

Because of their haste in packing the camp, Syn hadn't had time to break down his hunting rifle into his pack, the semi-automatic rifle was tucked into his shoulder while he quickened his significant stride to keep up with the small-framed girl who, despite her size, was setting an difficult pace for him to keep up with. If it wasn't so worrisome, it would have been amusing.

"Dian!" Syn didn't usually have to speak out loud to get her attention, but she was incensed and not listening to his presence in her mind. At the sound of his voice she whirled around.

"What, Pops?"

She was standing feet and shoulders squared. Syn was never afraid of his Psychic, but there were moments when he had a hard time seeing her as a teenage girl. He chose his next words carefully.

"Take a moment. Try to clear your–"

"I'M DONE TAKING A MOMENT!" She screamed at him. "Someone did this to us, Syn. Someone set us up, and I'm not waiting any damn more!"

As she turned back around to continue walking down the road, her stride was interrupted once again.

"Halt. Drop your weapons!"

The short, sharp bark surprised both of them. Syn could have kicked himself. He'd been so worried about Dian that he hadn't even noticed they were passing the mercenary camp that was stationed just a few kilometers from the Academy. Syn pressed his rifle tighter into his shoulder; this was going to be bad.

"I said drop your weapons!"

The man approaching them was in a pressed uniform that Syn recognized from the TITAN organization. His eyes were bloodshot, and his uniform looked slightly slack on his frame, as if he'd lost weight recently. He was being followed by half a dozen well-armed men who were having to trot to keep up with their commander. An additional commander was pulling up next to the man, shouting at him.

"Blaine, wait. We don't have the right to detain–"

"Quiet, Montez!" He cut the other man off. "Last warning. Put your weapons down, or we will detain you by force!"

The angry senior mercenary that Syn now knew to be named Blaine yelled. "I said STOP!"

"You first."

That was all Dian said before the fighting started. Blaine was stunned just long enough to delay the drawing of his sidearm. As soon as his hand touched the grip, the air around him became hot, and he felt every hair on his body stand on end. A pulse of electricity that felt like a kick to the chest sent him flailing backwards several meters. The sound of gunfire and men screaming was barely audible over the ringing in his ears and the burning over every inch of his body.

Syn's rifle was up in the blink of an eye. Firing hyper precise shots into the mercenaries. His bullets slammed into hips, knees and shoulders, doing everything he could not to kill these men whose only real crime was following orders, while knowing that even precise shooting wouldn't prevent all of them from dying.

Some were significantly better trained than others. While many of the TITAN operatives fumbled with their weapons at the sudden show of violence, many more were already returning fire. Bullets collapsed against Syn as he took aim.

Three of the mercenaries were circling to his left and hitting their mark with a great deal of accuracy. Syn pivoted and fired four rounds.

One found the foot of the first, causing him to stumble. The man beside him tripped over his fallen comrade and caught two bullets in the chest for his trouble. The third reached for his belt to what Syn could only assume was a grenade an instant before the fourth bullet ripped through his arm and out the back of his elbow.

The Hunter Leash turned back and caught Dian in his peripheral, an armored car bearing down on her. He began his attempt to dash in front of her, but his young Psychic's rage wouldn't be stopped by something as frivolous as a few hundred pounds of steel. She used her Psychic energy and pulled hard, ripping the front left wheel off the axle and causing the vehicle to flip onto its side.

The men inside the truck were trying desperately to climb out when Syn put a round through each man's head. The Leash spit out of the corner of his mouth in frustration. His attempt at mercy was rapidly failing. He and Dian both ran behind the flipped truck and used it as cover while they continued to fire shots and sling bolts of Psychic lightning at the hapless mercenaries.

Montez, who was still standing, was trying desperately to get his men to stand down. Chaos was all that ensued. Mercenaries were pouring out of their makeshift compound, armed and ready to fight. Montez was screaming at his men to little avail.

Dian was collapsing the awnings and tents, while bolts of white orange electricity scorched man and machine alike. Syn fired and reloaded as fast as he could. He knew that the Lightning Psychic would not be abated by words. Despite his impossibly precise aim and his years of experience, they were outmanned, several dozen to one, and his training had been shoot-to-kill, not shoot-to-wound.

The battle was brief but ferocious. In the span of just a few minutes the makeshift compound had been leveled. Men were lying all around them in heaps, those that were still alive were moaning and whimpering.

Dian spun on a heel, picked up her pack, and took off at a jog to the Academy. Syn surveilled what had been done and saw the young dark skinned Captain laying on the ground, he had drawn his sidearm in order to protect his men, it had earned him a bullet through the hand and shoulder.

"I'm sorry."

It was all the Leash could manage to say before he took off after his Psychic. This would have consequences, and he wasn't sure whether he or Dian were prepared to face them.

Tobias thought the entire process seemed a little bizarre. He had been greeted by Gregory and Zander in the hallway outside of the dorm room he called home.

"Mr. Marshall, we were wondering if you would assist us. We have a matter that needs attending to, and we are a bit short handed."

Tobias knew when an order was being posed like a question. Tobias turned back into his room to grab his gear.

"And Marshall," Zander added. "Bring your weapons."

The Academy had been - for the most part - a safe place. The violence he had been involved in had been part of training.

"What exactly am I assisting with?" Tobias asked, confused, as they exited the dormitory hallway and began the wide circle around the Academy's perimeter.

"We are performing a Wash today which requires a certain level of security. And because of the nature of this particular Wash, we need more than the usual," Zander answered curtly.

"Why me, in particular?" Tobias queried.

While it wasn't normal for him to ask so many questions when given an instruction, it didn't seem to be adding up. If a Leash was somehow dangerous while going through a Wash, why him? If it was a Level One or Level Two Leash, they could be easily controlled by a Level Three, and if it was a Level Three or stronger, Tobias would be of absolutely no use.

"You are remarkably difficult to influence, Mr. Marshall, and sometimes we need a stubborn spirit," Gregory answered.

Tobias couldn't tell which was more annoying. The way Zander never said anything, or the way Gregory always seemed to say too much. As they rounded the last corner to the elevators, Tobias recognized a girl sitting on the railing looking at her shoes. In addition to her Academy uniform, she also had a gun strapped to her hip, an old and frankly outdated 1911 style 45 that was obviously too big for her slender hands.

"Hey Al, waiting on something?" Tobias' voice made the young Psychic jump.

"Marsh–Tobias. What are you doing here?"

"Mr. Marshall is assisting us with today's Wash," Gregory responded.

Alyssia's eyes snapped to Gregory. "For a Level Four Wash? Mr. Gregory, are you certain?"

Zander let a flash of annoyance cross his face. "What happened to the days when soldiers just followed orders and did what they were told without a bunch of questions being asked?"

Gregory inclined his head toward his Leash with an amused smirk. "We started calling them students and giving them gold stars when they cleaned up after themselves, Zander."

Tobias snapped his attention to Gregory. "A Level Four Leash? There's only a few of those, and I wasn't aware any of them needed to be babysat."

Alyssia approached the ex-mercenary and spoke just above a whisper. "Angel. Angel needs to go through the Wash. He's dangerous."

Tobias raised an eyebrow but didn't speak. The missing Leash, Melania's partner who had been locked up. Tobias had only gotten the vaguest details.

As they entered the elevator, Tobias resisted the urge to demand more information. He did, however, pull his pistols one after another and checked them both, counting his ammunition and making sure they were chambered.

Aspis was sitting in a chair outside of Xiphos' cell. She had lined up three rubber balls on the ground by the cell.

"We usually only use two. Today will be a challenge, right?"

Xiphos didn't respond. His eyes were closed in concentration. He could however feel a mild shifting pressure on his eyelids and recognized it to be Aspis looking and the sensation registering on his body. He felt a shift in her mental focus and knew that Aspis was lifting the small rubber balls into the air. He bent his knees and extended the index finger on each hand. Aspis made a come hither motion with her fingers and all three of the balls began to spin and circle.

While gestures weren't needed for Psychic abilities to work, almost all Psychics used them as a way to center their thoughts and give them external stimuli to focus on while they were working. With the way

Aspis specifically used Psychic energy, she needed all the concentration she could muster.

"Volleys in odd numbers," Aspis said as she closed her own eyes.

Shh, Aspis. Don't tell me, show me, Xiphos whispered in her mind.

So she did. She planned out the next 300 moves based on 12 different geometric patterns in two dimensions. Then she pushed.

The balls flew forward and bounced off the cell wall. At every point of impact Xiphos touched the wall at the spot where the ball would have struck on the other side. The first several moves were relatively slow, but then they picked up to more than 12 or so a second. The sound of the balls bouncing and the light impact of Xiphos driving his fingers into the spot where the ball hit made the space around them sound like it was humming.

Fists.

Aspis reset her calculations in her head and turned all of her shapes from creating striking points in two dimensions to creating patterns in the air and rotated the shapes in her mind so that the impact pattern seemed much more random.

But it didn't seem that way to Xiphos. Her patterns flowed into his mind, and he saw what had once been a square, a triangle, and a rhombus become a rotating dodecahedron, spinning in the air in the space of an instant before launching out at lightning fast speed.

He had heard her instruction and had closed his fingers into loose fists. He took a stance, spreading his feet more than shoulder-width apart and bending his knees. Every time a ball hit the wall, his fist raced to meet it, slamming into the space where the ball would have come if it had the capacity to breach his impenetrable cell. The vibration grew in sound. like the steady drone of a saw being revved. They kept up their pace for three straight minutes before Xiphos missed a punch. Aspis had switched the pattern to be a Rhombicosidodecahedron with one of the three balls making the square shapes, one making the triangles, and one making the pentagons. All three balls fell to the ground and both Psychic and Leash stood still for several moments trying to catch their breath.

"Pentagons got you, huh?" Aspis asked as she wiped the perspiration from her forehead.

"I always think they're gonna have six sides. Correcting for an extra strike slows me way down," Xiphos said as he sat down and rocked back onto the cool stone floor.

Xiphos, he heard her call softly in his mind.

He opened one eye and looked at his partner. She smiled rather weakly at him.

"Just checking," she said aloud. Suddenly Aspis turned her head to the door, and Xiphos tried hard to steady his breathing so he could hear better.

Someone had walked into holding. Several someones, in fact. The young bespectacled guard was in the front of the group, his 6:1k rifle tucked into his shoulder. Behind him were Gregory and Zander. Gregory with his long comfortable strides, always made him appear like a man perpetually strolling through a park somewhere. Zander on the other hand was taking his practiced crisp steps, ever the soldier.

Behind them was Alyssia, the Energy Sync. Her long platinum blonde hair spilled over her narrow shoulders.

Aspis knew the girl's reputation, but it didn't bother her. The history of the Academy was drenched in blood. The first Mergers had been absolute slaughter before they had gotten the process more or less figured out. And 40 years was not enough time to get a process as advanced as Psychic Mergers perfect. Alyssia, in Aspis's mind, was just another significant anomaly that had to be worked out and understood.

Until recently nobody had thought that a Psychic could transcend their rank through sheer force of will and effort, but that was precisely what Aspis had done, and she had become the first Psychic to ever earn the rank of Level Four.

The most off putting thing about seeing her was the sidearm that she had strapped to her hip. Alyssia, to Aspis' knowledge, had never traveled armed. There had never been a reason for her to. But perhaps the most confusing thing was the man who was walking behind her.

His shoulders were set forward like a big cat's, and his eyes were sweeping angles around the room. He had a shaggy mane of dirty blonde hair and an unkempt beard that made him look even more like a lion.

Aspis instinctually reached out with her mind, but the moment she touched his mind his eyes met hers. Her mind flooded with a list.

Brachial, radial, femoral, dorsalis...

A smirk crossed her lips. *Listing arteries to block mental invasion. Clever.*

That must be the mercenary. He doesn't look like much, Xiphos thought to his partner.

Are you kidding? I can smell the blood on him from here.

Careful, Aspis. You sound curious.

How   dare   you.

Tobias stopped for a moment to look at the Psychic who had just tried to read his mind.

He could tell she was athletic and steady on her feet. Her mahogany skin and bright eyes made her look like a specter in the dimly lit hallway. She was standing outside one of the cells, three small rubber balls laid on the ground near her feet.

"Xiphos and Aspis," Alyssia explained quietly to Tobias. "The Sword Leash and the Shield Psychic. Our escort team. They specialize in protecting people."

"I was under the impression that there wasn't a Level Four team available for this. That's why they needed us?" Tobias questioned, only the slightest bit curious.

"Aspis and Angel hate each other. They would probably try to kill each other if they came in contact. He..." She hesitated, not sure if she should share so much information, while Tobias waited patiently for her to finish her sentence. "Well let's just say there have only been three or four Leashes ever held in our cells for any significant period of time, and except for his Wash, Angel will never get out of his again."

They arrived at the end of the hallway. Angel was leaning his forehead on the wall of his cell, wearing a set of ill-fitting pants and an oversized shirt that hung frighteningly loose off of his skeletal frame. The young Leash who was posted as a guard walked forward as if to assist in opening the cell.

"That won't be necessary, young man. You don't have access codes to this particular cell function. Just step back and stand ready," Gregory said with a reassuring smile.

The Leash nodded and hopped backward. "Y-yes sir," he squeaked.

Tobias was curious as to why they would put such a jumpy kid on guard duty, but these cells seemed secure enough that it probably didn't matter who was watching the door.

"Gregory, so nice to see you. Down for your weekly visit? I'm afraid I'm not prepared for you. But you also didn't bring me any flowers this time," Angel's raspy voice curled in the air, Tobias raised an eyebrow and Zander walked to the wall.

"I apologize it's been so long since I've been down, Angel. I honestly forgot you were down here," Gregory said. His voice was its usual warm tone, but his face was like stone.

Alyssa looked at Gregory with surprise, she had never heard him be cruel before or let someone's jeering make him angry. But even with his stone face, she could feel the rage spilling off of Gregory like dark wine from an overfull cup.

Zander pressed his palm against the access pad on the wall. It scanned his handprint, then opened up to a panel with a keypad. He hit several buttons then stepped back and turned toward Tobias.

"When he passes out, the wall will move. You will walk in and cuff his hands and ankles with these." Zander handed Tobias two pairs of semi-circle electric cuffs. "When the door opens, be quick. Bind both hands and feet."

Tobias turned the cuffs in his hands, they were heavy for their size. He had already seen firsthand how strong a Level Four Psychic was, and if the Leash was supposed to be the physical equivalent, well ...

"This shock collar is supposed to keep him contained? How?"

Gregory approached the keypad after Zander stepped away and entered several commands after scanning his palm. "Step one is depressurization of the room. Because Leashes have higher oxygen needs than your average human, this is actually a very effective way to render them helpless. When Angel passes out, you will apply the electric cuffs to him. The charge on them, once locked in place, is a constant steady shock to the nervous system. Not enough to cause significant harm, but it will force his body to constantly heal in order to maintain a state of consciousness. It would be enough to kill most non-Leashes."

Tobias scoffed his derision. "Thanks for the warning."

"Rude to talk about people like they aren't present, Gregory," Angel spoke, his cadence slow and deliberate as the rest of his body began to slump into the wall. "Why, if I wasn't such an empathetic per–person ... I might be inclined to be ... offended ..."

"Go to sleep, monster," Gregory spat in a rare moment of lost composure.

Angel smiled, his tattooed lips spreading into a maniacal grin before he passed out and slumped to the ground. Gregory opened the wall from the panel and Tobias hurried in, quickly and skillfully placing the bonds on his wrists and ankles.

It took less than a minute before the Shred Leash stirred. First a few twitches, then a deep, slow inhale. He rolled his feet underneath himself and stood slowly. Before his legs reached full extension, he lunged.

Zander moved in a blur, his large hand grabbing Angel by the throat before slamming him into the floor of the cell. The sounds of bones snapping and a high-pitched electrical hum from the charged shackles around his wrists and ankles filled the room. Alyssia had barely had time to blink, and Tobias had only just now gotten his weapon cleared from its holster. The guard had his rifle raised and aimed, and even Aspis had appeared at the back of the hallway, although she didn't have a weapon on her since she had had to check it at the door. But she was standing, knees bent, eyes laser focused on the open cell.

"He certainly is eager," Tobias said breathlessly, his weapon leveled at Angel's head.

Zander had stood and pulled a handkerchief from his back pocket to wipe his hand off.

"The first time we took Angel for a Wash he almost killed the Level Three pair we sent to retrieve him. We have since become more cautious and more familiar with his tactics. He has attacked every single time his cell has been opened. We were just more prepared than usual.

You can put your firearm away, Mr. Marshall. While in his diminished state a bullet could hurt him, I very much doubt it would do enough to stop him. Aspis please stand down. We don't need an incident. And Officer ... Cassius," Zander said, addressing the guard whose rifle trembled ever so slightly in the direction of the cell. "A hand tremor like that might end up spraying bullets everywhere. Please lower your firearm."

Aspis relaxed her stance but not her gaze as she returned to the intersection in the hallway between Angel's cell and Xiphos, posting herself there like a Nubian sentinel. The guard, Cassius, lowered the barrel of his rifle but kept it prepped in his hands.

Tobias slowly holstered his weapon. "A little warning would have been nice."

"What part of Level Four Leash locked in an underground detainment for violent criminals didn't sound like a warning?" Zander quipped while he dragged a very disoriented Angel to his feet.

The shackles around his hands and feet were glowing, and the smell of burning flesh was faint. Tobias couldn't help but admire the solution, generating a state of constant steady pain so that his ability to react to outside stimuli was nearly impossible. All of his reflexes would be slowed, all of his movements more labored. The Academy could spend every minute of every day for the next hundred years trying to convince people that they were a pinnacle of peace and that their military might was a deterrent for the evils of the world, but Tobias could see the brutal efficiency in almost all of their decisions. And while he would probably always have to resist the urge to find out exactly how bulletproof Zander was, or how truly gifted a reader of humans' murderous intent Gregory was, he had grown to admire both men for their efficiency. No move was wasted.

They turned to exit the holding facility. Zander had a grip on Angel's arm while Gregory walked several steps behind. The facility guard was to the left, gun at the ready. Alyssia walked near Gregory, and Tobias was in the front. Tobias shot one last glance at Aspis as they were walking out. She looked like a stone, hard and immovable, but she couldn't mask the slight tremor in her lip.

Inside the infirmary, Luke was busy organizing various containers of medical supplies. Catha was folding dressing gowns and sheets.

Rudra was sleeping peacefully, and Agni was nose deep in a scientific journal about hormone manipulation. Other than them, the only other occupants were two young female Psychics several beds over. One was reading quietly in a chair while the other was asleep and softly snoring.

"Catha, can you help me? I can't reach the–"

She took the container of pressurized liquid bandages from his hand and placed it on the top shelf above his head.

"Thank you," the skinny Psychic blushed at his tall silver-haired Leash.

"Pleasure. You won't pull?" she responded with a smile.

"If I had pulled it off myself I wouldn't have needed you to come get it for me," Luke flirted back.

If Agni hadn't at that moment been obsessively pouring over page after page in her science journal, she would have had to grin at them. As unusual as their pairing was, Agni had always thought of their relationship as beautiful.

The door to the clinic opened and one of the Leash trainees walked in looking rapidly around himself. "Hey, Doc, you got a minute? I'm kinda freaking out."

"What seems to be the problem, Simon?" Luke asked warmly.

Agni couldn't prove it, but it wouldn't have surprised her at all if Luke knew every single student in the Academy by their first name.

The young trainee shook his head. "I'm not sure. I just feel off, like my skin is crawling. I don't know what–"

Agni tuned him out. It felt rude to listen in on someone divulging medical issues, so she tried to give what privacy she could provide. She dove back into her journal. Agni was no scientist and certainly not a doctor, but she understood a great many things theoretically. She knew her brother wasn't into chemical stimulants of any kind, and besides the quantity of any of them it would take to give Rudra a buzz would probably be substantial enough to kill an elephant.

What's going on with you, big brother?

Agni had become aware of the volume in the clinic getting louder. She glanced up and saw that there were almost a dozen Psychics and Leashes walking in and jabbering frantically about needing medical treatment. Luke and Catha were patiently and gently finding them all seats, beds, or a corner to wait in until they could get to each one.

Rudra stirred in his bed, and Agni snapped back to attention.

"Doctor! Ru woke up."

Luke walked over to check his pulse and his vitals. Agni leaned forward while closing her journal.

"Ru, you ok?" she asked tentatively.

He grunted softly, but Agni was already reaching out to his mind. The fog that had been on him seemed to have lifted. When he had come into the infirmary he had been nearly incoherent, rambling and muttering all the while looking dazed and out of sorts. Luke had called Agni to come and sit with him while he drew blood and put Rudra to sleep.

"His cortisol and testosterone levels are off. Adrenaline as well. Like he just got out of a fight. His body is responding as if he just walked off the battlefield. What happened?"

Agni was trying hard to hide her concern and suspicion. "Not sure. Between your examination and Gregory saying he was acting peculiar, it almost seems like some kind of outside manipulation, but I'm not sure what could have created these specific effects on a human body, especially one as powerful as Ru's."

Luke looked grim. "I've seen these effects before, but not frequently from one of ours," he said as he checked all of his vitals again. "Everything seems normal now."

"What do you think it is?" Agni asked.

"I don't know. Give me a minute," Luke responded while he continued his exam.

"What's going on?" Rudra croaked, his voice scratchy and full of chemicals.

"You collapsed, Ru. As soon as you got into the clinic you–"

"You mind letting me do my damn job?!" The outburst from Luke has been so sudden everyone froze and looked at him.

Agni felt a prickle at the front of her mind. *Where does this little punk get off talking to me like that? I could burn this whole wing of the Academy down with my brain.*

She turned to face the young doctor, his eyebrows were knit and his teeth clenched in half a snarl.

Agni stepped forward before Catha intercepted. "Influence, aware."

"What the hell are you talking about?" Agni was reaching into her pool of Psychic power to turn these fools into a pile of ash when she felt it again. The pressure at the front of her mind, the vibration in her limbs wasn't coming from her.

"Luke." The doctor was shaking his head, willing the confusion out of his system.

"Yes, I can feel it now, too. It was faint, but now it's substantially louder. There is some kind of outside force pushing against–"

BANG

Agni and Luke jerked their heads toward the sound, and Catha blitzed to the other side of the room. She was holding down a young girl, a Psychic whose face was splattered with blood.

"I couldn't take it, I couldn't stand it anymore. The sound of her breathing was driving me crazy! I had to do something!" The young Psychic screamed and clawed at the ground with her left hand while Catha maintained pressure on her right arm and torso.

Agni's ears were still ringing, and she saw the pistol laying on the ground near the Psychic.

"Who did she–" Then Agni saw the bloodstained curtain around one of the other patients' rooms.

"She shot her?" The revulsion at the thought surged through Agni's stomach. But just moments before she had been ready to set Luke on fire.

"AWARE!" Catha shouted while still managing to keep the young Psychic pinned.

Luke shook his head. "Psychic influence this widespread, it has to be Melania. But if we are feeling the effects intensely at this distance, the rest of the Academy must be–"

The door to the infirmary flew open and a wild eyed boy tumbled into the room. "They're killing each other...they are ripping each other apart!" He had blood dripping from several lacerations and his arm hung at an extreme angle, but the fear and adrenaline seemed to be halting his pain response.

"Agni." Luke's voice seemed to come from far away.

The screams from the now opened doors reached their ears.

"AGNI!"

She snapped her attention to the doctor, she wanted to kill him much less than before. He was looking around the room, one eye closed tight as if he had a migraine and the light was making it worse. But now that he knew what was going on he was quickly trying to establish order in the room.

"Agni, restrain that Psychic and then contact support. We're gonna need all the help we can get. Catha, get the tranquilizers out of supply as much as you can carry. I've got a feeling we're about to be overwhelmed."

"What's happening?" Rudra asked, slowly trying to pull himself up.

"It looks like the Nightmare Psychic has just declared war," Luke said with grave finality.

CHAPTER 1.12
The Protocol

"The most important job of a Leash is also the least pleasant. If at any time a Psychic becomes a danger to the peace that the Academy has long established and it is decided that the Psychic cannot be reprimanded or brought back into the proper behavior by any other means, that Psychic's Leash takes responsibility for eliminating their Psychic. The Academy will then take full responsibility for housing and caring for the Leash. Every Leash must be prepared to make this incredible sacrifice, for the remainder of their days. These Leashes will be held in a place of honor for always."

The TITAN camp was in shambles, Blaine was sitting on the edge of his cot, his breathing shallow. His right ear was ringing, his right eye was a field of white, and his whole body throbbed with pain.

Montez was standing near his cot, arm in a sling pressed tight to his body. Nearly every bed in the medical tent was full. It had been a brutal beating. When the fight had started, an emergency broadcast had been sent to headquarters and the response had been immediate. TITAN was on its way.

The pain that wracked Blaine's body was a small consequence compared to the shame that pulsed behind his one good eye. "Montez..."

The younger captain turned to face Blaine, his expression hard and angry. Blaine had made a devastating mistake. It had cost lives, it was going to cost several good men and women their careers. He had advised against it and had been ignored. But the chain of command was to be respected, Montez wasn't about to throw away years of service by losing his cool on an incompetent commander.

"Montez, when reinforcements arrive, inform them of the ambush by the Academy, make sure they understand that when we attempted to..." he shifted painfully on his cot "...attempted to recover our asset that they refused and assaulted our outpost."

Montez stared for a long moment.

"Ambush, Blaine?"

"What else would you call what happened? We were assaulted by the Academy, which means they violated the standing treaties and we have the right to defend ourselves from hostile, rogue elements."

Montez stood in stunned silence for several moments. Did this idiot really believe the nonsense that spewed out of his mouth?

"Montez, confirm, or so help me god, I'll have you shipped to a recycling facility on the damn colony."

"Sir, you want me to lie to the Commandants?"

If Blaine could have yelled he would have. But he was too hurt, too tired. Even so when he spoke his threat was clear.

"You've been given a direct order from a commanding officer. Do you plan on defying it, Captain?"

Montez stood for a moment, then his heels came together and his face hardened. "Blaine, go to hell."

Blaine sat up on his cot and yelled for the guard outside the tent. "Arrest the Captain."

The elevator door opened, and Angel shuffled out, guarded at five points.

They made their way across the third level of the Academy. Tobias had to keep reminding himself to relax, the tension in his shoulders and hands visible. The Shred Leash had been muttering and giggling to himself for the majority of the trip, and it was making Tobias itch.

The door to the council chamber was guarded by a Level Three team. A tall skinny brown haired Leash with a serious face and a square jaw on the left of the door, and his small, dark skinned and somewhat easily distracted Psychic on the right.

"Nate, Caroline. Checking in for a Level Four Wash, will you two please assist?" Gregory asked in his deep, warm way. The Psychic and Leash looked hard at the Shred Leash who was more tattoo than skin.

"Sir, would you like us to request additional security?" the tall thin Leash asked.

"With you here? Who more could we ask for?" Gregory smiled warmly.

The door to the council chamber opened. Gregory went in first, Zander went in last. Angel's shifting shuffle step still bothered Tobias, but he wasn't making a move. The Level Three team took up their posts on either side of the door on the inside and the bespectacled Leash that was Angel's guard went to stand behind Tobias, his weapon tucked into his shoulder. The see-through glass coffins that the council called their home lined the outer circle of the room. The machines that monitored their vitals and their brain activity beeped and hummed in mechanical fashion.

"It's time for the Wash to begin, please wake the council," Gregory instructed.

The Psychic who was watching the door walked over to a pedestal near the far wall of the room and ran her fingers expertly over the controls, a hydraulic hiss was heard as all of the chambers began to open. It began slowly, then became louder and more urgent. The moans of the council began, their whimpers an unsettling chorus of despair and confusion. The hair on the back of Tobias' neck stood up, the pistol in his hand trembled slightly and when he felt slender fingers wrap around his bicep, he almost opened fire. His eyes darted down to see Alyssia's wide, focused eyes.

"Don't be scared, Tobias. The council members have all experienced mind death, their Psychic energy is unrestrained. It's going to feel heavy, but it shouldn't have any effect on you," she explained, glancing up at him sheepishly. "I could tell you were afraid."

Tobias didn't respond,but he didn't deny it. He was afraid. Less than 10 feet away was a monster in shackles that he still didn't understand, with a strength he couldn't comprehend. The two super humans who had subdued him were within a meter. The room was filled with wails and moans of people who were experiencing birth and death almost simultaneously, and now at his arm was a girl who had drunk several people dry and at their first meeting had almost killed him.

Suddenly amidst the wails of the council and the electronic buzzing of the machines a pulse issued outward. Zander was in the corner of the room, his face contorted in an active effort to focus, the Level Three Leash that was still standing by the door wavered, his knees wobbled and his eyes glazed with a dreamy look. Alyssia made a sucking sound through her teeth before exhaling sharply and slowly through pursed lips.

Tobias felt a heaviness in the air, it wasn't oppressive but he was feeling more than he thought. It reminded him of the feeling of cold water rushing down your throat and into an empty stomach, like some numb part was coming awake inside of him. The moments stretched on for a long while, Tobias could hear popping and clicking as Angel stretched and coiled his muscles and extended his joints, the glowing bracelets around his hands and ankles began to grow brighter but he didn't do anything that appeared aggressive. As far as Tobias knew, this was a completely normal way for things to go.

Suddenly an impossible pain slammed into his back. His breath caught in his throat and he knew a lung had been punctured. If he could have caught his breath he would have yelled for help, but then the pain changed as the weapon was withdrawn and stabbed into his other lung.

I'm dead, and I can't even see what killed me, he thought.

"Nice to formally meet you Mr. Marshall. My name is Donovan Al-lourai."

Agni felt the panic creeping up her spine. A spidery tickle of skin crawling. She could see the younger Psychics in the infirmary start to tick and slap at their skin as they looked around in a panic for the source of their discomfort. Rudra sat painfully up in bed, but his slow deliberate movement was offset by the anger that now burned in his eyes.

"I don't know what the hell Melania is doing, but she has officially pissed off the wrong Leash."

Luke and Catha had set about trying to calm the other Psychics and Leashes in the infirmary. Luke was handing out sedatives.

"Take it and try to find a quiet place to sit, it will lessen the effects. There is nothing wrong, you just have to try and stay calm. Agni, you have to go find Melania and figure out why she's doing this. Rudra, are you able to fight? If you are, you need to get up and go. Agni is going to need your help."

Agni and Rudra rushed out of the infirmary. It took a moment or two for Rudra to find his legs, but when he did he took off at a long strided jog.

"Agni, I'm going to go search the training facility, if I'm not back in two minutes come find me."

Agni wanted to protest. If Melania had to be restrained, she wasn't sure she'd be able to do it on her own. But Rudra was right, they had to find her fast, and the fastest way to do that was split up.

"Ok, but search quickly and hurry back."

He nodded before leaping twenty feet through the air to land lightly on the elevator platform to go down into the training room.

And Ru, we may need help. That may mean breaking rules, she thought of her brother.

Rudra knew she meant the Sword Leash. They broke in different directions, Agni continued to run around the circular walkway that went around the entirety of the Academy. She could almost feel his smile as a response.

She spent the next several minutes in a sprint, trying her best to avoid the mobs of panicking students, some of whom were clawing at their skin, others who were angrily accusing each other of things that they couldn't possibly have done.

"Why would you steal mission assignments from me? I'm up for discipline because you keep removing dossiers from my room!"

"You can't keep taking food off of my plate!"

"She left me for you!"

More than once, Agni had to fling a Psychic or a Leash overhead and into the Academy fountain in order to separate them for a moment. The panic became more and more prevalent, and she was having to actively fight her own paranoid urges. She couldn't imagine how powerful the effect would have been on her had she been unaware of what was actually going on.

"God, at this rate I'm never going to find–"

Agni's feet suddenly flew out from under her as she was slammed onto the marble floor. All of her senses fired at once and she threw herself backwards before a second Psychic assault could land.

She rose quickly to her feet, the wind gone from her lungs. Through her blurry vision she saw her, Academy uniform perfectly tailored, jacket on and stripes pressed, shirt tucked into her pants, pants tucked into her boots. Her hair was braided and swept into a tight bun. Melania the Nightmare Psychic was here, and she was dressed for battle. None of it had been a mistake or a temper tantrum gone wrong. This had been calculated. It was a war.

Agni wasted no time, she lashed out with her mind, sending a wave of raw Psychic energy at Melania. Melania flicked her wrist and the Psychic wave dissipated in the air. Agni felt as if her skin was burning, her breath coming back to her, but it was ragged. Her brain felt like it was swimming in molten lead, the heat behind her eyes blurring her vision.

Melania was striking on all mental fronts simultaneously and quickly closing the gap between them. Agni made a fist, but her fingers felt like they curled in slow motion. Melania was in her mind, the Nightmare Psychic was slowing her senses making her paranoid, pushing at the chemicals in the human body that make it weak, euphoric, frightened, and paranoid. Her senses began to overwhelm her. Agni tried to push again, but Melania pushed back, forcing Agni to the ground.

Stupid, Stupid! Agni screamed inside her own mind. *You let a more experienced soldier get the drop on you. Focus.*

Agni settled her breathing and began to reach out with her mind. The oxygen in the air compressed. "If you think I'm going to give you time to make one of your little fireballs, Agni of the Pyre, you're sorely mistaken."

Agni split her mental focus, still trying to compress oxygen while at the same time readying a Psychic defense, it was the wrong choice. Melania kicked out and sent Agni sprawling. It had been a calculated move, Melania knew that Agni wasn't used to actually being hit. Most of her combat training had been to stave off a Psychic attack, not a good old fashioned boot to the skull.

Agni sprawled but maintained her focus. As she rose to one knee she exhaled sharply. A rope of flame shot from her lips and scorched the air around her. Melania sidestepped but not fast enough. She had managed to evade the fire but in the process had lost her balance.

Agni was on her feet, her anger giving her focus. She created wind streams in the air that burned and raced toward Melania. The Nightmare Psychic evaded and then resumed her mental attack on Agni, pressing into her capacity, trying to blind her or force her hormones into overdrive.

But Agni was relentless and passionate. The more aggressive Melania's mental assault was, the broader and hotter the waves of fire became. Melania was being pushed back, and was rapidly running out of stamina, the heat was exhausting and oppressive. Melania could feel the moisture being sucked from her skin and her eyes. Nearly all of her focus had been on just trying not to get scorched, then a blast of fire finally hit its mark.

Agni's shot landed dead center in Melania's chest and sent her flailing backwards. She hit the ground and skittered several feet across the polished marble. She tried to stand quickly but a wall of Psychic energy pressed down on her.

"Surrender or die!" Agni spit out the instruction through bleeding teeth, her hands circled by intense flames, her hair singed in places and her lips blistered from the multiple blasts of fire that had issued from them.

Melania knew she was beaten, her weakness had always been in the face of brute force. And despite her impossible level of mental focus, and combat experience, she simply did not have the raw power to compete with the Fire Psychic and her unbridled rage. She had failed, and now she'd have to accept the consequences.

"MEL!"

Melania and Agni's heads both snapped toward the sound of the voice. There in a wrinkled uniform covered in dirt and scorched in several places was a petite, red-head, and a large grizzled man carrying a rifle that looked like it needed to be mounted on a tank.

"Dian," Melania smiled at the girl.

"Dian." Agni grit her teeth.

"Dian, WAIT!" Syn almost never yelled, but he had to stop her. She was out of control and if they got back to the Academy, and she was still this riled, she could very well hurt people that were their allies. He reached his hand out for her shoulder but snapped it back when a stream of electricity jumped off the Psychic's body and burned his fingertips.

The front gate was directly in front of them, he was hoping that the simple act of having to check in at the front gate would slow her down enough for him to get a word in edgewise, but that was not to be the case. They arrived at the Academy entrance to see the Psychic and Leash who were on duty arguing loudly with each other.

"Why are you doing this? Stay out of my head!" the Leash shouted at his Psychic.

"What are you talking about? I'm not in your head, besides even if I tried to read your mind I couldn't, we're a Level Three team, remember? I'd rip your head open if I tried!"

"Oh so you're a badass now, are you?"

"What are you doing?" The Psychic and Leash both raised their weapons at the same time, the anger outweighing their reason.

"Put your weapon down!" The Leash shouted.

"You raised yours first!" The Psychic responded.

"Both of you stop!" Syn shouted. But the startled Leash discharged his weapon, and the Psychic was dead before she hit the ground.

There was a moment of recognition and then fear in the Leash's eyes before they went blank and glassy. His mouth hung open and his knees wobbled. Syn knew the look. It was Mind Death. but it looked so different on a Leash than it did on a Psychic. Psychics lose their stability when their Leash dies. Their capacity to recognize differences in time, or space or moments. Leashes lose something else. They lose their humanity. They can still speak, still walk, still sleep and wake and function, but they are no longer human. They vanish behind a veil of emptiness.

Syn had seen it once or twice before, and it was always horrifying to him. The sounds from inside the Academy were now painfully obvious, war had broken out.

"I don't know what's going on, but I'm going in, Pops. Back me up," Dian bristled as she ran through the front gate. Syn stared for just a second longer at the now nearly catatonic Leash before rushing past him inside.

The scene inside was much the same, chaos had erupted from everywhere. People were fighting, some clawing at their skin, and others were curled up in balls in corners screaming. Dian was in a full sprint, she didn't know what she was looking for, but it wasn't long before she found it.

Dian watched as an explosion of flame slammed into Melania's chest and sent her sprawling. Agni was approaching, her fists wreathed in fire. Dian had served on assignments with Agni before, and knew exactly how dangerous she could be. Agni raised her hand palm out in a threat "Surrender or die!"

"MEL!!" Dian yelled. Melania and Agni both looked her way in shock.

"Dian, Melania has betrayed the Academy, she is a threat to our way of life. She has to be detained or else–"

"Dian, she's trying to kill me! Please help me, pet."

Through the heat and the smell of scorched clothing, Dian caught just the faintest hint of flowers and felt both her hands curl into tight fists and she launched herself forward. Not enough time for proper focus, but certainly enough for quick bursts, Dian wrangled all of the energy she could muster and unleashed it in bursts. Wave after wave of electricity fired in broad arcs from all around her, it made her hair stand on end and made her ears ring.

Agni had been the one who taught Dian how to fight. Helped her learn to focus and compress ions in the air, she also knew that a hot enough path would redirect her electricity. Agni whirled herself around and arched a stream of flame upwards, the white streaks of electricity encased the wall of fire and danced throughout it. With her second wave Agni fired stream after stream of liquid flame at the much younger Psychic, but the air was thinning and the fire was losing heat, on top of Agni already being tired from her bout with Melania.

Melania had managed to climb to her feet. The fight between Dian and Agni had only been going on for a few seconds but as fast as the two Psychics could attack, block, and counter it had seemed like several minutes. Melania reached with her mind to attack Agni but found her own energy store was depleted, her illusion over the entirety of the Academy had taken its toll. She was exhausted and her legs were barely holding her up.

"Syn, subdue Melania! I'll deal with Dian," shouted Agni as she roared a stream of flame that made her lips bleed.

"Hunter, protect her!" Melania yelled at Syn.

The Hunter Leash hesitated only a moment, his rifle snapped up and he took careful aim. He squeezed the trigger and the barrel erupted. Agni hadn't heard the shot, but she knew when she saw his rifle raised that he was aiming at her. She knew when he pulled the trigger, that was going to be it. She was going to die, and she was powerless to stop it.

I'm so sorry, Ru. I really did try.

CHAPTER 1.13

The Aftermath

"Psychics and Leashes are asked for more of themselves than any other citizen of any other nation and as such they must be cared for. In life, in death, and if the worst should happen, after mind death."

"Nice to formally meet you, Mr. Marshall. My name is Donovan Allourai."

Tobias heard the words as if they were far off, but when he felt the blade being pulled from his back, he managed to turn and see the face.

The bespectacled Leash in full Academy uniform was holding a five inch spike that was deep red with blood. "I've been chasing you for some time," he said as he smiled and raised his eyes to look Tobias in the face.

Tobias recognized him. The man in the suit vest at the hostage exchange. The one who had looked so out of place. *What is he doing here, and why did he stab me?*

Tobias felt his knees give out.

"Hey skinny, want those cuffs off?"

Angel looked up at the Specialist, his tattooed lips peeling back from his yellow teeth before lifting his hands. The Specialist threw a small rectangular box through the air which Angel caught with no effort.

Gregory and Zander began rushing toward him, but the Shred Leash was lithe and fast. Angel clicked the small handheld override and the restraints on his hands and feet fell away. Zander launched himself through the air at Angel, the young Leash that had been watching the door was less than a step behind him. Angel bent his knees and crouched until the back of his thighs nearly touched his ankles. He rocketed himself upwards, flipping backwards in a narrow arch to land by the female Psychic that had been standing guard. He raked his left hand down, fingers rigid and extended like a tiger's claw. Her neck spewed blood, her Leash had pivoted and was running full out toward the Shred Leash before he stumbled and his eyes went glassy.

The Specialist slipped out the door smiling at his handiwork. "No loose ends."

He slid out of the room and into the elevator, descending into the ensuing chaos of the Academy.

tat-tat-tat-tat

Angel looked like he had vibrated out of existence for a moment. In the split second before the female Psychic had hit the ground, Gregory had pulled her rifle to himself, chambered a round, and had opened fire on Angel. But the Shred Leash was simply too fast. He was on Gregory a moment later his yellowed fingers outstretched a millimeter away from a killing strike when Zander's cinderblock hard right cross slammed into Angel's cheek.

Angel hit the floor for just a moment. He twisted and contorted his body into a squat position, launched himself backwards, and landed on one of the pods that held one of the council members, their moans filling the air as their unrestrained Psychic energy flowed all around them.

"I guess this is the part where I make you make choices, huh?" Angel pressed his fingers together and slammed them through the back of the pod, his needle-like digits sticking through the right side of one of the council members chests. He then launched himself at another pod, and then another, all the while injuring members of the council.

Gregory dare not open fire or try to use his telekinesis to drag Angel to him for fear of causing more damage, and Zander simply wasn't fast enough to catch him.

"Zander, focus on saving who you can!"

"Then he will escape!"

"We don't have a choice. If the council dies, the whole Academy is in danger."

Gregory dropped the rifle and rushed to the nearest injured council member trying his best to patch the bleeding wound in his chest. Zander snatched up the rifle and aimed at the Shred Leash.

Angel sat planted above one of the pods coiled like a big cat, his teeth bared like a tiger. He knew Zander and Gregory were beaten, he had one last mission to complete before he was allowed to leave. He looked across the room at the blonde girl sitting against the wall shaking and crying.

"Melania needs you to be out of the way, little one. And I am her teeth."

He climbed down off of the pod and began walking toward Alyssia. Zander raised the rifle and fired until the bolt locked back, small rubies of blood covered Angel's skin, but none of the bullets had cut deep enough to do any damage. A Level Four Leash with a full Wash was nearly invincible.

Angel grabbed the dead Psychic on the ground and hurled them at Zander with enough force to kill any normal man. He didn't need those pesky administrators interfering with what he now had to do. Angel held up two of his fingers as if they were a knife. Both of the boney digits were already stained with blood.

"Now, little mouse. You die screaming."

Alyssia opened her mouth to scream as Angel lunged toward her, hands outstretched. He was a millimeter away from tearing out her eyes when he was was slammed into. The Shred Leash went skittering across the floor. He was on his feet in a flash and staring forward. The man in front of him ... it couldn't be.

173 cm

80 kg

Blonde Hair

Green Eyes

And now blood stained and incredibly pissed off, stood Tobias Marshall.

"Syn, subdue Melania! I'll deal with Dian." Agni shouted as she roared a stream of flame that made her lips bleed.

"Hunter, protect her!" Melania yelled at Syn.

The Hunter Leash hesitated only a moment, his rifle snapped up and he took careful aim. Agni hadn't heard a shot, but she knew when she saw his rifle raised that he was aiming at her. And she knew when he pulled the trigger that was going to be it. She was going to die, and she was powerless to stop it.

I'm so sorry, Ru. I really did try.

Syn squeezed the trigger and the barrel of the rifle erupted, but to Agni's ear it sounded almost like it had echoed. What was more amazing was that she didn't feel pain, or anything different at all.

You're hopeless, sis.

Rudra hit his feet but skittered several meters before he regained footing. He deftly pulled the bullet out of his forearm and dropped it on the ground. It was all the time the Hunter Leash needed to wheel on the much younger combatant and pull the trigger.

It would have been an easy and clear shot had Rudra's intercepting fist not bent the barrel of his rifle almost in two, sending the round into the marble floor. Syn dropped the ruined rifle and pulled a small baton out of his belt. It was made from Palladium micro alloy glass. It was harder than steel and more than capable of being slammed into another Leash without breaking.

The battle raged. Rudra dashing forward and attempting a strike while Syn calmly and expertly dodged and countered. It was an even match, and neither Leash was able to gain ground.

Dian and Melania had taken advantage of the momentary lull and had both resumed their attack on Agni. Agni was strong, but did not have Dian's youth and ferocity. Agni was experienced and intelligent, but didn't have the two decades of combat experience that Melania had. She was rapidly losing ground. And with Rudra unable to gain any ground against the Hunter Leash, she feared that her brother's help may have come too late.

"Krisha!"

Xiphos' voice was like music in Agni's ears. He landed with a roll and was on his feet in an instant. He launched his body through the air toward Dian. Melania yanked Dian back just in time to avoid having her be crushed by the Sword Leash.

Syn had slipped a blitz attack by Rudra, and with his offhand had drawn his custom 1911 from his belt. He aimed and fired at Agni, knowing his bullets wouldn't stop a Level Four Leash but would absolutely destroy the still quite vulnerable Psychic. The bullet shattered a millimeter in front of Agni's nose.

"You're a big girl, Agni. You can't keep waiting on big strong men to save you."

Syn's footing was ripped from him and he fell hard to the ground as Aspis jumped from the top of the stairs that led up to the elevator, caught herself on a pillar of Psychic energy, and then rushed the Hunter Leash.

"Ru, I've got your cover, come to me."

Rudra raced to Aspis' side, and Xiphos stood resolute in front of Agni. Syn had jumped to his feet, his baton in one hand his pistol in the other. Dian and Melania were shoulder to shoulder, heaving with exertion. The fight had been brutal, and most of them were exhausted.

"We have to run, Dian," Syn announced. "We can't beat them."

"Not without Angel!" Melania barked.

"Angel?" Dian cried, sparing only a moment to stare at the Nightmare Psychic.

"Yes! He'll be here any second now."

Tobias was watching from the ground. His assailant had tossed a small box at Angel, the Shred Leash dropped his cuffs and began his rampage around the room. None of it seemed very important. Tobias had, after all, died before. It was painfully obvious as his extremities went numb and his vision tunneled that he was, in fact, dying. He couldn't find anything significant to focus on. Several corpses, the faint smell of blood, the distant sound of weapons fire.

Dying.

No more than he probably deserved. How many men had he killed? How much blood had he shed? Death was, at the very least, a fair trade for the life he'd led. His broken vision landed on Alyssia, it would have made more sense for her to be staring at Angel and the carnage that was filling the room, but instead she had her eyes locked on him.

Tobias, I need your help.

I'm dying, I'm no help to anyone. At least this I will do peacefully.

Please forgive me.

Tobias's vision went black, his last conscious thought was that his body felt heavy, so very heavy. There, in the blackness of his mind, he felt calm swallow him whole.

"I don't like the dark," he felt his lips part as he muttered the words. The feeling of small warm fingers wrapped around his hand. He turned his head, but in the blackness he couldn't even see an outline of the owner of the hand. Then long hair tickled his wrist.

"I need your help, Tobias, and I found you. I found you in the dark. I'm sorry."

Tobias' eyes snapped open. Angel was advancing on Alyssia. Gregory and Zander had divided themselves in order to protect the Council. Gregory's eye contact was unblinking. He was trying to attack the Shred Leash mentally but was obviously making no progress. Zander had emptied an entire magazine at the monster but had barely made him flinch. Alyssia looked helpless and afraid, but she wasn't looking at Angel, she was looking at Tobias.

"Now, little mouse, you die screaming!" Angel lunged.

Tobias hadn't remembered moving, but he had lunged like a bullet. He lowered his shoulder and slammed into the slender Leash. The impact forced him upright. His collarbone had snapped on impact but almost immediately after the pain had registered his skin began to itch and the pain dissipated from the injury. The broken bone had healed. He turned his eyes toward Alyssia.

"What did you do?" His voice was hard and flat. He knew the answer, but couldn't believe it was real.

"Saved us both," she said softly.

Angel leapt to his feet and attacked with extended fingers like knives. Tobias coiled his body into fighting stance and, in a reflexive instant, became a blur of fists and elbows. Angel was flexible and unbelievably strong. He was personally responsible for the assassination of hundreds of people. Everything about him struck fear into every person he'd ever met. And he was losing.

Tobias bent his front knee and bobbed to avoid the head level kick. When Angel's foot planted, it was at the same moment Tobias was pivoting back up to his full height. He used forward momentum to slam his left fist into Angel's thin chest, expertly collapsing the diaphragm.

Angel dropped both hands to his chest, the blow had been bone shattering, and considering Angel's bones were several times denser and harder than normal human bones the force of the strike was even more shocking. As Angel's hands went to cover his chest Tobias's same left hand arched back and collided with Angel's chin. The Shred Leash was staggered, and his hands flailed wildly in defense but with his focus lost the incoming right cross couldn't be stopped. Tobias hit Angel with enough direct force to puncture steel, the resulting impact actually created a small concussive pulse throughout the room.

Angel crashed through the thick walls to the council chamber and splayed across the ground. Through a collapsed orbital socket he could see the enraged mercenary closing on him. To a normal human it would have looked like a blur of black uniform and dirty blonde hair, but Angel's fear and adrenaline made it look as if it was happening in slow motion. He forced himself painfully to his feet and did the only thing that he thought he was still capable of doing. He ran.

The battle continued to rage on the main floor of the Academy, with Melania distracted, her manipulation of the bulk of the members of the Academy had faded, and the Psychics and Leashes who were previously at each other's throats were now actively trying to care for the hurt or injured. Those who were in the blast zone of the super humans were doing everything they could to scramble out of the way.

Syn was maintaining a constant stream of assault on Aspis. Despite Syn's superhuman speed, she was managing to manifest shields in time to block each incoming impact, but she was wearing out. Rudra, panting with fatigue, tried to rush out from behind her barrier to help. But Syn was an old soldier, battle was his home front, his normally warm and kind eyes were hard and focused. He would break them both in time.

Agni was exhausted, her skin was covered in scorches and blisters from her own consistent cascade of fire. And as powerful and athletic as Xiphos was, he was being pushed back. Dian was no longer slinging bolts of lightning because of the confined space but that didn't stop her from attacking Xiphos' footing. He felt like he was walking in sludge and that the ground was shifting beneath his feet with every step. His reflexes and his speed had kept him on his feet but Melania was beginning to attack his mind. He began to feel almost euphoric and docile. The fight was rapidly leaving his body and he became sluggish and sleepy.

Dammit, just a little more.

There was a loud crunching sound, and the doors of the elevator were ripped off as Angel staggered out of the shaft. "Melania! We have to leave now!"

Melania didn't need to be told twice. "Dian, make a hole for us."

The Lightning Psychic spared only a glance at the lady of nightmares before she opened up all the reserves of power she had. Lightning blistered out of her body in a forward arch, Xiphos dashed to Agni and covered her with his body. Rudra pressed his body to Aspis and she shrank and compressed a shield around both of them.

"Hold your breath Ru," Aspis barked, taking one massive breath before tightening the barrier around them almost to their skin.

With an opening created, Dian, Syn, Melania, and Angel were dashing to the entrance of the Academy. No one stood in their way. They were out of the front entrance and out of sight before Xiphos and Aspis released those they were protecting. Rudra set off at a run toward the entrance but collapsed after several steps. The battle had taken its toll; he was exhausted and still not recovered from being bedridden. Xiphos was moving sluggishly, and Agni and Aspis were spent.

"We can't just let them get away!" Aspis yelled as she struggled to make her exhausted body move. But they knew that pursuit would be a waste. Every single step that Syn and Dian took away from them made them more formidable. Range was always the ally of a sniper. Luke and Catha ran from around the corner up to their comrades. "Is everyone alright? What happened? Where is Melania?"

"We're ok, doc, but Melania and Angel are both escaping," Rudra said breathlessly.

"Angel? How?" Catha shouted, already turning on a heel to pursue the escaping Psychic and Leash. "Wait Catha, Syn and Dian are with them, you can't fight all four of them by yourself," Agni said as she touched her fingers gingerly to her blistered lips.

"What do you mean Syn and Dian are with them?" Luke asked, his face rapidly tensing with confusion and rage.

"Four of the most dangerous people in the world just decided that they no longer wish to be governed. This is going to be awful," Agni spoke softly as she slid down the wall next to Rudra. "Awful."

Blaine had made the call some twenty minutes ago. Air support was on its way, he was riding shotgun in one of their armored trucks and prepping for a battle. Every man who was strong enough to walk, or ride, and hold a gun was on their way toward the Academy.

The news had not filtered through their small encampment exactly what had happened, and most of the TITAN personnel that were marching with Blaine believed, without much convincing, the story he had given them. But even though he had the full backing of his men, and had even earned enough trust that his air support hadn't been questioned, he still felt uneasy. He had provoked the attack against their encampment, he knew that. But his pride and his ego had to be answered in blood. His radio pinged.

"Captain."

"Go for Blaine."

"Got three Wasps coming in as backup for you, sir. Do we engage on sight?"

"No, hold for my order, but be prepared to–"

About that time, Blaine saw four figures race around an outcropping in the road. He could see that two of them were unfamiliar, but the other two, one of which looked like a man of middle age with a grizzled beard, and a broad strong frame. The other was a lean, small figure with hair that, in the sunlight, was a blistering red.

"Oh no," Blaine whispered, now acutely aware that he was trembling at the sight of the people who had demolished more than half of those under his command. He pinged his radio.

"Halt."

All of his troops stopped in their movement, and the vehicles rode into a U shape with Blaine in the middle.

"Stop!" He shouted at the evidently hurrying group of people.

They either didn't hear him or were completely ignoring him.

"I said stop!" Now rapidly he could hear the rotors of the incoming helicopter.

"Wasp requesting permission to engage, sir."

Bang

An arch of red light shot through the sky and Blaine whipped his head toward its source. Of the figures, three of them were still rapidly approaching his convoy, one had stopped and withdrawn, assembled, aimed and fired what appeared to be a cannon in a single hyper accurate shot. Accurate because the next sound he heard was the loud *clang* of metal striking metal at high velocity then, his radio pinged.

"What the hell was that? We're hit. The rear rotor is disabled, we're spiraling. NO NO N–"

All was static, and then the deafening crunch of metal and the screams of the pilots screeched through the radio before silence took its place.

Blaine whipped his head back to the four encroachers, the big one with the gun had rejoined the other three, he was reloading the gigantic cannon all without losing step. They were now close enough that Blaine could see the other two figures, a beautiful thin framed woman with black hair and a severe expression. And a man, or at least he thought it was a man, nearly every inch of exposed flesh was covered with tattoos or some other kind of markings.

"They are hostile. Fire at will!" Blaine barked the order into his radio and immediately his entire troop aimed their guns at the four.

All at once the rumble of gun fire was all around, in between lapses of rifle rounds he could hear the pump of rotors from the remaining two wasps that were now no more than a few hundred meters away, the sound of their guns whirring and then firing off thousands of high velocity rounds toward the rapidly approaching group.

Blaine turned back to face the four. Two of them were gone. The big man had dropped to one knee as was firing and reloading so quickly that the barrel of his rifle seemed to be issuing steady tongues of flame. The tattooed man was darting in a zigzag pattern up the road, but changed direction so quickly that he appeared to fade out of existence for moments only to reappear several meters closer and still driving forward fast.

Suddenly the tattooed man was on them, he used his body and smashed through the ballistic windshield of the left most vehicle, shattering bulletproof glass and metal, and landing in the broad cab. Blaine turned his head in time to see the interior windows splattered with blood. One of the doors came flying off of the vehicle, smashing into several TITAN members who were trying to react to the sudden assault. The tattooed man emerged from the vehicle, covered in blood and holding a TITAN operative's body aloft like a human shield as he rushed the soldiers who were on foot.

Blaine saw that he was closing the gap, so he opened his own door, raised his rifle and tried to get a bead on the superhuman before he could kill any more of his troops. But the blood drenched nightmare squatted like a frog and lept high into the air over Blaine's back, landing in the gun nest of the vehicle that sat on the far side of the semi-circle. With a swipe of his hand, he removed the gunner's head from his body.

Blaine shouldered his rifle and fired several times, and even though his aim was good, the bullets bounced harmlessly off the tattooed monster as he continued to rip his way into the armored vehicle. Blaine could see his men's faces as they tried to fire up into the encroacher. A blinding flash of light dazed him, followed by a loud concussion, and when his vision cleared a second Wasp was crashing 50 meters away. Fire coated both the outside and the inside of the helicopter.

Blaine gripped his rifle in shaky fingers. He looked up and noticed, for the first time, the black haired woman several paces in front of him walking in the direction of the tattooed man. He raised his 6:1K and aimed it at her back.

"S-Stop!" He shouted his command. At least he thought he shouted, he tried to sound forceful when he said it. Felt the air pass his lips but either because of his shock, or the noise of combat around him his ears did not register the words. He took aim and squeezed the trigger.

But the trigger wouldn't depress. It wasn't stuck, his hand simply wouldn't respond to his instruction. He couldn't believe how very tired he suddenly was. He recognized the indifference must have been coming from an outside source but couldn't make himself care enough to continue the fight.

What's the point? I'll just lay down right here.

His heavy eyelids began to close as the black haired woman shot a glance over her shoulder. Her beautiful, stern face surveyed the absolute destruction they had left in their wake. The red headed girl ran up to her, took her hand, and glanced back at Blaine for a moment. She looked sad, almost heartbroken.

And then they ran.

EPILOGUE

"Tobias Marshall. The tradition, laws, and reputation of the Academy are now your responsibility to bear as it has been for a generations of Leashes before you. Carry your title with pride."

Gregory and Zander had given half a dozen or so speeches exactly like this in the last few minutes to various, newly Washed Leashes. The difference here was that Tobias was a level 4. A god amongst men. And he was very unhappy about it.

He hadn't spoken to Alyssia since the initial Merger. A freak happening, an impossible occurrence that Gregory could not explain and that Luke could not reverse. Tobias and Alyssia were now Merged.

He had been dying, bathing in a Psychic Wash, his mind too weak to fight off Alyssia's probing mind, and the Merger had just occurred. They were now a Level Four team, with the same level of power and responsibility as Agni and Rudra.

He looked straight forward, avoiding Gregory's gaze during his speech. The new uniform was comfortable, the white and blue bars across his shoulder indicating that he was Academy personnel and an instructor. After an additional trial period, he had been told he'd be given a gold bar to go with his blue that indicated he was back in the field.

"As is tradition, we have selected titles for you as a Level Four team to differentiate you from your peers. You, Tobias Marshall, because of your extraordinary capacity to adjust to the tempo of battle, to initiate and engage without command instruction, and your ability to anticipate the greatest threat near you and react accordingly, your peers have given you the title of Reflex Leash. Wear this badge of honor well."

Gregory continued to speak as he moved to the next Leash. Tobias kept staring forward. Alyssia was at his shoulder, terrified to look up at him. Even her new Psychic name wasn't enough to shake her from her nervousness. Sync Psychic did have a nice ring to it, though.

She had wanted to give him space but had found that to be impossible with their new found connection. He had spent the first several days trying to lock his mind away from her but the harder he tried, the more obvious it became that he couldn't.

The next several days had been rage and confusion glancing through their shared link. He had briefly considered killing himself, and considered killing her several more, but these were passing thoughts. The last week, though, had been fairly quiet. He had resumed his training duties as had she.

Her classroom students couldn't stop asking her about her new bars and her new Merge. They all wanted to meet the Leash who had finally been able to Merge with her. But she was afraid, afraid of this cold man with the monster inside his head. And now as Gregory was walking back and forth giving a speech she had heard a hundred or so times in the past, she found herself wanting to talk to her Leash but was petrified to do so.

If you can hear me, nod.

She almost screamed but managed to contain herself. The voice had been in her head. It was his voice. She tilted her chin up, then back down slowly. She heard the slow exhale from the newly dubbed Reflex Leash.

Good, then just listen. I can feel how nervous you are. So let me clarify, I'm not going to kill you. I'm not going to do anything that would make MY life more difficult and being one of those brainless zombies you have stocking shelves or cooking meals doesn't strike me as any kind of life. So listen to me when I say, I will never stop looking for a way to end this merger without it harming us. In the meantime, as long as I'm alive, I will protect you exactly the way I'm supposed to. And I promise you that as long as I've got my feet underneath me, the only thing you will ever have to be afraid of again, is me.

Alyssia couldn't stop shaking. She knew he wasn't bluffing, she knew he was far more dangerous than any person she had ever met and, without thinking of the consequences, she had made him a super human. She couldn't help but wonder if she had accidentally made a monster too much like herself.

She could feel his eyes boring into the side of her face and timidly raised her eyes to meet his. He wore his same hard expression except for a ghost of a smirk on his lips. "Ready to go for a ride, doll face?"

And all at once, Alyssia was at peace.